Dollmaker

Dollmaker

J. Robert Janes

First published in Great Britain by Constable & Company Ltd.

Copyright © 1995, 2002 by J. Robert Janes
All rights reserved.

First published in the United States in 2002 by
Soho Press Inc.
853 Broadway
New York, NY 10003

Library of Congress Cataloging-in-Publication Data

Janes, J. Robert (Joseph Robert), 1935–
Dollmaker / J. Robert Janes.
p. cm.
ISBN 1-56947-285-8 (alk. paper)
1. Saint-Cyr, Jean-Louis (Fictitious character)—Fiction.
2. Kohler, Hermann (Fictitious character)—Fiction.
3. World War, 1939–1945—France—Fiction. 4. Police—
France—Brittany—Fiction. 5. Germans—France—Fiction.
6. Brittany (France)—Fiction. [1. France—History—German
occupation, 1940–1945—Fiction.] I. Title.

PR9199.3.J3777 D65 2002
813'.54—dc21

2002017560

10   9   8   7   6   5   4   3   2   1

*This is for Gracia who fights the good fight
and never quits but is always there when needed*

Behind the face of innocence,
the hardness of the firing

Author's Note

Dollmaker is a work of fiction in which actual places and times are used but altered as appropriate. Occasionally the name of a real person appears for historical authenticity, though all are deceased and the story makes of them what it demands. I do not condone what happened during these times, I abhor it. But during the Occupation of France the everyday crimes of murder and arson continued to be committed, and I merely ask, by whom and how were they solved?

Acknowledgement

All the novels in the St-Cyr–Kohler series incorporate a few words and brief passages of French or German. Dr Dennis Essar of Brock University very kindly assisted with the French, as did the artist Pierrette Laroche, while Ms Bodil Little of the German Department at Brock helped with the German. Should there be any errors, they are my own and for these I apologize but hope there are none.

1

As they moved in single file through the night, the rain of bombs continued. Now the crump of an explosion, now a series of brilliant flashes to the east over Lorient and the submarine pens, now the throbbing of heavy aircraft among the constant bursts of flak.

'It is nothing,' said the police chief, lifting the hand that held the shaded lantern. 'It happens all the time now. You'll get used to it.'

'Of course,' grunted St-Cyr. 'We're old hands. Nothing troubles us.'

'Not even the murder of a shopkeeper in the middle of nowhere,' sang out Kohler acidly. 'Christ, this wind would chill a polar bear, Louis! Couldn't Boemelburg have made things easier?'

As Head of the Gestapo in Occupied France, Hermann's chief had other matters to keep him busy. 'I'll speak to him,' said St-Cyr, tossing the words over a shoulder.

It was always the same for them. Finish one case and start another. No time for a little holiday. No time even for a decent piss.

'Turn away from the wind,' shouted Kohler. '*Don't* splash me this time!'

'Pardon. That second bottle of Münchener Löwen you insisted I drink at an altitude of 5,000 metres has short-circuited my bladder. A moment. That is all I ask.'

Victor Kerjean waited in the pale lantern light.

'Shouldn't you douse that thing?' shouted Kohler nervously – a 2,000-pound bomb had hit something important, causing secondary explosions. 'Hey, my fine, I thought it was illegal to show a light?'

'Especially at times like this,' grunted St-Cyr under his breath. 'Go easy, Hermann. Kerjean is good. It's his territory and he knows it.'

Threading their way among the gorse and bald boulders of granite, they continued out across the irregularities of the moor, went down into a low, rocky defile and came, at last, to the railway spur.

Again the hand with the lantern lifted. 'He is just along a little way. One cannot miss him.'

Blood everywhere probably, thought Kohler grimly. 'Any idea why he was out here?'

'Yesterday,' muttered St-Cyr. 'Friday, the 1st of January, 1943. At just after dusk.'

'Give or take a few hours,' sternly added Victor Kerjean, pausing to face them and raising the lantern so that they saw again the resolute dark blue eyes and rounded cheeks that were grey with the evening's shadow. A Breton, fifty-eight years of age, big-shouldered and far taller than his peasant ancestors, the Préfet of Morbihan had come all the way from Vannes. Come personally, since the two detectives were from Paris Central and the Admiral Karl Doenitz, C.-in-C. U-boats, had summoned them.

Lorient, the telex had read. *Dollmaker arrested in murder of shopkeeper. Most urgent you send experienced detective immediately. Fragments of bisque doll not – repeat not – his.*

'Dollmaker,' said St-Cyr more to himself than to the others. 'Paul Johann Kaestner, Kapitän zur See of U-297.'

'Ah, *yes*, and that one is not going anywhere,' said the police chief firmly, 'even if he *is* one of the Occupiers.'

'You're certain it was him?' asked St-Cyr.

'Positive!'

'Good. That's what we like to hear. It makes things easy for us.'

A hand was tossed. 'Ah, Paris! You people . . . You'll see.

You will have no doubts. He was out here at the time and has confessed to this.'

'The fool!' snorted Kohler under his breath. Murder was holding up the U-boat war in the North Atlantic and never mind that January and February were the stormy months and things ought really to have slackened off. The Führer must be pressing Doenitz to get the boys out there. 'A good shot with the torpedo, is he?'

'A hero. One of the best. His victim is at the next bend in the tracks, where the spur divides into its two branches and the iron switch-bar he has used to crush the skull, lies cast aside.'

Merde, another messy killing, thought St-Cyr, and Hermann's stomach not right from the roller-coaster flight: Le Bourget to the nearby aerodrome courtesy of the Luftwaffe in a requisitioned Dornier without passenger seats or heat of any kind. The time was now 9.30 or 10.00 in the evening.

A shabby square of faded, wine-red sailcloth, pinned by stones, covered the corpse. When this was removed, they saw that the shopkeeper was indeed sprawled face down across the tracks. The tan-coloured trench coat had long been used, the coarse homespun scarf of beige wool was teased by the ever-buffeting wind.

Again and again the crump of exploding bombs came from the city and its dockyards. The brilliant flashes momentarily lit up the moor and the spur as if trying to lift a darkness that was too heavy.

'Take the black-out tape off the lantern, please.'

'Louis . . .' began Kohler, alarmed.

'One lonely light will not matter,' said the police chief. 'It will all be over in a split second.'

Was he some sort of humorist? 'Twenty kilometres are nothing to those boys,' grumbled Kohler passionately. 'All they want is to drop their bombs and get the hell home.'

'They are already leaving. They have made the circle, yes? and are now heading back out to sea so as to avoid the batteries of Finistère and the Côtes-du-Nord.'

3

'Then give me the fucking lantern and let us have a look at him.'

Blood and brains and chips of bone were matted by glossy black hairs some of which stuck out oddly in clumps the wind played with. One hand, the left and out-thrown, had clawed at the pale, pea-sized granitic gravel, digging its fingers in deeply. The right hand, also thrown out, had swung back towards his assailant as if driven by impulse.

Glazed and wide, the eyes stared at the rusty iron sleeper-bolt that was not twelve centimetres from the face and held the burnished rail the forehead had struck as he had fallen.

Blood had run freely from a flared left nostril and, now congealed, webbed the coarse black hairs and made a little puddle on the gravel next to the larger mass from the mouth.

'A man of between forty-five and fifty years,' said St-Cyr. 'Not old, not young. Not wealthy but not so poor he could not afford a pair of glasses.'

Both lenses were broken, and in the right lens, gaps had appeared where the shards had fallen away.

'The frame is bent in the middle, Louis. Whoever did it, stepped around the poor bastard for another look.'

'In panic?'

It was but one of many questions.

'In panic, yes,' said Kohler. The glasses lay on the shoulder of the railway bed about a metre in front of the corpse and slightly to its left. The last bombs fell. One by one the anti-aircraft guns ceased. Then distant on the air, came the sound of the all-clear, and finally only the sounds of the wind and the breaking seas.

'Inspector . . .'

'In a moment, Préfet. Please,' said St-Cyr. 'The Admiral mentioned fragments of bisque?'

'Over here, then. Just along the tracks towards the washing plant. About twenty metres. Sous-Préfet le Troadec, my assistant in Lorient, has been most observant.'

4

The town cop. 'Big Foot,' grunted St-Cyr under his breath as they followed. 'That's what it means in Breton.'

'But intelligent,' offered Kerjean, not turning to confront these two from Paris. 'He will not have trampled a thing. Believe me, Chief Inspector, the Sous-Préfet Big Foot knows his business and so do I, as you yourself have confided to your friend not long ago.'

Did the moor pick up sounds and magnify them? wondered St-Cyr. Somewhat miffed, he said, 'Of course. Now the shards, please, and the lantern. Hermann, lift the glass a moment. Let the wind touch the flame and banish the soot of unfiltered paraffin.'

Flesh-coloured and thin, some like broken pale shards of rose petals, the bits of bisque huddled among the granitic chips which, pale and flesh-coloured too, had all but hidden them. 'Part of a doll, all right, Louis.'

'The face, I think but someone has collected several of the pieces? Your Sous-Préfet?' he asked, looking up into the light.

Kerjean shook his head. 'He has touched nothing. This is exactly as it was found.'

'Then who dropped the doll and who took it away?'

'This we do not know.'

'Then who picked up the pieces and who informed your Sous-Préfet of the murder?'

Kohler watched the two of them closely. The brown ox-eyes of the Sûreté's Chief Inspector never wavered nor did the gaze of the Préfet.

'The Kapitän Kaestner,' said Kerjean firmly. 'That one has refused to hand over the pieces but has shown them to myself and the officer in charge of U-boat operations, the Kapitän Freisen. It was Herr Freisen who informed Herr Doenitz of the matter.'

Hence the Admiral's insistence that the bisque was not Kaestner's.

'And when was Sous-Préfet le Troadec summoned?' asked Louis.

5

Kerjean hesitated. A pause would suit best, perhaps the wetting of the throat so as to drive home the point. 'At 3.10 this morning, the old time.'

'Three?' asked Louis, surprised.

Not a flicker of triumph appeared though Kerjean hesitated again before saying, 'Yes. That one waited for several hours both here and at their headquarters in Kernével before addressing the problem. Six cigarettes were stubbed out just over there against the flat rock upon which he sat to think it over.'

'What was he doing out here?'

'Gathering clay from the pits. At least, this is what he steadfastly claims though he could purchase all he needs for a few francs. Ten perhaps, or twenty at the most.'

'Clay?'

The Préfet crouched to touch one of the thin, whitish streaks that lay atop the gravel and parallel to the tracks. 'Spillage from the railway trucks. Kaolin for the dolls he makes. It's very slippery when wet.'

'And the shopkeeper?' interjected Kohler.

'Was the one who sold them for him here in Brittany and was his agent with the faience works in Quimper.'

'So they met out here to place a new order or discuss a new design? Come off it, Préfet. How long has Kaestner been stationed in Lorient?'

The Gestapo was a big man, far taller than Jean-Louis, even taller than himself, and from the Kripo, from Common Crime. 'Just over two years,' said Kerjean levelly. 'Almost right from the beginning.'

'And he's still alive? The son of a bitch must have the luck of the gods.'

'Or the skill, is that not so?' asked the Préfet, not wavering. 'The Kapitän Kaestner is well liked by his men, Inspector Kohler. Indeed, they count it a great privilege to be with him.'

Was it a warning? wondered Kohler and decided that it

was. 'They'll lie for him, Louis. They'll bend over backwards to help us.'

'Perhaps, but then perhaps not. When forced to live so closely for months on end, little animosities can assume the size of mountains. A Dollmaker?' he asked.

Kerjean nodded. 'That is his nickname. That and Vati – Daddy, the Old Man – though he is not quite thirty-two years of age.'

'And has sunk how many ships?' demanded Kohler swiftly.

'Twenty-seven for a total of 164,000 tonnes.'

'At a cost of how many lives?'

Was the one from the Gestapo feeling guilty or merely saying, If one could kill so thoroughly, why mess around with an iron bar? 'Five hundred and forty, maybe more. Oh for sure, who's to say exactly, since the British fail to tell our German masters? But it is enough to warrant the Admiral wanting him out there again.'

'Then we will get to work,' said St-Cyr guardedly, 'and we will not bother to sleep tonight.'

'But I have arranged the rooms . . .'

Was it such a catastrophe? 'Those will keep. Now see if you can find us another lantern in that washing plant you spoke of. Hermann, go with him. This lantern will do me until you return.'

'You sure you'll be all right?'

Hermann always had to have the last word. After nearly two and a half years together one did not argue. One simply let him have it.

Besides, Hermann would begin to sort out the Préfet. '. . . *Our German masters* . . .' How could Kerjean have been so bold? Surely to use 'our German friends' would have been far wiser and Kerjean fully cognizant of this?

'Either he is very troubled and distracted by this matter,' muttered St-Cyr to himself, 'or he wanted us to clearly see he was no collaborator, even though, as I myself, he must work for the Occupier.'

Always these days one had to be so very careful, and always such things cast their reflections on the matter at hand.

One dead shopkeeper.

'You are like a fly in a whorehouse, Victor. You buzz when the moment is inappropriate and a swatter nowhere to hand. You say a stupid thing like that. You let me guess at this one's age to see how close I'll come, yet you do not tell us his name, though both must be known to you.'

It was a puzzle particularly as the Préfet really was good at his job, one of the best.

Kerjean was not forthcoming. As they walked in single file through the night, and the beam of the Préfet's torch shone on the tracks, the spur came ever closer to the sea and soon the booming of breakers against rocky cliffs filled the air with its loneliness.

The line turned west. They were still in moorland – coarse grasses, broom, clumps of gorse and more boulders, thought Kohler. Lots of cover, lots of ups and downs but on a low plateau of some sort perhaps forty or fifty metres above sea level . . . 'Christ, what are they?' he blurted.

One by one and sentinel nearly five or ten metres high – yes, at least the nearest of them was that high – the standing stones gave their uncomfortable silhouettes to the darkness. Ah *merde*, they were like ancient gods standing in judgement of all that was around them.

The Préfet waited. The one from the Gestapo was suitably impressed – caught completely unawares, which was good. Yes, very good. Terrified a little perhaps by the unexpected. Was Herr Kohler superstitious? Would he now comprehend just how primitive a place this was?

'Wha . . .' began Kohler again.

It would be best to enlighten him. 'The first of several alignments in the Morbihan Jean-Louis will, no doubt, introduce you to.'

'How old?'

8

Had the voice grown smaller? 'As much as or more than four thousand years. Late Neolithic, yes? They go with the menhirs, the single standing stones, the dolmens also, and the passage graves.'

And you wanted me to be startled so as to betray my innermost feelings, thought Kohler uncomfortably. Were all Bretons so wily?

They continued on. The sea was now very close. The smell of rotting fish and kelp, of iodine and salt, filled the air and mingled with that of sea birds and their dung and something else, a musty dustiness he could not explain.

'The pits are just around this bend.'

'You know the place well.'

'I make it my job, Inspector. Prepare yourself. *Regardez*.'

Suddenly dizzy, Kohler drunkenly caught himself, for the line hugged the edge of a precipice. Stark white but ghostly grey in the darkness, and with splashes and wounds of deeper grey, the cragged and hollowed unending expanse of the clay pits fell away for ever from the spur, but glowed eerily, while up from the tortured ground came the sounds and thoughts of long-lost miners and those of nearer times. Of flint and copper and bronze on rock, with fire perhaps and water to shatter things and, more recently, dynamite.

Kohler found the presence of mind to offer a cigarette and a light, both of which were gratefully accepted as if the lesson was now over, though they had to huddle from the wind. 'Our friend the Captain took his clay from the far side, nearest the sea,' said Kerjean, looking up from the flame as he held Kohler by the hand to steady it. 'That one claims the kaolin is better there than anywhere else, a rich pocket. It is all a residual deposit, the kaolin having been produced by the chemical weathering in place of the feldspar in the granite.'

Louis should have heard the lecture, since he was always pounding his partner with such improvements of the mind. 'How far are we from the murder?'

'About a kilometre and a half. It's a good walk. He was all

9

alone. The plant has been shut down for the holiday. He was seen leaving the pits at 3.20 our time.'

The old time. Not Berlin Time, which was now the order of the day and in winter, one hour ahead: 3.20 p.m. becoming 4.20.

'Still lots of light?'

And just past the winter solstice, was that it? 'Enough.'

'Then the killing was done in daylight?'

Was it so surprising, this little token of co-operation? Kerjean drew on his cigarette and tried to assess Jean-Louis's partner, a giant with bare head, the Fritz haircut, puffy, faded blue eyes, a storm-trooper's jaw and big shoulders. Were all Bavarians so unconsciously menacing, or was it just the shrapnel scars, the graze of a bullet wound on the forehead and the slash down the cheek? 'To hit a man that hard and only once could easily have been done in darkness, yes, or daylight. Until the coroner establishes the time of death, the matter must remain in the lap of the gods.'

But whose gods, was that it? wondered Kohler. Trapped into betraying his eagerness, he said. 'But you think it was done in daylight perhaps up to an hour after the Captain was seen leaving the pits, so at about 4 p.m. your time?'

Was it a small offering of peace, this Gestapo's use of the old time? 'At a prearranged spot and with the victim's back turned so that the Captain did not have to see his face.'

'Then why the killing?' asked Kohler levelly. 'What was the motive?'

'You will see. The washing plant is over there not far from where the Captain took his clay. That large silhouette on the horizon, yes? The granite is crushed and screened to remove the coarsest material, after which the clay is separated by washing and allowed to settle into two products. Coarse kaolin, at up to five microns in particle size, and the fine at below one micron. When dried, most of it is sent to Quimper for the making of faience.'

'Why not admit it doesn't make a bit of sense Kaestner's

killing that shopkeeper? Not here, not anywhere. There's no money in dolls – there can't be.'

And you have fallen right into my little trap, thought Kerjean. 'Oh but there is, Inspector. Herr Kaestner comes from a very old family in Waltershausen, Thuringia. His grandfather was *the* famous Kaestner, one of the finest dollmakers in Germany. The Captain dreams of revitalizing an industry he knew and loved as a boy but which fell prey to the last war and the hard times after it. He and Monsieur le Trocquer, our shopkeeper, were partners in this little venture. Kaestner and his crew put up the money, since Monsieur le Trocquer had none. Absolutely none, you understand.'

'How much?'

They had not moved in some time, so intense was their conversation. That, too, was good. '300,000 marks to get things started.'

'Reichskassenscheine?'

'The Occupation marks, yes. Yes, of course. None other can be used, isn't that correct?'

'6,000,000 francs. That's one hell of a lot to entrust to an impoverished shopkeeper.'

'Monsieur le Trocquer was perhaps on his way to tell the Captain the money was still missing. One cannot say at the moment just why he came out here. It is too early in the investigation.'

'Missing?'

'Yes. Since at least the 5th of November.'

A decisive man, the Captain – was that it, then? A simple matter of money? 'You're not exactly happy to see us, are you?' asked Kohler cautiously.

'Should I be? The Captain killed him, Inspector. Justice has to be done no matter how difficult or on which side of the fence one sits.'

'I could have you shot for that.'

'You won't. You are not like the others, Herr Kohler. Even here in the Morbihan we have heard of you.'

'But you wanted to get it straight between us?'

'That and my knowledge of Jean-Louis. He's one for the truth, as is yourself apparently, for you wear the scars, particularly the one down the left cheek from eye to chin, a rawhide whip and a little matter in Vouvray, I believe, that was settled regardless of the status quo.'

And now you're trying to make me think you like me, thought Kohler warily.

'Inspector, who is to say how the wind blows in these troubled times? For myself, you will understand, I had to be certain. If, as your reputation says, you seek the truth, then you and Jean-Louis will have my entire assistance no matter the consequences. If not, then rest assured justice will find its way. Ask the stones. They will tell you that here in the Morbihan we do things a little differently if necessary.'

All alone and happy about it, St-Cyr carefully set the lantern next to the fragments of bisque, then retraced his steps to the corpse. Though the light flickered over the edge of the embankment and into the nearby gorse, he could no longer see the lantern due to the bend in the tracks, and when he stood all but where the killer had delivered the death blow, he could see even less of the light.

'So, good. Yes, that's good,' he said to himself, and taking out his pipe and tobacco pouch, stood a moment in quiet contemplation. Somewhat corpulent, not tall, but not too short either, he was a solid trunk of a man with broad shoulders, a wide brow, thick bushy dark brown eyebrows and a moustache grown long before the Führer had taken up the fashion. A muse, a lover of books and of gardening and fishing, a lover of many things, a cop.

The thin trails of spillage from the railway trucks glowed a ghostly white, emphasizing the blind spot most definitely. 'Kerjean should have noticed this,' he said aloud. 'There is no way such a one could have missed it, yet so far he has said nothing of it.'

And what of the Sous-Préfet le Troadec? he asked himself. An unknown quantity, though to his credit he had noticed the fragments, ah yes. But had he noticed the most important thing of all?

Between the fragments and the corpse someone had stumbled and fallen, then, still on his or her seat and in terror perhaps, had frantically pushed themselves away and back around the bend and out of sight. A full twenty metres. The clay was often smeared. Sporadic threads and clots of coarse black wool – an overcoat no doubt – had been caught on some of the sleepers. The heels had been dug into the gravel to give purchase and at one place, a sharp bit of granite had punctured the left palm. There would be scrapes and bruises. Blood and kaolin were smeared on the outermost rail nearest the fragments, red against stark white and the burnished grey of the iron.

Whoever had backed away from the shopkeeper had then stood and had dropped the doll, which had hit that same rail and had showered its fragments inwardly at that person's feet.

One tiny fragment – a portion of the cheek, he thought – revealed a smear of blood, indicating that just before falling, the doll had been gripped in the left hand by the head.

'Either this visitor discovered the body and retreated from it in horror or there was an altercation of some sort with the shopkeeper just prior to his death and this drove the visitor from him.'

After dropping the doll, the visitor had left the railway spur and had wandered out into the moor next to the innermost part of the bend. Had he or she then killed the shopkeeper?

Most of the terrain was either covered by gorse and bracken or was of bare rock with rare pockets of coarse granitic sand, so footprints were not easy to find and only with daylight could they conduct a thorough search. But was the presence of this visitor the reason the Kapitän

Kaestner had been so diligent in collecting the pieces of the doll, and why, please, had Kerjean not looked more thoroughly?

There was still no sign of Hermann and the Préfet. Though the Bavarian was easy-going and no man's fool, still it was sometimes a problem for others to accept their having to work together. Kerjean could well have thought it best to keep things close until he could speak privately with the Sûreté.

Again St-Cyr looked along the track into the night but saw only the flickering of the light. In spite of the war and animosities that were only natural, Hermann and he had got on splendidly. Well, most of the time, and had done so since the fall of 1940. A trick of fate God had played on him. A *friend* among the enemy! God often did things like that to his little detective. 'So, what have we here, then?' he asked, throwing a look up into the heavens. No answer would be forthcoming. There never was. God wanted detectives to think for themselves.

'Did you confront this visitor?' he asked the shopkeeper. 'Did you challenge him or her, and force them to retreat from you in horror?

'Or did this visitor kill you and then retreat in horror at what they had done only to return for a cautious look and to inadvertently step on your glasses? And why, please, did you remove them? You were holding them in your left hand when struck, is that not so?'

Retrieving the lantern, he again located the place where the killer had stood to deliver the blow. It had been a ruthless, downward swing of the switch-bar with both hands no doubt and the weight so totally behind it, the shock had driven the toes of the killer well into the gravel. Craters of several centimetres' depth marked the places where the shoes or boots had been planted. Kerjean should have noted this too, yet had chosen to say nothing of it.

An open and shut case. One U-boat captain. Must things always be so difficult?

When the Préfet and Hermann finally arrived, he had them place extra lanterns round the bend. Lit up, there was no dispute. 'The shopkeeper, the Captain and at least one other person,' he said gruffly.

'There, what did I tell you, Préfet?' enthused Kohler. 'It's not for nothing that Louis was chosen to work with me. Right, Louis? Boemelburg knew him from before the war. The IKPK, the International Police Organization.'*

'Yes, yes,' said Kerjean testily, 'but I still say the Captain killed that one.'

'Perhaps,' said Louis – Kohler held his breath and waited for the oft-pronounced disclaimer – 'but perhaps not, Préfet. For now the Kapitän Kaestner can keep. The time of killing, please?'

Ah *merde*, thought the Préfet. Now it's serious. 'At dusk, or just before it.'

The ox-eyes of the Sûreté swept emptily over him. 'And when did the watchman see the Captain leaving the pits? Remind me, please.'

One would have to face it. 'At 3.20 in the afternoon, the old time, as I have said.'

'Perhaps an hour before dusk and almost exactly twelve hours before reporting the crime.'

Light from one of the lanterns etched Kerjean's shadowed cheeks and watchful gaze. 'Who was this other person, Préfet?' asked Louis severely.

The one called Kohler was now out of sight behind himself. To shrug would be stupid, thought Kerjean, but he would do so anyway. 'I do not know. I only got here this afternoon, Jean-Louis. I have barely had time to find accommodation for you and your colleague.'

'My partner and my friend.'

'If you say so.'

'I do!'

'Good. Then if you have no more need of me, Chief

* The forerunner of Interpol.

Inspector, I will see if I can find the coroner and a photographer.'

'Good! That is exactly what we need and the next time you lead us to a murder, Préfet, be so kind as to use the most direct route. I think you will find your car is much closer and the walk across the moor, though edifying, an utter waste of our time.'

Normally the diplomat even in the toughest of situations, Louis had let things get the better of him. Kerjean merely nodded curtly then turned abruptly away to vanish into the moor.

'Louis, who the hell is he trying to protect?' hissed Kohler, not liking it one bit.

'I don't know, my old one. I wish I did. We worked together on several things before the Defeat of 1940. Always I have found him absolutely forthright and efficient but then, ah what can I say, I did not have a partner such as yourself.'

'Sorry.'

'Don't be. We will find things out now because he has made it imperative!'

'6,000,000 francs are missing.'

'Six?'

Kohler quickly told him that the Captain had entrusted the shopkeeper with so much. They set to work, were very thorough. Some fifty metres beyond the fragments, Kohler found where the Captain had swung his satchel of clay aside. The bag was still there on the edge of the embankment. 'We walked right past it, Louis. Kerjean said nothing of it.'

'Yes, but from here, Hermann, could the Captain not have left the tracks to strike overland to the site of the murder?'

It was all so dark but for the lanterns. Dark and eerie. The wind wouldn't stop. There was the feel of rain in the air. They found a boot print, a smear of the white clay and then another and another, then no more of them. 'Did he kill

16

the shopkeeper, Louis? Is that what Kerjean wanted us to see? He and that watchman spoke Breton. I couldn't understand a word but am certain the bastard could speak French as well as I can.'

Which was pretty good for one of the Occupiers, most of whom couldn't understand more than a few words and couldn't have cared less, since the French willingly ran things for them. But, then, Hermann had been a prisoner of that other war from 1916 until its Armistice and had used the opportunity to learn a cultured language. Which was entirely to his credit and fortunate, since that was the way one found things out. Well, sometimes. Besides, how else was he to have conversed with his little Giselle and his Oona?

'Hey, if it makes you feel any better, I can't understand Breton either,' confessed St-Cyr.

'Even though Marianne was one of them?' Uncomfortably Kohler offered a cigarette. 'Sorry, Louis. I shouldn't have reminded you, should I?'

'Of my dead wife? My second wife?' retorted St-Cyr. 'She never spoke Breton at home, even to our son, since to do so would have been to admit of that shameful ignorance the rest of France have tarred such people with. Which reminds me, if I can do so, I had best pay her parents a visit.'

'They'll only blame you and you know it. Why punish yourself?' The Resistance in Paris had accused Louis of being a collaborator – still did for that matter – and had left a bomb for him which his wife and little son had inadvertently tripped a month ago almost to the day. She'd been coming home to him from the arms of her German lover who'd been sent to the Russian Front. The woman unrepentant, no doubt. Still defiantly independent and proud of it, as most Bretons were. 'Look, I really am sorry I mentioned it,' said Kohler.

'So am I.'

'Why didn't the Captain return for his satchel?'

'Perhaps he was too shaken and forgot it,' offered the Sûreté.

'Then Kerjean really did leave it there for us to find.'

'Perhaps.'

They worked in silence, each taking a side of the tracks and retracing their steps to the fragments and beyond them to the Captain's collecting bag.

'An ammunition satchel,' grunted Kohler, looking down at the thing. 'Regulation issue. Kriegsmarine blue. Stores must be tolerant of heroes. Quite obviously he saw something up ahead and eased this thing aside.'

'Yes, but *what* did he see? A broken doll on the tracks? The visitor sitting there or standing? Or both the doll and that person?'

'Whatever it was, it caused him to make a little detour.'

'And that detour could just as easily pin the murder on him.'

It was only as they retraced their steps and searched along the tracks well past the body, that they came upon an abandoned shed and found in the scant gravel nearby, the marks of a bicycle's tyres.

'Both coming and then leaving,' murmured Kohler, running fingers lightly over them. 'The leaving in haste, I think. The road is just beyond the shed. That's where our friend the Préfet should have left the car and led us to the railway spur but decided not to.'

St-Cyr heaved a troubled sigh. 'Then he knew of the cyclist but has made no attempt to remove the evidence.'

A strange man. One up to his ears in something. 'There are no footprints,' said Kohler. 'Whoever pushed the bicycle into that shed, took the trouble not to leave any.'

'Perhaps . . . but then, ah *mais alors, alors*, Hermann, were they removed later?' There was plenty of bare rock, so the task would not have been difficult. 'Was the owner of the bicycle the visitor?'

'Or someone else? A fourth person.'

*

One by one the lanterns went out of their own accord and still there was no sign of the Préfet and the coroner. Only the sound of the breaking seas kept St-Cyr and Kohler company but this was soon muffled by dense fog that came in of a sudden and decided to stay.

Beaded mizzle broke on icy cheeks. Noses constantly dripped. Kohler wiggled his toes trying to find a particle of warmth. Far out to sea, the long lament of a fog horn sounded faintly.

'That's the one on the Île de Groix,' commented St-Cyr grumpily. 'A good ten kilometres. Dead flat and painfully mournful, as is appropriate!'

'Let's find that shed. Maybe it's dry.'

'Is Kerjean deliberately leaving us out here to stew in our own juice?'

'Maybe the coroner likes to sleep in? Maybe he had to come all the way from Vannes, eh? Hours, Louis. It could take the son of a bitch all day to get here!'

'*Nom de Jésus-Christ*, Hermann, what is it this time? A photographer without a film? Some argument as to bills unpaid – a last job perhaps? Or is it that the Admiral Doenitz needs to be informed of recent developments and has demanded one of his photographers assist?'

These days there were always complications. Others always had to get in the way. 'The shed, remember?' snorted Kohler and when they found it, he held the door open and from some hidden cache among his inner pockets, offered a flask of peach brandy, though God knows how he had obtained it and one did not often ask such questions.

There were two upended wooden kegs that had once held sleeper spikes. These they used as stools, resting their backs against the bare cold boards and sharing a last cigarette in silence until Louis was moved to say, 'Misery unites us.'

Kohler ran his eyes over the inside of the shed. It was nothing much. Bare pine poles clad with boards. Tarpaper on the roof, thank God. No leaks. Just room for a bicycle or two and, in a corner, lots of flattened, clean straw. No sign of sheep dung or any other such item . . .

'Don't even *think* of bedding down!' seethed St-Cyr acidly. 'You do and they will be *certain* to arrive.'

'Hey, I thought that's what you wanted?'

Did Hermann always have to grin at adversity?

The Bavarian leaned over the straw, and from a niche on one of the cross-timbers, plucked a package of cigarettes. '*Voilà*, Chief. Lucky Strikes.'

'Pardon?'

He pulled down a lower eyelid in mock salutation and rubbed his frizzy, fast-greying hair that was not black or brown but something in between. 'Nineteen of them, my fine Sûreté *flic*. One is missing, in case you wondered.'

They lit up, savouring the blend of fine Virginia tobaccos. They drew in deeply and looked at each other for the longest time. 'U-boat cigarettes?' asked Kohler.

'From an American freighter or a downed aircraft from North Africa? Could it be possible?' suggested St-Cyr, examining the glowing end of his cigarette. Marvellous . . . They were absolutely superb.

Kohler shook his head. 'A freighter. My gut tells me our friend the Captain left this little souvenir for the owner of the bicycle.'

St-Cyr drew in deeply. When the fog had arrived it had made him damned worried, for with it would come the rain to wash everything away. Now he found a contentment which, though he knew he ought to be wary of it, he welcomed. 'Our Captain is turning out to be quite interesting.'

'Aren't the sinkings of twenty-seven ships and the deaths of five hundred and forty men interesting enough? Or the more than two years of surviving what must be a damned desperate war?'

'Or the 6,000,000 francs? He seeks only the richest pockets of clay – is so anxious to get at them he arrives back from Paris and wastes no time in coming here.

None at all apparently. He must have had a car at his disposal.'

'An expert, and not just with the periscope.'

'A dollmaker whose grandfather was famous for it.'

There was silver foil in the cigarette package and an aroma that was still so superb, Kohler had to have Louis sample it. 'They come in cartons of twenty-four packs, I think. Maybe someone on one of the lifeboats handed them over after the Captain blew their ship right out from under them.'

'Honour and courtesy on the high seas or the threat of U-297's deck guns?'

Deep down in the straw there was a lady's crumpled white handkerchief. So hard had the fist been clenched, the handkerchief had to be tugged at to open it but there were no initials and only the faintest trace of perfume. 'Sandalwood, rosemary, lemongrass and bitter orange,' said St-Cyr. 'Something quite old and expensive, I think. A woman, then, who values herself, is valued by someone else, or both. Let me keep the cigarettes and this, Hermann. Let me add them to the tufts of coarse black wool from the tracks and the shards of bisque, particularly the one with blood on it. Say nothing of these to our Préfet or anyone else. Not for the time being. Let us have our own surprises.'

At a shout, they returned to the fog which was now so thick, they could barely make out the Préfet's lantern.

Six men were with him and their shapes grew but slowly. The Sous-Préfet in his blue uniform, cape and kepi, the coroner looking more like a startled grey-brown mouse in a heavy brown tweed overcoat, scarf, no hat and seaboots, two photographers, one German, one French, the latter decidedly uncomfortable, the former quite content.

And two workmen in dusty, tattered blue denim jackets, black corduroy trousers with coarse black woollen pullovers and heavy wooden clogs, their black berets absolutely filthy, their expressions impassive. Had they seen so much, these two, nothing surprised them any more?

21

The workmen had a stretcher between them and both coveted it so much, the gnarled hand of one was placed firmly above that of the other.

'Inspectors, if you will be so good as to tell these gentlemen what you want photographed, they will do their utmost while the coroner examines the body.'

'Why not let them shoot it first?' hazarded St-Cyr, surprised.

The Sous-Préfet, a serious and uncomfortable forty-year-old, threw the Préfet an uncertain glance. 'But . . . but Monsieur Tessier, here, he has already photographed it several times?'

'Why were we not informed of this, Préfet?' demanded Louis sharply.

Ah, Paris, why did they have to think each little oversight an insult? 'There seemed no need. After all, they were only preliminary shots. I knew others would be required by such as yourselves.'

The bastard! Was it now to be open hostility? wondered Kohler. 'Louis, let me handle this. Take a hike. Go and have a look at the clay pits, eh, and pick up the Captain's satchel.'

'In this?' snorted Kerjean, flinging a hand up in disgust. 'Ah pfft! Jean-Louis will see nothing of the pits today. *Nothing!* Besides, there is nothing there to interest you.'

'But all the same, I will do as he suggests, Préfet. Hermann, see that the photographers capture all the footprints and give us a shot or two of the bicycle tracks.'

'*What bicycle?*' demanded Kerjean swiftly. 'There was no bicycle.'

'Oh but there was, Préfet. Show him, Hermann. Let him see this one thing the gumshoes from Paris have discovered. Nothing else. Keep him in suspense. Let him worry about the rest. It'll be good for him.'

The light was now a pearl grey, with everywhere the fog so close it was not until St-Cyr was almost at them, that he saw the standing stones and sucked in a breath before hastily crossing himself. Then he left the railway spur and went among them to touch their clammy surfaces and say to no one but himself, 'How many murders have you witnessed down through the ages?'

Like Hermann, he came upon the edge of the clay pits quite unexpectedly and, leaning back, for the precipice at his feet was sheer, gazed dizzily down and then out into the fog.

As if with open hands, their fingers claws, the pits stared up at him and he saw at once how difficult it would be to find a man down there. And even as he tried to see further into the maw of the place, the rain began and made the ground below run with milk. 'It's slippery,' he said and turned uncomfortably away.

At 10 a.m. Berlin Time, 9 a.m. the old time, they left the place in the Préfet's little Renault, all crammed together and with the ambulance and the body behind. In the centre of Lorient, perhaps some ten kilometres from the clay pits, they let the Sous-Préfet and the photographers out at a bomb-damaged square, then dropped the coroner off at a shattered railway station. Devastation was everywhere. The homeless were on the road *en masse* to friends and relations in the countryside: hand-drawn carts, wagons and baby carriages heaped with belongings, children, old people and blank stares when confronted with the Préfet's incessant honking.

Then they took the road from Lorient to Quiberon and its peninsula, a distance of at least fifty kilometres through fog and rain and finally wet snow that did not hang about but melted instantly.

There were farms, salt marshes, bits of pine forest – other alignments, yes, and dolmens – along the way but nothing to alleviate the depressingly cold grey landscape.

'You are booked into the Mégalithe,' said the Préfet. 'I hope the accommodations are to your satisfaction.'

A twenty-five room hotel in which they were the only guests.

'It's the off-season, Louis. We ought to be grateful they've opened the place up for us.'

'Of course.'

2

When one single set of shutters was opened, a grey and dismal light washed into the massive dining-room of the Hotel Mégalithe whose legions of empty tables still held the white linen cloths and settings of the late summer of 1940. Every sound echoed. The place was freezing. Dust clung to the bread-and-butter plates and overturned coffee cups, the knives and forks and spoons.

Even the menu had to be blown off. St-Cyr threw the girl in black broadcloth and black velvet, with the white lace apron and the giant stovepipe coif of starched white lace, an uncertain glance. 'A dozen oysters,' he said, his words crashing on timid ears that were all but hidden by curls. 'A bottle of the Muscadet, the sole *meunière, pommes à l'anglaise* – ah, I know it is heresy to ask for English-style potatoes. Cauliflower and Brussels sprouts, I think. Cheese and dessert. Oh, and coffee. The real stuff if you have it.' He'd ask. These days one could only dream but Herr Doenitz might have interceded on their behalf. It was just possible, wasn't it?

The girl, no more than seventeen, blurted something unintelligible and, with moisture rushing into her stark blue eyes, turned and raced from the dining-room.

'Can I do nothing right in this place?' he asked himself. All of the other windows were shuttered tightly. He had had a battle just to get this one open and had finally done it himself.

Sitting down with his back to the alcove's sombre panelling, he passed uncertain hands over the table-cloth which was not just cold but insufferably damp and likely mildewed.

'*Inspector, what is the meaning of this?*'

The sharp voice of the owner's wife shattered the silence. St-Cyr picked up the menu and, gazing across the room, heaved a futile shrug. 'Some oysters?' he winced.

'Don't be absurd! You may have the *cotriade*' – the fish soup that was more like a poor man's stew – 'and the bread if you have enough tickets.'

Shit! 'I . . . We . . . that is, my partner and I have none, Madame Quévillon. Are this week's orange, lime or yellow? I can never remember which is which and am seldom home in Paris long enough to update my ration booklets.'

'Paris, hmph! They are chartreuse and you must ask the Préfet to supply you. No food can be given without them. This is *not* Paris!'

Formidable in severe black, ankle-length voluminous skirts, and without the benefit of an apron but with a metre-high coif of stovepipe lace – was it that high? – she looked like the warder of a medieval prison for women. 'A glass of the Muscadet, then?' Would it be possible?

'Forget it,' she said tartly. 'It is not a day for alcohol.'

'Then please tell my partner I have gone for a walk to seek nourishment from the fog!'

'As you wish. It's just as you please, monsieur.'

'Inspector! It's Chief Inspector St-Cyr!'

'Of course.'

He caught himself at the door, forced humility into his voice and begged the location of Monsieur le Trocquer's shop.

The woman drew herself up so that she towered over him with that ridiculous coif. Her shoulders were every bit as wide as his. 'It is on the rue de Port-Haliguen not far from the cathedral. You cannot miss it, since the door will wear the wreath of black and the shutters will be closed.'

'And the cathedral?' he asked. Was she always so forbidding?

'Follow the promenade to the rue de Lille. Go up it to the cathedral, then turn right.'

'*Merci.*'

'Will you be taking supper?'

Carelessly he tossed the hand with the shabby, wet fedora. 'I doubt it. The meals leave much to be desired. Please do *not* expect a tip!'

The fog didn't want to leave, and with the snow, it made more forlorn what had once been a thriving seaside town of three thousand in winter, some eighty thousand in summer.

All along the promenade behind that great, sweeping curve of sand, the grand hotels and boarding houses were shuttered and, if not empty, occupied only by their owners and/or perhaps an ancient retainer or two. Hardly a soul stirred. Beached sardine and tunny boats huddled as if so leaky they dared not put to sea and feared the highest tides. Flaking paint marred the wet, fine sand with its bits of shells, while here and there on weathered signboards frayed notices cried out the delights of former days. *Palms read and fortunes told. Young ladies and gentlemen need the truth about embarking on their futures before it is too late.*

Swimming lessons were given by a Professor Armand of Paris, who was also assistant instructor at the Lutétia Pool and the Cité des Sports. A busy man. Children under five had to be accompanied by a parent or guardian, those from five to ten and older would come themselves but all were to bring their butterfly floats. Strict obedience was imperative. Dismissals were not uncommon. There were no refunds. Absolutely none.

Ballroom dancing competed with moonlight cruises to Belle-Île and other places. *Boules*, croquet and tennis were by floodlight if one chose. There was gambling. There was even a cinema but the title of its last feature film in the spring of 1940 had been picked away by curious boys determined to undress its leading lady.

Excursions to view the megaliths – the 'druidic' stones – were common and recommended the picnic lunch or moonlight supper. Bathing was not encouraged and most certainly not recommended except for those sites where the ruins entered the sea and the currents allowed of safety.

Marianne and himself had spent their honeymoon here. Her choice of location. He had looked forward to their exploring the megaliths. Four days between cases and hardly time to get to know each other better.

As he plodded up the rue de Lille, St-Cyr vowed not to tell Hermann how disastrous that honeymoon had been. He'd never hear the end of it if he did. Marianne had had a severe allergy to scallops, discovered on their very first night – God did things like that to detectives. Robbed them of simple pleasures. Her family's farm was inland near Ploërmel, well away from the fruits of the sea, so no one could have blamed her for not knowing. 'Yet she tried her best to make our visit enjoyable,' he said. 'The poor thing. Life isn't fair.'

She had been absolutely lovely and of a very quiet, gentle nature, with soft blonde hair and large blue eyes just like that young girl in the dining-room. A woman so lonely in Paris, she had succumbed to the attentions of the Hauptmann Steiner.

Love? Had it really been love? he asked himself and fortunately could not answer since the shop was now in view.

A nothing place – one could see it at a glance. Faded letters – second-hand goods. Teacups and teapots, probably. Bits of glassware and china, old lace, costume jewellery and dolls, yes, dolls. Yet the place had so little of the look of prosperity, he was forced to wonder why the Captain would have taken on such a partner.

When he rang the bell there was silence. When he rapped on the window of the door, he widened a crack that had been there for ages.

At last a figure appeared behind the wreath, a blurred

shadow in black wool with a slim waist, flared hips and a left hand whose fingernails had just been painted.

'Monsieur?'

The sill was warped. The door came unstuck . . . 'Pardon, madame. I am the . . .'

'It's Mademoiselle Paulette, monsieur. My father . . .'

The door began to close. 'A moment, please!' He leaned on it. 'I am the Chief Inspector Jean-Louis St-Cyr of the Sûreté Nationale. A few questions to help us with the investigation. Nothing difficult. I promise.'

'The Sûreté? Was he so important? I . . . I never knew. He . . . he never said. What's he done then, eh? Come, come, Monsieur le Sûreté, let us have the evidence of it!'

'Nothing that we know of but it's interesting his family should think he had been up to something.'

'I *didn't* steal the money!'

'Then you have nothing to worry about. Now, please, a few questions, that's all.' He'd leave the money for a little.

The shop was musty and cramped and not very tidy either. One by one the girl switched on a scattering of table lamps and the light within a tiny carousel which soon began to rotate with the convection and threw its shadows over an array of seated dolls who all seemed to be watching the proceedings intently from their shelf. Exquisite clothing on them. Perfect in every way and far, far better than anything else in the place.

'Mademoiselle Paulette, may I . . . ?' He took out his pipe and tobacco pouch, having opened his overcoat, and she saw that he was about fifty or so years of age and that he wore a light brown suede vest whose buttons looked as if ready to burst. An old vest, and much loved.

'Mademoiselle Paulette, on the day your father was killed – please, I am sorry to have to mention it but . . .'

She trailed a fingertip across the glass countertop through the beads of summer and gave him such a disconcerting look, he was forced to rephrase his question. So, that was good, she thought, and she had put him on the

29

defensive. It was marvellous what one could do to men if one was pretty.

'When did your father leave the shop to find the Captain Kaestner? It's a long way to the clay pits, mademoiselle. One has to ask how he managed to get there.'

She would smile softly at this teddy bear of a detective and she would gaze frankly at him and choose her words most carefully. Yes, that would be best. 'My father left the shop at just before noon, Inspector, so as to catch the *autobus au gazogène* to Lorient. He said he had business to attend to and that I was to mind the shop and see to mother. She's ill. She's been ill for years. She's in a wheel-chair and can't get about. Someone always has to take care of her.'

As you should – he wanted so much to say, to chastise the impish look in those china blue eyes, to wipe the smart-assed cheekiness away. 'Don't play with me, mademoi-selle,' he said severely.

'I'm not. He told me not to pay any attention to Préfet Kerjean, if that one should return.'

'Pardon?'

Was the detective so caught off guard? 'They had an argument, Inspector. Lots of shouting. The Préfet was very angry and threatened my father with all sorts of things including . . .' She paused to search him out and touch the beads again. '. . . including the asking of the tax officials to look into his accounts.'

Ah *merde*, the money . . . ? Had she been ten leagues ahead of him? 'They argued?'

'Violently. Several things were broken. Mother heard them shouting and very nearly came down the stairs in her wheelchair. The brakes are broken.'

'And yourself?'

'I heard them too.'

The girl was no more than twenty years of age. The black woollen dress clung provocatively to every feature even though she was in mourning.

There was a Peter Pan collar of white cotton with a bit of pale blue embroidery. Nothing special. Practice needlework perhaps for a girl who obviously would care little about such skills.

'Exactly what did they argue about?' he asked cautiously.

Again she would gaze frankly at him. Again she would run her fingertip through the beads, touching them one by one as if they were those of a fecundity meter. 'Madame Charbonneau,' she said and shrugged. 'That's all we heard.'

'Madame Charbonneau?'

Was it so puzzling? 'Yes. The big house that overlooks the sea near Kerouriec. She's a friend of the Captain's. Well, he . . . he fancies her but she's married and has a little girl.'

The urge to shake some manners into this . . . this budding *fille de joie* was almost too much to bear for St-Cyr. Sporting herself like this when she should be . . .

'Are you certain that is all you overheard?' he asked harshly.

Her answer must be modest – shy like a schoolgirl whom a priest was instructing. 'She's a friend of the Préfet's too, Inspector. A good friend, if you know what I mean.'

The bitch! 'So, they argued. Where were you? In the shop, outside or upstairs?'

'I was in the cellar at the back. That's where he puts me from time to time. At least, that is where he used to put me but no more, I guess. Is he really dead?'

'Very much so.'

'Good! Then as soon as mother goes I can begin to have a life of my own. Aren't you going to light your pipe?'

Ah *Nom de Dieu, de Dieu*, he thought, this one, like so many Breton girls he had come across over the years in Paris, was heading straight for the streets. 'Yes, I will light my pipe and stay awhile, I think, and you will answer my questions both truthfully and succinctly since my partner is from the Gestapo and no doubt now on his way to find us.'

31

'The Gestapo . . . ?'
'*Yes!*'

The Mégalithe was just that, thought Kohler grimly. A great barn of a place. Stone Age in its outlook and with glass display cases in the upstairs hall, of all places. Stone axes, flint arrowheads, shards of primitive pottery and a couple of skulls whose teeth, due to the coarse diet of rock-ground wild grains and chewing leather, were blackened stumps. Ugh!

'Look, Madame Quévillon, I'm asking you once again. Give us something else. My partner had his honeymoon in Quiberon. His wife's dead. Let him at least have a . . .'

'All rooms overlooking the sea are reserved.'

'But you have no guests?'

'You are our guests.'

Ah *Gott im Himmel* . . . 'But . . . surely we could have a couple of rooms with a glimpse of the sea? What could be nicer?'

She would look at this one from the Gestapo, noting the dissipation of sagging jowls, puffy eyelids and faded blue, unfeeling eyes, the long scar on the cheek, of course, and the graze across the forehead – had it been from a bullet? she wondered and decided that this must be so. A hard man, hard-living. A womanizer and fond of drink and tobacco as well. 'It is the threat of spying, Inspector. The Admiral Doenitz has ordered that all rooms overlooking the sea be closed and placed off limits.'

'Oh for God's sake, the damned U-boats don't even use those waters out there. They approach the base well to the west of the peninsula. There are far too many islands, too many shoals.'

'That does not matter and please do not raise your voice at me. The ordinance is for all hotels and places with rooms for rent and it has been in effect now for the past year and a half.'

Kohler let a sigh escape. 'But you have no guests other than ourselves?'

32

'That, too, does not matter. The Admiral believes perhaps – who is to say with such a one? – that there are those among us who give the British very up-to-date news of the comings and goings of his submarines.'

'By clandestine wireless?'

'Or by fishing boat. Some leave and fail to return.'

'In those crappy little *sardiniers* and under sail?'

'That is what I have just said.'

'To England?'

'Ah, now, that is another matter and of this I would know nothing.'

'Spying . . . But we're on Herr Doenitz's side? Louis . . . ?'

'Your associate is French and a Parisian, is he not?'

'From Belleville, yes, but he loves the sea, madame. At least a few oysters, a bottle of . . .'

She drew herself up. 'I have already discussed the impossibility of such things with him.'

'Then tell me where Doenitz beds down his U-boat crews between operations?'

'The Hotel of the Sunbathing Mermaid. It is on the boulevard Chanard overlooking the beach. Their shutters are all open, of course.'

'And the Captain? Where is he being held?'

'At the jail – yes, even here in such a place as this, in summers we found the need for one. It is on the rue de la Côte-Sauvage, not far from the Port Maria and right between the sardine canneries.'

The stench must really be something. 'If Louis comes back, tell him I went to see the Captain.'

'Of course. And which of you will be paying, monsieur?'

Were all Bretons so practical? 'Neither of us. You're to bill the Admiral and that's an order right from the top, from Gestapo Mueller in Berlin.'

God curse the Nazis. 'You could telephone your friend?'

Was it a crack in her armour at last? 'It might disturb him. He gets miserable when interrupted. I want him

33

happy, madame. He works much better and . . . why, then our stays are so much shorter.'

She knew he would be grinning like a wolf. She listened as he left the hotel by the front door and only then did she hastily cross herself and find in the skulls of others a quiet moment of contemplation. Everyone knew things had not been right in the household of Monsieur le Trocquer. Several would most certainly have wanted that one dead. He had *not* been a nice man. Uncouth, a drinker, a visitor of certain houses whose women should be driven into the streets and sent to prison. Why even at the best of times, he had resented the shop of his dear wife and she, poor thing, was now in such constant pain from a crippling arthritis of the hips, she could no longer walk and must leave her chair only for her bed.

'That daughter . . .' began Madame Quévillon. 'That Paulette . . . What will she do without the father to put her in her place?'

Everyone said the Kapitän Kaestner's money was missing. 6,000,000 of the new francs. A fortune.

'That girl will vanish,' she said on seeing Ginette le Gonidec come up the stairs to find her. A good girl, Ginette, one given to much piety and very dutiful. 'That Paulette will take the money and disappear or someone will think she has it and kill her when she fails to tell them where it is. Then that person or persons will hide that body she loves to sport so much, and those two from Paris can look all they want but they will never find her. Not in a place like this.'

Not along the Côte Sauvage where the cliffs held caves no one could see from above. Not with the tides in the Baie de Quiberon either, or the salt marshes and tidal flats of the Golfe du Morbihan or the presence of bogs no one chooses to enter. Not with the passage graves of such as these, she said, looking at the skulls. Yes, there were so many secret places none of which would be known to those two from Paris or many others for that matter.

*

St-Cyr could hear the mother complaining upstairs as the daughter got her ready to receive him. He thought to leave it and concentrate on the daughter and the money – after all, was it right to disturb the woman so soon after the death of her husband? She wasn't going anywhere, was trapped. He thought to call an apology up the stairs, then thought better of it.

The trap door to the cellar was behind the counter, under a frayed runner the cat must often use at night. The staircase was steep, the timbers low. Boxes, bales, old trunks and suitcases were crammed with things the shop might or might not sell.

Picking his way through the rubbish, he passed the coal bin and noted that it was empty, most probably not entirely due to the rationing but from sheer parsimony. Though coal was exceedingly difficult to obtain, there ought to have been a little driftwood. There had been perfectly suitable pieces on some of the beaches Marianne and he had visited on that last day when her stomach had settled a little and the blotchy attack of hives and the temperature had abated somewhat.

Right at the back there was a small, dark storeroom, quite empty and without an electric bulb in its overhead socket. High on the wall there was a ringbolt and from this dangled a length of rope.

'*Jésus, merde alors!*' he sighed. 'Le Trocquer tied her up, then left her in the dark to punish her.'

There was no stick with which to beat the daughter, only that rope. No gag. No chair or stool of any kind, and the rope not long enough for her to have sat on the floor. 'The bastard,' he said and knew then that the daughter had had every reason to have wanted her father dead.

'Does she have a bicycle?' he wondered. 'Did she go after him?' She could have hitched a ride with the Germans perhaps. They'd be going to and from the base several times a day. Pretty girls were always in demand. She could have taken another *autobus*. He must find the schedule.

'Lorient,' he said, 'and then the road out to the airfield and from there across the moor to that shed and then along the tracks, or perhaps she simply followed the tracks right from the city?'

But had she done so?

Reaching up, he touched the knot in the ringbolt and let his fingers trail down the rope. The things one discovered about others. Death often hid so little.

Then he went upstairs to the shop to find the dolls all looking at him with widened eyes of blue or brown, and long dark lashes or blonde ones. Their cheeks were touched with the pink flush of health, their lips were so beautifully red.

'Fashion dolls,' he murmured to himself. 'Exquisite needlework. Everything perfect. Some with many skirts and billowing evening gowns, others in capes or simply dresses.'

The colours of the fabrics glowed with quality in spite of the severe shortages. Cashmere and lamb's wool, silk, satin and cotton, with lace petticoats beneath and, he thought, everything precisely in order. Everything exactly as it should be, 'because that is the kind of man the Captain is.'

'Inspector . . . ?'

'Ah! Pardon me. I was entranced by the Captain's dolls.'

She would give him a coy look and delicately brush a curl away from her ear. 'So was my father.' She threw the fullness of her china blue eyes at him. 'Entranced – fascinated and so eager, for you see, Inspector, the Captain modelled his dolls after people he knew.'

Merde . . .

She gave a nonchalant shrug. 'Oh for sure he dressed them up. What man wouldn't enjoy such a thing? Some ladies in Paris make the clothes for him. They're very good and quite expensive, isn't that so?'

What was the girl driving at? he wondered. 'Exquisite,' he said warily. She grinned but then grew serious and went over to take down two of the dolls.

'But the faces, Inspector, the figures, they are from memory. His two sisters.' She held the dolls up. 'His mother and his aunts when they were young ladies, his cousins, a lover or two or perhaps those were just girls he desired but could never possess. Yes, that is how it must have been, for he would not otherwise have made them into dolls.'

She turned and, stretching on tiptoes, replaced the dolls and tidied their dresses. Then she stood there looking at him across a clutter of pressed glass and paste. 'Others too, from around here. Yes, of course *they* must not be forgotten. But if you ask me, Inspector, it's a queer enough thing for a man to want to make dolls, let alone to make them of people he knows, especially if they are from around here and can be identified by others.'

Ah *Nom de Dieu*, what had they found themselves in this time?

'The men from the U-boats and the other Germans come here to buy things, Inspector. Sometimes one of the dolls if . . . if they think it will amuse their fellow crew members to undress it on a long voyage or they have children or girlfriends at home.'

The girl went on, this time shamelessly tracing a fingertip over a suggestive vase of pale yellowish-green Depression glass and not looking at him. 'Me he would not use as a model, though I offered the use of myself many times. He said he understood me only too well and that the expression on the doll's face would betray my innermost thoughts and that . . .' She paused to suck in a breath and look frankly at him. '. . . and that he wanted no more trouble with my father since he already had enough of that.'

The missing money – was this what she meant? – or did she go with men from the Captain's crew? he wondered. Had she thought it best to hint at this since he'd find out soon enough? 'Your mother, mademoiselle. We had best not keep her waiting.'

How cautious of him!

Half-way up the stairs, she turned so swiftly at some thought, they all but collided and he felt her sudden breath on his brow and pulled an accidental hand from her hip. 'Please try not to upset her, Inspector. Right now she is beside herself with worry about the future and very depressed.'

Their eyes met. St-Cyr searched hers deeply, asking himself, Why is it you think it so necessary to tell me this?

Then they went on up the rest of the stairs and into the flat.

Kohler was taken aback. The *gendarmerie*, a skinny, two-storeyed affair of soot-encrusted grey granite block, was squeezed between two rusty, corrugated-iron sardine canneries that stank to high heaven of fish boiled in their own oil. The din was unbelievable. Legions of young girls and older women, some wearing the stovepipe coifs or others of starched white lace, worked, sang, gossiped and threw curious glances at him through the wide-open double doors.

He thought to light a cigarette but found he had none and wondered why, if Doenitz valued the hero of U-297 so highly, he had allowed him to be incarcerated in such a place? Surely house-arrest at one of the *Ubootsweiden*, the U-boat 'pastures', the rest centres in the countryside, would have suited better? The Captain could not help but have a constant headache. Whistle blasts would wake the dead and if not the whistles, the wooden clogs of two hundred hurrying females every change of shift.

'Trust the French to put a police station here!' he snorted. They never ceased to amaze him and were always throwing up some new twist of character.

Expecting to find a surly *flic* on duty, he was brought up sharp. Three pairs of U-boat eyes stared at him through the layered haze of tobacco smoke. The oldest of them, a man of no more than thirty but looking fifty, had a thick black

Vandyke and the perpetually haunted, sorrowful expression of death perceived.

The youngest, a boy of seventeen, had the ever-moving, furtive gaze of one who has stood at death's door and been suddenly reprieved but for how long?

They had been playing a favourite board game, *Mensch ärgere Dich nicht* – Man, don't 'shoot' yourself. All wore, at rakish angles, the dark blue forage cap with submariner's badge and the faded blue coveralls that rumour said had been modelled after the British Army's battledress for its ease of getting about, especially when firing torpedoes or their 88-millimetre deck gun.

'Kohler to see the prisoner.'

The one with the beard took the stem of a cold pipe from between his teeth and got slowly to his feet. 'Herr Kohler, ah yes. We've been expecting you. Obersteuermann Otto Baumann at your service.'

The accent was definitely of Lower Saxony and Bremerhaven most probably. Chief Helmsman of U-297 and no doubt one of the Captain's Watch Officers. As if to emphasize this to all and sundry, even though it wasn't dress-up time, the Ritterkreuz, the Knight's Cross, hung on the left breast pocket below the Atlantic U-boat badge. There were also two of the black-and-white wound badges and the underwater escape badge, this last signifying a real test of luck and skill and just plain guts.

'Obersteuermann . . .'

'Otto, *please*, Herr Kohler. Rank means certain things, yes, of course, but in the Freikorps Doenitz we prefer not to stand on ceremony.'

The U-boat Service . . . 'Good. All I want is a few words with the Captain just to introduce myself and to make it clear my partner and I are on his side.'

'We're not guarding him,' offered the boy tremulously. 'We're looking after him.'

'Then why isn't he playing?'

'Because he's busy,' said Baumann unwaveringly. 'Vati doesn't want to see anybody right now.'

'Oh, come on now. How else can we begin to . . .'

'Establish his innocence?' asked Baumann.

'Yes.'

The Chief Helmsman pocketed a ring of keys that had lain on the table and picked up what was obviously the Captain's Luger. 'It's loaded, I think,' he said non-committally. 'It always seems to save argument. You tell him, Martin. Martin, here, is our Second Engineer, Herr Kohler. You wouldn't know it to look at him but he can make our electric motors whisper like a woman in heat and whose whispers, my friend, have saved our balls many times.'

The one with the clean-shaven, prominent jaw, wide lips, high, bony forehead and big hands still could not find the will to smile. 'Herr Kohler, the Captain isn't to be interviewed without Special Officer U-boats Kernével being present.'

Verdammt . . . 'Do you mean to tell me we can't talk to Kaestner *without* Freisen being present?'

Baumann hefted the Luger. 'Martin, be so kind as to ring up Base Kernével and ask the Kapitän Freisen to drop everything so that he can join us. That'll solve Herr Kohler's problem and we can get back to our game.'

'But it's more than fifty kilometres . . . ?'

'Vati has no legal counsel, Herr Kohler,' offered the Second Engineer. 'In the absence of one we, who owe our Dollmaker so much, are insisting all interviews be in the presence of our Special Officer.'

Shit! They had kicked the French *flics* out. Either the crew were making a circus of it or they were trying to save the Captain from himself. 'Then while you're at it, ring up the Admiral and tell him my partner and I are off the case as of right now, eh? Then call le Trocquer's shop and ask the Chief Inspector St-Cyr to pick up two tickets for the evening train to Paris.'

'Don't be difficult,' sighed Baumann. 'Humour us. Vati's special.'

'Piss off! You're keeping us from talking freely to the one who needs us most. He could have done it, my fines. We've evidence to suggest he damned well did!'

It was the Second Engineer who said levelly, 'Then that is ample reason why the Kapitän zur See Freisen must be present. Please, it is but an hour or two, yes? It is not for nothing that we call our C.-in-C. Base Kernével the Bullet. He'll come, and when he does, you can talk to Dollmaker all you want.'

'He did it, didn't he?' swore Kohler exasperatedly. 'You bunch think the Captain slammed that shopkeeper so you want to give him every bit of help you can.'

Baumann shrugged, the boy wet his lips and nervously brushed the faded blond hair from his brow. The Second Engineer merely picked up the dice and shook them.

St-Cyr sat uncomfortably in the straight-backed, uncushioned chair the daughter had fetched from the tiny kitchen. No more funereal a bedroom could be imagined. Madame le Trocquer wore black lace over a black robe and nightdress. Exquisite black lace flowed from her withered, white-dusted, blue-eyed face like an ancient spider's tent to cover the ample double bed. Black pillows and cushions propped her up. She even wore a square of black lace over her head whose iron-grey and yellowish hair was like wire and braided into two tight pigtails that were tied with black ribbon. The hair was short, so the pigtails stuck out a little.

Having enjoyed her illness, she was now to enjoy her grief. A widow at what? he asked and put her age at sixty and a good ten years older than her husband.

He would try again. 'The woman at the big house near Kerouriec, madame? Your husband and the Préfet argued. Her name was . . .'

'Mentioned? Is that what you told him, Paulette?'

Dutifully the daughter stood with downcast eyes like a

handmaiden across the bed from him. 'Yes, *maman*,' came the whisper.

'You little fool! Préfet Kerjean and your father were the best of friends. The woman was nothing to them. *Nothing*, so why should they have argued about her?'

Livid, Madame le Trocquer hunched her thin, bony shoulders. 'It's cold,' she said spitefully. 'There never was enough heat. That's why I *have* the arthritis. There'll be heat enough now, Paulette.'

'Yes, *maman*.'

St-Cyr heaved a desperate sigh. 'Madame, there was an argument. So violent was it, several items in the shop were broken. Your daughter has said she overheard Madame Charbonneau's name.'

'That's all I heard.'

'Yes, of course. It's enough for me to demand the truth.'

'The house is by the sea and some three kilometres from the main road, Inspector. The bus does not always go to Kerouriec. The woman is from Paris. The husband was a famous pianist, though there is never much work for such as those. You're from Paris. How is it, please, that you do not know of him?'

Charbonneau . . . The Rachmaninoff and the Schubert. The Palais de Chaillot in mid-April 1940 with Marianne at his side, a rare evening out. She had worn the azure blue silk dress with matching high heels. She had looked even younger. 'I do remember, madame. Yvon Charbonneau . . . the critics were most unkind to savage him. He was marvellous.'

'Humph! Marvellous or not, he and that new wife and child of his elected to come here for the Duration to that house his Great Aunt Danielle foolishly left him some time ago. Such legacies only produce indolence. Now he no longer plays the piano but searches the megaliths for clues to the past while the wife, she . . .'

'She *what*?' he asked.

Ah! the detective so wanted to hear scandal he was leaning forward in his chair and Paulette was nervously touching the base of her beautiful milk-white throat and looking pale. 'People say she is the Captain's mistress, Inspector. Others say she is the Préfet's and since my husband was sometimes asked to deliver messages for either of those two, well . . .' She sucked in on her cheeks. 'One cannot say what one will find.'

Was the woman naked, madame? Was she fornicating on the beach with the Captain perhaps, or the Préfet? 'There was a doll?' he hazarded.

'Not one from the shop. Paulette would have seen that it was missing. None are.'

'But did you hear either of them mention this doll?'

The woman shrugged and kept her shoulders up tightly like the folded wings of a vulture. 'I heard nothing, Inspector. *Nothing*! These old walls may not be much but they are soundproof, thanks be to God!' She crossed herself.

'As is the room in the cellar?' he asked.

Her eyes narrowed with suspicion. 'What room?'

Must they do this to her? wondered Paulette. 'He knows, *maman*. The Inspector will have visited my little cubicle when I was upstairs here with you.'

'Then perhaps he will understand that young girls who disobey their fathers need to be taught a lesson and that even though it can tempt a man to baseness, beauty means nothing and soon fades.'

Ah *merde* . . . Had the father abused the daughter or was it that the woman only suspected this?

'Some money is missing, madame. A lot of money. Is there anything you can . . .'

'Tell you about it? Only that it was a piece of foolishness. The Captain Kaestner may be good at U-boats but he's an imbecile at business. Reviving his grandfather's dollmaking has become an obsession. If you ask me, he uses it to take his mind off things.'

It was the daughter who hesitantly confessed, 'Everyone knows their chances of survival are less than two in ten

43

now. U-297 has been through a lot, Inspector, and very nearly didn't make it home the last time.'

The woman gave the daughter a scathing look. One could hear her shouting, You little fool! Why not tell him everything then? That those men are using you!

The girl dropped her hands to her sides in defeat at that look and stood with eyes downcast waiting for the rebuke.

It was not long in coming. 'Well, tell him then, since you're so proud of it. A boy of seventeen, Inspector, a *first* time for that one, I believe.'

Jésus, merde alors, did they hate each other so much? Fists were clenched, a foot was stamped. Tears rushed into the girl's eyes. 'I didn't do *anything* with him! He . . . he was dancing with Renée when . . . when suddenly the drummer hit the cymbals and . . . and Erich went all to pieces and began shrieking for his mother.'

The girl wiped her eyes with her fingertips, then used the back of a hand for her nose. 'Some of the others held Erich and pulled his pants down. Their . . . their Chief Engineer gave him a needle to calm him. He . . . he wasn't allowed to go home on leave this time.'

'He still pisses himself,' seethed the woman acidly. 'He says he's not going back to sea but everyone knows he'll have to, otherwise they will shoot him.'

And those are the kind of friends your daughter seeks, thought St-Cyr. War made instant friends and lovers, often turning young girls and housewives wayward because there was little future for them and the Occupier had everything, as well as being handsome and exciting and from faraway places.

'The Captain saved them by taking the boat well below its maximum diving depth,' said the girl softly and not looking at him. 'They got stuck in the bottom muds and the RAF rained depth charges all around them for more than an hour.'

'Where?'

It was such a gently given question. Was the detective so

sensitive a man? 'Off Lorient, on their final approach after being nearly two and a half months at sea. The men now call the Bay of Biscay the RAF's playground. U-297 was already very badly damaged. They . . . they didn't think they could dare to go so deep but the Captain, he . . . he insisted it was their only chance.'

A man of steel then. A Dollmaker.

'The money, madame. The 6,000,000 francs.'

Must they come back to that? 'It was to be used in large part to purchase and improve one of the faience works. My husband kept it in one of the cardboard shipping boxes they use for the dolls. He refused to let the Crédit Municipal keep it. Taxes . . . he was worried about their having to pay taxes on it.'

'And the Préfet threatened to bring the tax collectors.'

'If *she* says so,' the woman indicated the daughter. 'For myself, I heard nothing, as I have said.'

'Yes, but what do you think became of the money?'

Fiercely she darted a look at him. 'How should I know? I can never leave my bed or chair. *Never!* Perhaps someone broke into the shop and stole it, perhaps my husband took it to Quimper on one of his so-called "business" trips and lost it there. Who's to say?'

'Quimper?'

'Yes. That is where the dolls are made. The faience works. Did you not listen to me? They are then sent to Paris to be clothed.'

'But . . . but I thought the Captain made them?'

'Only the first ones, the prototypes. He makes the head and then the mould, isn't that so? And from the mould, fifty or so copies are made and fired. One of the faience works in Quimper allows the use of a kiln. The heads are then painted, given hair and eyes and attached to their bodies before being shipped to Paris for completion. In time, the Captain hoped it could all be done here in Brittany but, though we are good at making lace, we apparently lack the necessary imagination for fancy clothes.'

Whores was what she meant, and loose women.

St-Cyr glanced over his notes. Visits to Quimper and Paris would most probably be necessary but would there be time, and would they turn up any answers?

'The child of Madame Charbonneau . . .' he began.

'It's not hers, it's the pianist's. A girl of ten. Her mother died when she was seven and a half.'

'In the blitzkrieg?'

Was it so terrible? 'Yes. A Messerschmitt took her.'

Ah *Nom de Dieu*, the poor thing. 'Would the child have a doll perhaps?'

Did the Inspector think she was such a fool as not to realize which doll he meant? 'All girls of such an age have dolls they used to play with when little.'

'Yes, of course. How stupid of me. Did the child and her stepmother ever visit the shop?'

'And leave behind a doll that was not like one of the Captain's? If they did, I heard nothing of it, Inspector. She was of money but has fallen on hard times, though still for such a one to visit our shop . . . Ah, that one would not do so even if reduced to her last centime.'

For a woman who was bedridden, Madame le Trocquer was exceedingly well informed. The town gossip perhaps or certainly included among them.

Paulette looked as if wanting to say something about Madame Charbonneau and the child but at a glance from the mother, held her tongue.

'Inspector, I do not know why my poor husband was killed nor who would do such a horrible thing. He was a good man, the soul of consideration. I never wanted for anything, did I, Paulette?'

The girl stood like a pillar of salt with head bowed.

'Paulette?' said the mother sharply. 'Please answer me.'

They broke down then and hugged each other with a show of wet kisses, much weeping and protestations of loss and everlasting love. Heaving an impatient sigh, St-Cyr

46

muttered, 'I will show myself out and will put the lock on, have no fear.'

The girl's bedroom door was tightly closed and as he passed it, he thought to duck in for a little look. Clearly she knew far more than she was letting on and just as clearly things in the household had been far from what they should have been.

The door was locked. Alarmed, he threw a look back along the all but barren corridor, then gave it up and went down into the shop. They would have to get a magistrate's order to search the place. Days . . . it could take weeks!

A last glance about revealed the row of dolls all looking at him with the widened eyes of innocence betrayed.

Reaching up, he took down one of them and, shutting his eyes to better concentrate, ran a fingertip delicately over a cheek.

'The bisque is very fleshlike, very lifelike,' he muttered to himself. 'Hard and yet soft feeling, finely porous like skin and cool, and that is why the Captain sought only the finest kaolin.'

Taking out the shards he had picked up from the railway bed, he was saddened to find them too small to compare, or the one too smeared with blood.

It wasn't hard to find the Hotel of the Sunbathing Mermaid who gave her favours to lonely sailors and tourists who might well lose their wallets. Her pale blue tail fin, voluptuous body, bright blue eyes and extra long lashes, sparkles and ravishingly long blonde hair added that little touch of whimsy to the stark façade of a fifty-room hotel that had been built in 1890 out of granite and given Gothic spires to make it interesting.

Like Madame Quévillon had said, all the shutters were open.

Kohler grinned appreciatively. The mermaid was at least five metres tall and had, before the war, been neon-lighted so as to make her visible from well out to sea. 'I like it,

47

Louis. Yes, I can see why the Freikorps Doenitz chose the place.'

'A few oysters, a bottle of the Muscadet, some lobster perhaps and the fillet of sole or turbot.'

'Stop whining like a collaborator! Hey, I'll see what I can do.'

The plate was heaped with sauerkraut around whose soggy, steaming nest a curve of coarse, thick, boiled sausage huddled.

Boiled potatoes lay pathetically to one side, a sort of hors-d'oeuvre perhaps. No one else was in the mess, the former dining-room. They were to be fed a submariner's standard fare after thirty days at sea. There was even black bread with a suspiciously thick crust of mould.

Kohler took up his knife and fork then reached decisively for the mustard.

'Your stomach, idiot!' shot St-Cyr testily. '*Don't* scorch it and bellyache to me.'

'I'll see if there's any tomato sauce.'

Sacré nom de nom!

'So, Louis, what's with the stovepipe coifs?'

It was too good an opportunity to miss. Besides, Hermann would file the information away. His curiosity about the French was like that of a man in a flea market. Everything of interest was a bargain to him.

'The stovepipes, yes,' began St-Cyr. 'The Bretons are Celtic but due to the absence of phosphates in the soil, most are not so tall – you will have noticed.'

He hacked off a chunk of sausage and examined it suspiciously. One never knew these days. Cat, rat, fishmeal, sawdust – edible seaweeds perhaps . . .

'Eat it, *Dummkopf!*'

'The Bretons, the Armoricans, Hermann, they wanted their women taller so they bound their heads with wire as the ancient Chinese did the feet of their princesses. When France took the region over, of course the practice was stopped, but . . .'

'But the stovepipes remain,' breathed Kohler. 'I think, I've got it, Louis. The influence of Paris and of refinement.'

'Yes, you've got it.'

'Then it's just like the Captain must have said. The dolls had to be dressed in Paris because only there would they know how to do things properly.'

The sauerkraut was salty. Beer was called for but it was deliberately thin and flat, and by the time Kohler had managed it, his sausage was cold.

They ate in silence. Not another soul ventured into the darkly panelled dining-room. Though there must be other U-boat crews on rest and recupe, there wasn't a sound but that of the wind which had decided to bring more rain.

'We're being shut out, Louis.'

'Ostracized is the word you want.'

'No matter. U-297's crew are convinced the Captain did it and *that*, my fine Sûreté, is *not* something they conveyed to the Admiral.'

'What of Freisen? Wouldn't he have informed the Admiral of this?'

'We'll find out later. He'll be there at 1530 hours.'

The potatoes were without butter, margarine or even a sprinkling of parsley but when salt and ersatz pepper were liberally added, a tiny particle of taste crept forward to remind one of the past. Poor Marianne had not been able to keep even potatoes down. Four days of agony and then . . . why then Paris and life with a man who had seldom been home for more than a few days at most and had neglected to think his absence might have been troubling. Young and healthy women do need sex. When denied it, they crave it and who can blame them if they are tempted by another?

'We have also the distinct possibility of a marriage of convenience, Hermann. A Madame Charbonneau is married to a Parisian concert pianist who has a ten-year-old daughter whose mother was machine-gunned to death during the blitzkrieg.'

Marriages of convenience these days were so often done

to hide one's identity or past. *Verdammt!* 'Does the kid still have nightmares?'

It was spoken like a father. 'Probably. Was the doll hers, Hermann? That is what I want to know since the Admiral insists the bisque was not the Captain's.'

St-Cyr dragged out his pipe and tobacco pouch only to gaze ruefully at the few remaining shreds. Hermann mopped up the last of the juice with a bit of bread from the inside of the loaf. Like many who had once been in the front lines of that other war under intense bombardment, he ate stolidly.

He was really a very uncomplicated person, this former detective from Munich and Berlin, a man who had seen so much of death, his stomach had finally rebelled. A man who had two sons at Stalingrad . . . Ah *merde*, the telex Boemelburg gave me, thought St-Cyr guiltily. The boys were missing in action and presumed dead, and Boemelburg, being the Chief, had left the dirty work to Hermann's partner who was a coward, yes, when it came to such things.

'The Captain must have told Freisen the fragments weren't from one of his dolls,' said Kohler. 'Bullet then passed it on to the Admiral.'

Did they all have nicknames? 'Why don't they simply let U-297 put to sea without the Dollmaker?'

Kohler found his *mégot* tin and made the supreme sacrifice of sliding it across the table. 'Because, my fine friend, if you ask me, the men won't sail without him. They must have had such a bad time on their last cruise, the Admiral is willing to humour them by asking for a couple of detectives to prove his boy is innocent.'

The tin contained Hermann's collection of cigarette butts, most saved, some picked up from God knows where. Several had lipstick on them, that last case? wondered St-Cyr. A cache of butts in a Louis XVI-style concrete urn that would hold geraniums in season. The garden of the Palais Royal, a missing eighteen-year-old girl and a bank robbery . . .

He heaved a sigh. 'More than two years of constant stress, never knowing if the next moment would be their last. Even Paulette le Trocquer was sympathetic to their plight and knew the odds.'

'Obersteuermann Baumann wears the look of death, Louis. He knows he's going to die no matter what, so it's all to the good if the Captain's case keeps them ashore for a little longer.'

Packing his pipe, St-Cyr lit up, coughed suddenly at the hot fire, and, wincing, tried to settle down. 'Please clear the plates,' he choked, and when this was done, laid out his little bits and pieces: the fragments of bisque, the clots of coarse black wool, one packet of American cigarettes, a crumpled white handkerchief and lastly, wrapped in paper, a small and much kneaded wad of kaolin no doubt taken from the Captain's satchel.

Reluctantly he withheld the cigarettes, forcing Hermann to clumsily try to roll one from the contents of his tin. *Mon Dieu*, it was cruel. The Bavarian's fingers, which could defuse even the most clever of tripwires or fuses, could not seem to control the cigarette paper or its tobacco. 'Here, let me. To think that you, a former artilleryman and bomb disposal expert, never learned the art even in that French prisoner-of-war camp you managed to find refuge in.'

Deftly St-Cyr rolled the cigarette, licked the paper, smoothed the thing out, pinched off both ends, tapped them and returned the recovered tobacco to the tin.

'We must offer a Lucky Strike to Freisen and the Captain,' he said by way of apology. 'It may be our only hope of driving a wedge between them.'

Kohler lit up and blew smoke towards the ceiling then indicated the handkerchief. 'Things the Bullet wasn't told, eh? A cosy ride in the hay and the woman forgetting a little something?'

The shed and the bicycle tracks . . . 'Then why was the handkerchief crumpled so tightly unless she wanted only to resist but found she dared not do so.'

'Did that belong to the piano player's wife?'

'And these?' asked St-Cyr, plucking at the tufts of wool. 'Is it that this Madame Charbonneau, who it is rumoured is both mistress of the Préfet and the Captain, witnessed the murder or committed it?'

'Or were the shopkeeper's wife and daughter simply lying to you about her being the mistress of anyone?'

'The pianist spends all his time searching the megaliths for clues to the past. They would not have lied about that. It's far too easy to check.'

'Driven to it, is he, by the wife's fooling around?' shot Kohler.

'Perhaps.'

'Then he'd be out and about a good deal and that, my fine Sûreté, is what those two wanted you to think. Besides, clots of wool like that could have come from almost any female here, or hadn't you noticed? The men even have black overcoats.'

'But would a man have retreated? Would he have pushed himself away on his seat, or dropped the doll and then, yes then, returned to step on the victim's glasses quite by accident?'

'We'll interview the Captain first, then borrow a set of wheels and pay the pianist and his wife a little visit.'

3

Kaestner's look was piercing. It was as if the Dollmaker could not stop himself. Sharp grey-green eyes sought the absolute truth with a frankness that was disturbing.

A man of thirty-two, of medium height, he was slight, not unhandsome, though the face was narrow, the chin pointed, the lips thin and often tightly parted showing the crowns of clenched teeth, the ears prominent.

The thick brown hair had been cut short, boyishly parted on the left and given but the whisper of a hasty brush. When he spoke, he did so with clarity and pointedness. More intent on observing, he kept his own counsel with good reason.

Préfet Kerjean had seen fit to be present.

On the other hand, the Kapitän zur See Freisen, the C.-in-C. U-boats Kernével, would always be the man in the background. Ever watchful of the Captain, he was suspicious of everyone, under orders from above and intense in his own way. A man of thirty-four perhaps, and with a short-cropped sandy beard, moustache, high forehead, prominent brows, blue eyes, large blunt nose and crinkly hair that was parted on the left and closely trimmed.

Somewhat taller than the Captain, the Bullet sat more stiffly, rocking back in his chair when the notion took him. Was he not a little impatient? wondered St-Cyr. Did he really mind so much the stench of sardines, sewage, iodine and lifeless air? If so, why hadn't he insisted on moving the prisoner elsewhere?

Neither of the captains were in uniform except for their

white *Schirmmützes*, their caps, which sat formally to one side of each of them on the table. Their dark blue turtle-neck sweaters, heavy dark blue corduroy trousers and boots were the essence of informality and comfort.

One of the *Blitzmädels* from Base Kernével sat primly at the opposite end of the table from the Préfet with a pad and pencil in her lap and still wrinkling her nose distastefully. Blonde, curly, wavy hair, serious blue eyes, soft pink cheeks, lovely red lips, a trim, neat twenty-two-year-old in a snappy blue Kriegsmarine uniform. A telegraphist.

Everything was to be taken down in shorthand to be later transcribed and telexed to the Admiral at the U-boat Command Centre in Paris.

The cell was cramped. There was barely room to stretch one's legs. The racket from the canneries intruded but would just have to be ignored. Kohler longed for a cigarette and coffee, even the ersatz garbage of ground, roasted acorns, barley and chicory, but none had been offered and no one was suggesting it. The generalities over, they'd now get down to business with the decisiveness of battle.

The Préfet launched into the coroner's preliminary report.

'Time of death approximately 4 p.m. the old time, 1700 hours Berlin Time on the afternoon of Friday, the 1st of January. The force of the blow strongly suggests the assailant was a man in his prime. Both hands grasped the switch-bar and this is evident from the smearing of soot and grease. Gloves were, however, used.'

He paused to look at each of them in turn, nodding finally at the *Blitzmädel* to signify he would continue. 'These gloves were of black leather, probably of light weight, that is to say, not insulated with a thick cotton liner.'

'A moment, Préfet,' interjected St-Cyr. 'How is it that the presence of such gloves was determined?'

'Tiny shreds of leather were torn from the gloves by rasps of metal on the bar. These shreds were examined under the

54

microscope, at a magnification of one hundred. I myself have witnessed them.'

It was Freisen who, rocking back in his chair, told him to continue. No diplomat when it came to the French, the C.-in-C. U-boats Kernével had allowed his impatience to show. He'd tolerate Kerjean's presence only for so long.

Ignoring him, the Préfet laid the report on the table and decisively pressed it flat. 'They were dress gloves similar to, if not the same as those worn by officers of the Freikorps Doenitz when ashore and in uniform at this time of year.'

Ah *merde*, thought St-Cyr, how could they possibly tell from so little?

'I wasn't wearing uniform,' said the Dollmaker. 'I was in my spare coveralls and sheepskin jacket. The watchman will confirm this. We shared a cigarette and a few words about the weather.'

'I have already asked him,' said Kerjean levelly. 'He is not certain, Captain, if you wore gloves but thinks . . .' The Préfet lifted a cautionary finger. '. . . that perhaps the gloves were in the pockets of your jacket.'

'Then he is mistaken. I would not gather kaolin while wearing them, since I have to use them on parade, yes? Nor would I wear them afterwards without first washing my hands.'

Kerjean sat back to survey him. The girl's pencil was poised. She hardly breathed. She was really very pretty but professionally intense like so many Germans. Did she have an interest in the Captain? he wondered and thought it likely. 'But . . . but you did wash your hands? You apologized for the state of them? You grinned, Captain, and shrugged it all off, and Monsieur le Pennec, who speaks about as good French as you do yourself, poured water from his kettle over them and offered the use of his towel with apologies of his own, is that not so?' The Préfet looked at Louis and shrugged open-handedly. 'The towel, my friends, was filthy but what can one say since it was the only one the watchman had?'

Verdammt! thought Kohler. This thing . . .

Freisen turned to the Captain to confer earnestly and quietly. It was Kaestner who said, 'I did not have my gloves with me. They were in my bag which was on the bed in my room at the hotel here.'

'The gloves can then be examined,' grunted the Préfet as if it really did not matter.

Freisen leapt in. 'They'll be torn. They're not new. This is crazy, Préfet. Crazy! You're mad.'

'Mad or not, I aim to continue.'

Ah *Nom de Dieu*, thought St-Cyr, does Freisen also think the Captain guilty?

The Captain watched the Préfet with that same decisively piercing look as if through the periscope and Kerjean the enemy tanker.

'The conclusion?' asked Kohler.

Were the Bavarian's eyes always so lifeless? 'Ah yes, Inspector. The coroner concludes that as Monsieur le Trocquer stood near the inner rail of the spur, he was approached from behind and to his right. You yourselves found evidence of the Captain's having left the railway for the nearby moor some distance towards the pits.'

Shit, thought Kohler, he means to pin it on the Doll-maker even if the Captain didn't do it!

The Préfet continued. 'The shopkeeper was challenged. He did not turn. He removed his glasses, isn't that so, Chief Inspector St-Cyr?'

Louis nodded curtly. The girl was ready to pounce again on every word. Her whole being was focused on the end of her pencil.

Kohler thought her perfect. Naked, she'd be absolutely delightful but probably kept it all locked up for some lucky guy.

'The victim whipped off his glasses,' said Kerjean decisively. 'No doubt he was planning to pocket them for safety's sake but . . .'

Again the girl waited. When the pause grew, she glanced up, giving the Préfet the fullness of her eyes.

He met her gaze with an emptiness of his own that said so much about where he really stood with the Occupier. 'But the blow came, the glasses flew out of his hand. He collapsed and was carried forward and down by the force, thus striking his forehead on the outer rail, something that would most certainly have killed him had the other not done so.'

Louis took out the cigarettes and offered the Captain one but if he knew of the package and the shed, the Dollmaker was far too clever to let on.

Freisen, apparently, didn't even notice they were American cigarettes nor did the girl who refused with a shake of her pretty head and said a quiet, 'Not when I am on duty.'

'There is one other matter,' said Kerjean, saving the cigarette for later but noting its origin. 'The briefcase he was carrying is missing.'

'What briefcase,' demanded Kaestner swiftly. A rise at last? wondered Kohler.

There was a sigh from the Préfet. 'That I think you know only too well. Of old brown leather and shabby, isn't that so? Nothing special because not only had he been a man of little means all his life, Monsieur le Trocquer had not cared much about his appearance.'

'A moment, Préfet. How is it that this matter of the briefcase came to light?' asked St-Cyr.

It would not do to smile as the mackerel was pulled from the basket of sole to lie stinking on the cutting table. 'The wife has said that before he left to catch the bus, her husband came upstairs to get the case. He was in a hurry and upset but did not say what was the matter or why he needed it.'

'But you and the victim had only just had a violent argument?'

'An argument? Ah no. A discussion perhaps. Yes, that's the way it was. The money was missing, isn't that correct? Monsieur le Trocquer was not forthcoming. I urged him to speak up so as to leave no suspicion in anyone's mind.'

'But the daughter has told me several things were broken?'

'The daughter? Ah, a few bits of glassware. Monsieur le Trocquer got in a huff and threw out a hand. It was nothing.'

But now you are afraid, thought St-Cyr, glancing at the Dollmaker and the Bullet. 'The value, please?'

Nom de Jésus-Christ, what did it mean, this attack? 'A few francs.'

'And the reason for his "getting in a huff", Préfet?'

Jean-Louis was serious. 'This I have already mentioned, Chief Inspector. The money, yes? Is time of so little value to you?'

'Time is to murder what salt is to an open wound. One or both of you cried out the name of a Madame Charbonneau. This was heard by the daughter and the mother also, I believe, though that one steadfastly denies it.'

Exasperated, Kerjean blew out his cheeks and tossed the hand of inconsequence. 'And the former, Jean-Louis? That little slut? Paulette le Trocquer would lie for the sheer pleasure of seeing if she could get you to believe her!'

'What do you think was in the briefcase?' asked Kohler.

Startled by this new direction of attack, the Préfet's eyes narrowed swiftly. 'The money? Is this what you two think?'

'I'm asking.'

'Then I do not know, Inspector. Since the Captain's money has been missing for some time.'

'How long, please?' asked St-Cyr.

Would the two of them keep it up? wondered the Dollmaker. So far so good.

'I . . . I can't be sure, but at least eight weeks. Its absence was discovered by Monsieur le Trocquer just before U-297 returned to the Keroman bunkers on the 5th November. Privately he accused his daughter of the theft. The girl still denies it and did so then.'

It would be best to shift the direction of attack. 'Was the submarine badly damaged, Préfet?' asked Louis.

Again there was that swift, dark look from Kerjean. 'Why not ask the Captain? Let him tell you.'

'Perhaps I will,' said St-Cyr, moving the cigarette package until it was directly in front of him. 'I want first to settle one thing, Préfet. Since you and Monsieur le Trocquer argued about Madame Charbonneau what, please, is your relationship with her?'

Me, a married man with six children, is that it, eh? wondered Kerjean. It was. Ah, Jean-Louis, how could you do this to me? 'That is a private matter, Chief Inspector. I am not on trial here, nor am I under suspicion, or am I because of the word of a girl who wants only to escape the boredom of her little life?'

Why must he be so difficult? wondered St-Cyr, greatly troubled by him and saddened, too, at the thought that perhaps the Préfet was trying to protect someone or had done the killing himself. 'It would help if you told us.'

Ah damn that girl Paulette. 'Madame Charbonneau is a friend, that is all. I have many friends in the Morbihan. I make it my business to know the people with whom I may one day have to deal on matters of the law.'

It had been spoken like a good cop, yes, of course, but . . . 'And the husband of this woman, Préfet,' asked St-Cyr, 'is he a friend also?'

Prepare yourself then, Louis. Prepare yourself my fine little buzzard from Paris. 'Both Sous-Préfet le Troadec and myself have many times returned him to her, Chief Inspector, and *that* is the extent and the beginning of my friendship with them. They are lost, yes? Like so many who ran from the invasion of 1940, they cannot find the will or courage to return to Paris. Like all great artists, Monsieur Charbonneau seeks in the things around him the inspiration for his work and the reason for his being. He "hears" a symphony he wishes to write. Who am I, a simple policeman, to question such as him? But when the weather is very bad and I find him out in it digging for bits of pottery and old bones or flint axes among the megaliths, I take him home to his wife and daughter.'

'You did it,' said Kaestner flatly. 'You killed that shop-keeper.'

'I did not. I had no reason to but it's interesting you should think to try and put the blame on me. You who are on such familiar terms with her, Captain. You who do not go home on leave to see your family but spend all your free time making dolls or visiting the wife of another.'

Kaestner sprang. So swiftly did he lunge at him, Kerjean had only time to grip him by the wrists as the Captain's hands closed fiercely about his throat.

The table went over. The girl shrieked, Kohler rammed the two of them, sending them into the wall. '*Enough!*' he shouted.

Choking, plum-red in the face and clutching himself by the throat, the Préfet sat on the floor slumped against the wall. '*Bâtard!*' he raged. 'You've been fucking that poor woman against her will. Admit it! Fucking her, you bastard! Forcing her! Le Trocquer found out and tried to blackmail you into forgetting about the money or giving him more time to find it.'

Merde, thought St-Cyr, what have we now? Kaestner backed away as if struck. Freisen said, 'Johann, is this true?'

The girl tried to find her pencil and pad.

'A glass of *marc*, I think,' breathed Kohler, 'and some coffee. Louis, ask the Obersteuermann to see that we get it and are not disturbed otherwise. No one is leaving.'

'I . . . I must.' Embarrassed, the girl looked so helpless.

Kohler gave her a nod. 'Take a few minutes. Here, have one of these. You're due it.'

Fortunately no one had stepped on the cigarette package and when she timidly took one, her big blue eyes glanced uncertainly at him before flicking warily to the Captain.

You sweet thing, thought Kohler. That's just what I figured you would do.

Freisen had noticed her reaction too and so had the Préfet.

Louis was pleased but chose to hide this by brushing himself down and finding his chair. And when the coffee and the brandy were brought in steaming mugs, he asked Baumann for enough tobacco to fill his cherished pipe. 'It helps me think, and that is something we all must do.'

At a nod from his Vati, the Obersteuermann yielded up his tobacco pouch and muttered in German, 'It is okay, yes? I have another somewhere.'

St-Cyr wondered if they were going to have to take on all fifty-two members of the crew.

French toilets were always filthy but the boys from U-297 had made this one spotless, which only proved – yes it did, thought Elizabeth Krüger – that the French were inferior.

Yet I cannot stop myself from shaking, she said and bit a knuckle.

It had been clever of the Captain to have done that – a desperate move, yes, of course. But he was like that. He took chances. He assessed things coldly, rapidly, thoroughly, then, having weighed up each situation, struck when and where least expected.

The Préfet, fool that he was, had blurted out his feelings for this Madame Charbonneau who spoke German so perfectly, the Captain liked to visit her. A touch of home.

The Préfet had as much as confessed to the murder. Now everyone would think he had done it. Yes, everyone. So, good. Yes, good.

But me? she asked, nervously drawing on the cigarette and wishing that the Captain would see how she felt about him. 'I, Fräulein Elizabeth Krüger, Special Assistant to the Kapitän zur See Freisen, am afraid.'

Toilets did that to one sometimes, made them confess things best left unsaid. Had he really been fucking the Frenchwoman against her will or with it? Did it matter so much to herself? It could not last in any case. No, it couldn't.

The dossiers of the two detectives had not been good. Herr Kohler, in spite of having two sons missing in action at Stalingrad and presumed dead, had a reputation for going against authority. He was no Gestapo, no Nazi though a member of both by force of circumstance.

And his friend, his partner? she wondered. That one was even more so a hunter of the truth. A patriot even though the Resistance still had him on their list and had killed his wife and little son.

He had a new girlfriend in Paris, a chanteuse, a Gabrielle Arcuri whom he had met on a case at the time of his wife's death, which only showed that war speeded such things up greatly and there still might be hope for herself.

But did St-Cyr feel guilty about it? Could this be used against him? His wife had been unfaithful, a German, a Hauptmann. Most Frenchmen would hate their women for such a thing, a patriot only more so. The wife had been a Breton. The mistress was a White Russian who had fled to Paris as a teenager at the time of the Revolution.

Herr Kohler had two women in Paris. A twenty-two-year-old former prostitute and a forty-year-old Dutch alien he had rescued and would shelter even though by rights she *ought* to be deported. His wife back home in Wasserburg was suing him for divorce so as to marry an indentured French peasant.

But could the Captain use the information in those dossiers? Could she somehow see that he got it without anyone else knowing?

The cigarette was from the American freighter, the *Esther B. Johnson* out of Charleston, South Carolina. The Captain had found her alone and drifting off Cape Hatteras and had used his last eel on her then had finished her off with the deck gun. 8,000 tonnes right to the bottom.

But first they had boarded her and had found such treasures everyone still got a laugh out of it. Lipstick and silk underwear for British girls her crew would never meet. Silk stockings, her captain's wind-up Victrola and phonograph records, ah such records. Benny Goodman, Artie Shaw, Bing Crosby, Glenn Miller, Tommy Dorsey, Billie Holiday and others . . .

They had returned in triumph with their loot stuffed into every nook and cranny, having spent all their torpedoes, eaten nearly all their food and burned up virtually every last drop of fuel.

August 7th of last year. She had been among the welcoming party that had crowded the *Isère*, the old wooden ship that had once taken convicts to Devil's Island but now served as a tender to U-boats tied up to before finally slipping into the bunkers.

The band from the garrison had filled the harbour with the sound of the *'Siegfried-Line'*. There had been flowers and French girls too. Girls who gave themselves willingly to members of the crew and even had had children by them. No whores among them. Those the boys saved for later as a warm-up to the homecoming party in the Café of the Three Sisters which was now no more due to the bombings. Now the homecomings were not so nice and the parties had been moved here to Quiberon for safety's sake.

The bombing raids had spoiled things in Lorient. The Happy Days of 1940 were long since over. One whole wall in the Bar of the Mermaid's Three Sisters here was covered with photographs rescued from the other place, photographs of those who had been lost. Karl Jahrmärker of U-192, Otto von Jacobs of U-200, Franz Kellner of U-187, all of them gone within the last ten days. One hundred and fifty-six men sunk 'with man and mouse', as the boys would say. And to dance in the presence of those photographs, while she waited for the Captain to show up, was a bad thing. Yet no one would take the photos down. They had a thing about it. They honoured their dead.

'While fucking some drunken French girl in the toilets!'

she said bitterly. 'Why is it that most men are so coarse they would even take turns?'

Not all of them were. The Captain seldom stayed long at these parties or at the Saturday-night dances. Oh for sure he would always put in an appearance unless something came up, but he preferred to keep to himself ashore and sought diversion elsewhere or with his dolls.

The cigarette was now down to its last but still she held it cupped in her hand and stared emptily at the thin trail of smoke until awakened to its threat. 'The cigarettes should have all been used up by now. The detectives will have realized this but have said nothing of it.'

Ah damn, what was she to do? Would they discover she had kept a carton for the Captain so that he could dole them out as he saw fit? Cigarettes for the husband of that woman and cigarettes for the Préfet.

Crumbling the last of the cigarette to dust, she let the remaining flakes of tobacco fall into the toilet and stood a moment staring at them. The RAF had rained depth charges on the boat that last time in early November. U-297 had had a gaping hole in her bow, no deck gun – a British destroyer had rammed them in the North Atlantic some 1,327 kilometres to the south-west of Iceland and just outside the southern limit of the Greenland pack ice, but even *that* damage had not stopped the Captain from putting her on the bottom.

'The *Totenallee*,' she said in a whisper. 'Death Row, that's what they now call the final approach to Lorient.'

There had been panic aboard. Four had been killed. One had had his head crushed to a pulp. Gas had escaped from the batteries. Its deadly hiss had been heard all the time, the air choking . . . Sweat had run into their eyes as they had all looked up and had hung on in the darkness waiting for the next explosion. Dear God, why must it end for them this way? Obersteuermann Baumann knew it would. No one could escape that look of his, not any more.

She vomited. She gripped her stomach and, kneeling, threw up everything. Gasped, 'Sweet Jesus, spare him.'

Kohler heard her gagging. The chain was yanked and he wondered what had upset her so much. Nerves of course. It didn't take a donkey to see she had the hots for the Captain.

But there must be something else. The truth? he wondered.

Préfet Kerjean withdrew into that dark, brooding silence so typical of the Breton. The Captain remained intensely aware of everything around him. His very being evoked command.

Freisen was perturbed and, unlike the Captain, betrayed a sour disposition. He and the Captain had used the interlude to exchange a few words in confidence. None the wiser, the C.-in-C. U-boats Kernével was not happy.

Dollmaker would go his own way as in everything else. That's what it took to survive and he was a survivor most certainly.

The girl waited tensely. Unable to lift her eyes from the pencil and pad, she knew the Chief Inspector was looking her over slowly and that . . . Ah what is it that troubles you so, Fräulein Krüger? wondered St-Cyr. Love rejected, truth denied or something you yourself have hidden? A spare key to this cell perhaps? A little something you can slip to the Captain if necessary?

'So, let us begin again,' he said magnanimously the peacemaker. Relighting his pipe, he puffed happily away to show that there were no hard feelings and that it was all just routine.

Kohler smiled inwardly but remained outwardly impassive. Apart from Kerjean, none of them could possibly know what Louis was really like.

'A matter of blackmail . . .' began the Sûreté.

'It's impossible. I wouldn't have stood for it. *He* wouldn't have had the guts. A shopkeeper? Le Trocquer? Most certainly not!'

Louis tossed the hand of dismissal. 'Good. Then let us turn to something else. The fragments of bisque you collected, Captain? Since they are the proof the Admiral wishes us to see, might we not examine them?'

Kaestner gave him a curt nod and, digging deeply into a trouser pocket, brought out a crumpled white handkerchief and laid the ball of it before him.

No one moved to open it, most notably himself.

'The bisque is French,' he said at last. 'Though it might be from a Bru doll or a Steiner, I am inclined to believe it is from a Jumeau.'

'Perhaps *the* most successful of our dollmakers,' breathed the Sûreté and, setting the pipe aside, reached for the handkerchief and began to unravel it.

Kaestner watched him like a hawk, noting every nuance no matter how insignificant, thought Kohler, but at the same time, recording the reactions of everyone else. He seemed to have antennae even in his fingertips which favoured the edge of the table and tapped out the Morse of a keyed-up nature.

But even this outward sign of agitation could simply be to put the Gestapo's Bavarian detective off. *Verdammt*, what was it with him?

St-Cyr spread the fragments. Some were up to two centimetres across, others but a few millimetres. 'There are some shards of blue glass?' he said, looking up and across the table while reaching for his pipe.

'The eyes – an eye,' said the Captain. 'Blown glass, not enamel, though it was sometimes used. The doll had dark blue eyes and almost certainly thick blonde hair.'

'Human hair?'

'Or dyed mohair. Angora, silk and the wool of Tibetan goats were also used at various times. Inspector . . .'

'It's Chief Inspector.'

Again there was that nod, this time of acquiescence,

thought Kohler, though Kaestner must wonder why the Gestapo's French counterpart exceeded him in rank.

'Why not ask how it is I know those are *not* from one of my dolls, Chief Inspector?'

Louis drew on his pipe in thoughtful contemplation of the Captain and the fragments. Kohler could hear the question running through the Sûreté's mind: As in the sinking of Allied shipping, so in the making of dolls, Captain, is there that same inner search and demand for perfection?

The answer came with that little nod Louis sometimes gave, Yes, it is as I thought.

'The white bisque my grandfather was famous for, Chief Inspector St-Cyr, was known as Parian. The name is taken from the marbles that are found on the Greek island of Paros. The heads and sometimes the other body parts are made of a hard paste and it is this that makes it possible to capture great delicacy and detail.'

Like a conjurer willing to challenge the doubts and snide remarks of all who would question his making dolls, the Captain produced a small head and set it carefully on the table between them.

'Ah *mon Dieu*,' sighed St-Cyr softly. 'Hermann, it is absolutely exquisite.'

'A girl of ten,' came the Bavarian's stony reply, 'with light brown hair.'

'It's real hair,' said Kaestner. 'It's her own. Angélique and I agreed on this.'

The child was looking down at something that intrigued her greatly. The expression was one of wonder and fascination. It was obvious her little mind was racing but what was far more important was that the Captain had captured the look. It typified the child. It was of her, and this is what made the head come to life so well.

The softly red and very natural lips were parted slightly, the aquiline nose was pinched as breath was held and one could see this clearly.

'Touch her,' said the Dollmaker. 'Go on. She won't bite, though she's very capable of doing so!'

He could laugh, this captain and when he did, it was with the conjurer's delight. He had proved beyond a shadow of a doubt that not only was he a master sculptor but that the fragments were definitely not his and beneath him.

'It is the same as in the dolls I saw at the shop,' said St-Cyr greatly humbled.

'And that, Herr Chief Inspector, is why I insist on only the finest kaolin. It occurs in pockets. Nature saved those small places from the ravages of minute traces of leached iron which would stain the clay and spoil things for me by giving it a faintly pinkish cast. I then produce my own slurries and refine the clay by settling and decanting. I work only with the finest clay, which is that below one micron. I mix it with ground feldspar and some other things, yes? then knead it and finally steep it in water before using.'

Elizabeth Krüger waited for them to continue. They were like two men who would challenge each other constantly but first must feel the other out. And the head of that child? she asked herself. It was so beautiful it brought tears into her eyes, for the stepmother was so very beautiful too. Dark-haired and dark hazel-eyed, that one, and how is it, please, she asked herself, that he can remember them both so clearly during the months at sea of never knowing if he would return? The months in which, for a few brief moments each day if he could get them, he would close himself off in his tiny cubicle separated only by . . . that thing? Working on its blank with fine sandpaper and a jeweller's file so as to get the mould exactly right, then touching up the eyes, the lips. The stepmother too – oh yes, he had made a doll of that one before he had ever made one of the child.

The one from the Sûreté spoke, startling her and causing her to panic and blurt, 'A moment, please!'

'Captain, there is no blood on any of these fragments?'

'Blood? Why should there be? The body was nowhere near them.'

'You saw the body?'

'Of course I saw it but not from where I found the fragments, and only later.'

The Préfet could not help but watch him closely and hang on every word. Kohler pitied Kerjean. He was up against a formidable adversary but what was worse perhaps, was that the Préfet knew it only too well.

The girl softly blew her nose. 'The start of a cold, I think,' she said, blushing. 'Please forgive me. You may continue.'

Why must innocent young girls always wear their hearts on their sleeves? wondered St-Cyr sadly. She was pretty enough but no match for the Captain, who would want someone not only very beautiful and sophisticated, but also very intelligent and creative in her own right. Ah yes, most certainly.

'There was blood on one of the fragments I found, Captain,' he said. 'Whoever dropped the doll had cut themselves on the gravel of that railway bed. Why is it that you washed these off, please? That is a matter of destroying evidence, a matter for the courts. Hermann, please make a note of it.'

If he thought to disturb the Captain, Louis was sadly mistaken, thought Kohler. The bastard was just too decisive, too intent.

There was a brief grin. 'All right, I washed them off but only to examine them. I didn't think. Is there harm in that?'

Louis laid his pipe aside in the ashtray the girl had slid his way. Kohler could hear him saying to himself, Men like you never stop thinking, Captain. Even your C.-in-C. questions your saying such a thing.

He gave another sigh and let his fingers trickle away from the fragments. 'Not unless you were trying to protect someone, Captain.'

'Who?'

Préfet Kerjean did not look up. Freisen silently swore and then finally said, 'Out with it, Johann. That is an order.'

The Captain shrugged. 'There was no one with the fragments when I came along the tracks from the pits. I was hurrying. I did hear someone up ahead but could not see who it was. An argument. Two men . . . in French.' He looked at the Préfet and said. 'Why not ask him?'

Kohler thought Louis would ignore the inference and nodded inwardly when he did.

'French? What did they say, please?' asked the Sûreté.

'I couldn't tell. A challenge perhaps.'

'And then you found the body, Captain, yet you did not immediately go for help? You waited almost twelve hours?'

The table-edged Morse stopped. Suddenly there was a brief pause and then a decisive tap. 'Chief Inspector, I knew I would be blamed. I hadn't done it. Indeed, if I wanted to recover our money why, please, would I kill the one man who could help us get it back?'

' "Our money?" Please explain this, Captain.'

Fräulein Krüger hesitated. Kohler knew the point of her pencil had just stabbed itself through the paper.

The Captain heaved an impatient sigh. 'Very well, if that is what you wish. I'm not alone in this venture. I myself put up . . .'

'Is this necessary?' demanded Freisen. 'It really has no bearing . . .'

'Everything has bearing, Herr Freisen. That doll's head, those fragments – blood not on them. Twelve hours of delay you yourself were a party to.'

'*Verdammt*, the French! How dare you?'

Louis paused, Kohler could see him impatiently debating whether to answer. 'I dare because in murder, Herr Freisen, that is so often the only way to uncover the truth. Now, please, allow the Kapitän zur See Kaestner to explain since he is the one we are here to interview.'

And you have set them at each other's throats by downgrading the C.-in-C. to Mister and using the Captain's full rank, thought Kohler, pleased.

Kaestner budgeted a tiny smile of understanding and threw the girl the briefest glance as if to say, Relax, Elizabeth. Everything will be all right. You will see.

'As Captain and Managing Director, I invested 100,000 marks. Each of my officers came in for 25,000 of their hard-earned savings. That makes 200,000 except for . . .' He paused. '. . . my Obersteuermann who sees in the venture a place for 50,000 of his carefully hoarded savings. You must remember, gentlemen, that none of us can send our pay home. It all has to be spent in France, yes? so the venture offered not only an avenue of investment we could control but also a very good chance to multiply that investment many times over. No one is making dolls at present, and certainly none of such high quality.'

'That is a total of 250,000, Captain,' said Louis.

'The rest is in shares among the crew. The men of U-297 are solidly behind reviving a business that up to the Great War made *the* most perfect dolls in Europe. The Royal Kaestners.'

'And after the Great War?' asked Kohler, breaking his silence.

'It was soon all destroyed but for myself, Inspector, who listened to the pleas of an old man and chose instead to go to sea.'

'Did you kill that shopkeeper?' asked St-Cyr.

'I most certainly did not. I found le Trocquer lying on the tracks. I waited, yes, both there and then at HQ Kernével with my C.-in-C. with whom I had, as one of his captains, to confer.'

'And I had to notify the Admiral,' said Freisen tightly. 'My advice was to go carefully. Johann felt that since he was the only one the watchman would have seen, he would be blamed. Now if you don't mind, it is getting late. I must make out the daily dispatch to the Admiral. Fräulein Krüger, if you would be so good as to join me. I am afraid we must hurry, yes? I'll dictate on the way. You can then transcribe and bring it to me for signing. Gentlemen.' He indicated the cell door with an extended hand as he stood up.

'The fragments and the head, Herr Freisen, might I keep them?' asked St-Cyr.

'Yes. Yes, of course. There can't be any harm in that, can there?' The C.-in-C. flicked a glance at the Captain, whose expression told him nothing. 'For the moment,' stammered Freisen uncomfortably. 'Yes, that will be all right. Please do not lose them.'

'Of that you may be sure,' said St-Cyr. Hermann would have to find them a set of wheels. The Freikorps Doenitz would be unlikely to offer help of any kind; the Préfet even less.

'Until tomorrow then,' he said in his finest Sûreté voice.

'At the same time, if the war does not interfere.'

'And if it does?'

It was Freisen's opportunity for revenge. 'We will let you know.'

'Monsieur, this bus is finished for the day.'

Vehemently the driver pointed to the *Défense de monter* and indicated the door. Kohler took in the pancaked Basque beret with its bird droppings on black wool and the cold, wet remains of a hand-rolled cigarette. The lips were thin, the face pinched. Stiff, grey whiskers emphasized a belligerent chin. The dark eyes were fierce. Acid exuded. So be it then.

'Get out. That's an order. Kohler, Gestapo Central, Paris. *Don't* switch it off.'

The scar on the giant's face was terrible. 'But . . .' began the man.

St-Cyr tried to squeeze past and only succeeded in getting his head round his partner. 'Hermann, must you? Monsieur, we need it only for a little, yes? Transport. An important case. The murder of . . .'

They meant it. There was no hope. Well, okay then. Good! *'Le Trocquer,'* hissed the man. *'That bastard deserved everything he got and you two deserve what you are taking!'*

He coughed and spat fiercely to one side, hitting the side window. Grabbing a filthy jacket, he tucked it under an arm, swept up the cancelled tickets, drained the fare money from its steel tubes, and squeezed past the two of them in a heated rush. 'I fart at you!' he shouted angrily. 'I *hope* you obtain the king-sized headaches too *and* the influenza!'

'Ah *merde* . . .' began St-Cyr, suddenly worried they might catch it.

'What was that all about?' asked the new driver.

The only passenger threw his eyes up to God in question and alarm. 'I think we will find out soon enough.'

It was twenty-five kilometres to the house near Kerouriec and the sun had all but set. Kohler tried to slam the thing into gear.

'Double clutch it!' seethed the passenger. 'It's like a woman, idiot. It *needs* to be caressed before being driven.'

'Since when were you an expert on women?'

St-Cyr shuddered as the gearbox complained. With a jolt, the unwieldy bus yielded. 'We'll take the road along the Côte Sauvage, eh?' shouted the driver. 'It'll be shorter.'

'There . . . there are no headlamps. The cliffs . . .'

'Don't panic. I know what I'm doing. Sit back and relax.'

Nom de Jésus-Christ! Must God do this to them? Like all *gazogènes*, this one's firebox would have to be fed and must nearly be out of fuel. Ruefully the passenger hung on and looked around at the slatted wooden seats that had seen decades of use. Rubbish was everywhere. Old vegetables lay on the floor, squashed beneath careless clogs. There were bits of paper – even a shawl of black lace that had been torn so many times, it had been left in silent tribute to public transport.

During the day, cages full of chickens, ducks and piglets, destined only for the Occupier, would crowd the roof up in front of the tank that stored the wood-gas which powered the engine when it wanted to. Bicycles would be tied up there too, if they weren't very good and the Occupier was certain not to steal them. Suitcases, bags of potatoes and seaweed, ah so many things. But the mess, the refuse? How low have we descended? he asked of the Occupation. Cruelly blatant posters cried out for silence. One never knew who might be listening. Spies were everywhere.

Out over the sea towards Lorient the night was fast hurrying while down below them at occasional intervals, the land fell sickeningly to angry breakers and rocks that were anything but friendly. Oh for sure there were little coves, tiny fishing ports and bits of secluded beach where in summer one could perhaps have bathed in the nude with one's new wife but . . .

'How long has Baumann been with the Captain?' he shouted – one could not talk normally.

'I wish I knew. Death approaches yet he invests in a hopeless scheme. I've seen that look before,' sang out Kohler.

'In the trenches, yes, so have I. Did he kill le Trocquer?'

'Was he even near the clay pits?'

'He guards the Captain as one would a brother but is there a spare key to that cell?'

'A spare key . . . ?'

'That stenographer-telegraphist, idiot. The one with the moon eyes for the Captain.'

'Oh her. Perhaps. But Baumann and that Second Engineer guard the boy too, or hadn't you noticed?'

Kohler glanced questioningly into the rear-view but found he had to adjust the damned thing. For a moment the bus was left to navigate on its own. St-Cyr caught his heart as they headed for the cliffs. 'Hermann . . .' he began.

'Hey, it's okay, eh? It's all in the driver, Louis. You should take lessons.'

'If only you would let me,' muttered the Sûreté's little Frog under his breath.

Kohler could see him scowling at the thought of having

lost his great big beautiful Citroën to the Occupier. The car was, of course, parked in a locked garage nowhere near the courtyard of the rue des Saussaies in Paris, formerly head-quarters of the Sûreté but now that of the Gestapo in France. No way would he leave it there and yes, a private lock-up too and the keys right where they belonged in a certain partner's pocket. Keys . . . there it was again, the possibility of a spare key and the Captain locked up tighter than a drum, or was he? Ah *merde* . . .

'You can drive us back,' he shouted encouragingly. 'Hey, I'm going to let you.'

'Be quiet. Let me think in peace. I will close the eyes, so as to shut out the infamy of darkness that has found us on the road without headlamps, or had you forgotten the Wehrmacht must have removed them for security's sake?'

'*Verdammt*, this old girl is throwing enough sparks out behind to let the whole world know!'

So she was.

Just outside the tiny hamlet of Kerhostin, on the spit of sand that joined the once-severed island of Quiberon to the mainland, they ran out of fuel and were forced to smash up several of the seats. Chilled by sweat, St-Cyr cursed the blitzkrieg pace the Germans always demanded. No time for an apéritif and simple contemplation, no time even for a piss.

'Don't even think of it!' snapped the driver. 'I'm not stopping.'

Kerjean's evasiveness was troubling, but did it stem from guilt or worry over something else? Something between himself and the shopkeeper – the contents of that missing briefcase perhaps? Or was it something Paulette le Trocquer and/or her mother could well have overheard and might at any time reveal to others?

Victor had a son in the army. Had the boy been badly wounded and sent home, or was he in a POW camp in the Reich? If the former, Victor would want him out of France; if the latter, why, out of Germany for a fee of at least

100,000 francs, the going rate. Money would be needed. Had money been found?

What was it Madame Quévillon had said to Hermann about the fishing boats? 'Some leave never to return.' For centuries Bretons in the north had been sailing to England to sell onions, other produce and lace, to smuggle also. But Vannes and the Morbihan were so much farther south.

Yet from here they had sailed in their simple craft to Portugal, Morocco and Mauritania to collect *langoustes*, the spiny-lobsters which they then had stored in tanks at Concarneau and other places.

It was something that would have to be checked out. That blind spot on the railway spur, that shed and the bicycle tracks . . . the denial of these.

And a violent argument. The threat of tax assessors and a girl who heard only one name but was certain of it.

'But if you ask me,' the girl Paulette had said, 'it's a queer enough thing for a man to want to make dolls, let alone to make them of people he knows, especially if they are from around here and can be identified by others.'

By the Préfet, he asked, or by the husband of Madame Charbonneau? and knew now that this was what Paulette had meant.

'*Merde*,' he murmured sadly, 'that girl had best be careful lest the odds of her surviving equal those of the U-boat crews.'

4

'The house near Kerouriec . . .' began St-Cyr. 'It's magnificent, Hermann. Grey granite block that faces the sea and
softly glows in the pitch darkness while the sound of
breakers is constant. All of the shutters are open but the
black-out curtains pulled. Not a sliver of light escapes.'

'Quit going on about it. Let's get this over with. I'm
hungry and tired.'

'And impatient. A moment, please, my old one.'

They had walked up the road from the bus and now stood
beside a granite pedestal on which, in addition to its bronze
sundial, there were several seashells and pebbles, and the
bleached remains of a gull. 'The child,' murmured Kohler,
fingering the collection.

'Yes. Is she the one to check for escaping light? If so, then
her stepmother is willing to place great trust in her and is
very astute. It is a thing most parents fail to do.'

The house rose up from the grassy moorland perhaps one
hundred metres from the shore and clustered pines. It had a
narrow, older, taller wing to the left, one of two storeys
with tall, thin chimneys and a circular dormer in the attic
in which there was a spy-hole window the child must love.

The rest of the house was much more recent – perhaps
three hundred years old, thought St-Cyr. Of one storey with
flanking gables and an attic dormer dead centre.

Tall French windows were set below and equally spaced
on either side of the front entrance. Above this entrance, at
the end of the main hall, or off the largest bedroom, there
was a small porch with a Louis XIV iron railing so that the

mistress of the house could open those doors in summer and stand looking out towards the sea.

That sigh Kohler thought he knew so well came, prompting him to say tartly, 'If not a return to some lousy patch of soil your ancestors might have tilled, then retirement to a place like this, eh? We're wasting time, Chief.'

A cinematographer at heart, St-Cyr gave another, deeper sigh. 'Time is never wasted when atmosphere is absorbed. To understand a suspect or possible witness, understand the place and the surroundings in which he or she lives. Try to learn, Hermann, so that when this war is over you will have something tangible to take home with you.'

'Piss off! We're here to stay in France for ever and you know it. Stalingrad means nothing. It's just a setback.'

The Sixth Army were surrounded and all but being annihilated. Hermann knew it only too well and was a realist but one must not argue with him now.

They pulled the bell chain in unison. From behind a black-out curtain came a shrill challenge as the door opened a little. 'Who is it, please?'

'Two detectives from . . .' began St-Cyr.

'*Detectives*? You had better come in then. *She* did it. She *crushed* his head with a rock until the blood *spurted* from his nose.'

Ah *nom de Jésus-Christ*. 'Of course. That is just as we have thought.'

The beam of a torch blinded him. Pushed from behind, he brushed the curtain aside and blinked.

Stunning, wide-set grey-blue eyes met his from under a cascade of light brown hair. The delicately chiselled face, with its lovely smooth brow and cheeks, was intensely serious.

'*She's* in the kitchen. Use the bracelets. Have you guns? She might be difficult and will need restraining.'

Merde . . . 'Your stepmother?'

'*Yes!*'

'*Angélique*, what have you been saying? *Pour l'amour du*

78

ciel, child, why must you do this to me? I *loved* your mother as a sister. She was my dearest friend.'

'Madame . . .'

The woman dried her hands on the tea towel she held then didn't know what to do with it. 'Inspectors . . . Préfet Kerjean warned me you would come, but tonight? After dark? So soon? I . . .'

'*There*, what did I tell you?' spat the child, stamping a foot.

The woman was tall and in her late thirties or perhaps early forties, it was hard to say. Of Paris most definitely and proud of it. Defiantly her dark hazel eyes refused to retreat from the Sûreté's surveillance though conscious also of the Gestapo's.

The dark, almost black hair was long and loose and thick and a little untidy for she'd been busy but she'd not trouble to tidy it in front of them. The forehead was clear and smooth and wide, the eyebrows decisive. The dark eyes were serious and unwavering, the lips exquisite, the chin smooth. A very attractive woman who would keep her looks for a very long time if allowed.

'You had best come in then,' she said at last, giving them a non-committal shrug. 'Angélique, please go and watch the stew. We can't burn it.'

'I won't. *You* can't order me around *any* more!'

'*Angélique!*'

The child fled. In shock, the woman fought to get a grip on herself and at last succeeded. 'I can offer little, Inspectors. There is some cider. It's really very good. She made it.'

St-Cyr shook his head. 'We're not spongers. We know the times are hard.'

'Then at least come in and sit by the fire. My husband . . . he isn't well. He . . .'

'Has not yet returned?' asked Louis.

What was it about him she both liked and feared? His sensitivity? she asked herself as she started for the living-room, and found the will to softly smile for it could do no harm. 'Yes. I'm afraid Yvon is really not himself. He's out in all weathers and at all times. This war, this place,' she gestured with a hand, 'the stones . . . they've got to him. Even the curfew means nothing.'

'Didn't the fact that there had been a murder bother him?' asked Kohler.

For a moment she paused to look steadily at him, then said, 'Yes, the death of that poor unfortunate man, this, too, has greatly disturbed him but there are no doctors here to deal with what troubles him, Inspectors. My husband is so utterly lost in the past, he can't or won't find his way back to the present. Unlike so many, he is not content to simply read of it and dream of better days and better food but must dig his hands into antiquity, cutting them repeatedly as he searches with the desperateness of a demented treasure-seeker who finds only old bones and bits of pottery when,' she waited for them to sit down, 'when those same hands could so release our souls, the war would be banished if only for the moments he played.'

There was a grand piano in a deep, dark rosewood that glowed from among the clutter of easy chairs, sofas and lawn chairs, throw rugs, shawls, books – great stacks of them here, there and on shelves too – a stuffed red hen, a net bag of seashells, the tattered remains of a wasps' nest, a collection of butterflies, photographs both old and much more recent, little things, things of the seaside and summer. Dried wild flowers too.

'It's lovely, madame,' enthused St-Cyr. 'I commend you. Comfort is everywhere, contentment in simple things revered.'

'I've changed little, Inspector. It's almost as Adèle left it.'

He arched his bushy eyebrows in question at the name and she nodded towards the stone mantelpiece above which hung an oil painting of two women on the beach. Both were sunbathing in the nude and looking towards the artist as if the one to say, Come and join us then; the other, Please, can we not have a moment's privacy?

'Adèle is lying on her towel with her back to us,' she said. 'Me, I am the one who is sitting and is not too happy about the intrusion.'

Both women had their long hair pinned up. Adèle Charbonneau had had a gorgeous posterior, one worthy of committing to canvas. Every supple curve was there, even a glimpse of a breast behind the arm upon whose elbow she had leaned to look back.

'She was very beautiful,' said St-Cyr. 'The daughter is very like her.' Marram grass encroached the sands on which the women sunbathed. Waves gently lapped a pebbly strand and beyond this, curled over and broke well offshore. 'It is like the place I dreamt of when my second wife and I came to Quiberon for our honeymoon.'

'It was lovely. It still is. Angélique and I . . . we used to go there sometimes in that first year but now . . . Well, you've seen how she is, I didn't kill Monsieur le Trocquer, Inspectors. It's monstrous of her to say such a thing.'

She wrung her hands in a gesture so instinctive of the futility of arguing with such a lie, it betrayed her innermost feelings for the child.

'We did get on fabulously when Adèle was alive. Angélique was the daughter I never had but always wanted. My first husband was . . . was unsuitable, who's to say? Then Yvon and I . . . Did Préfet Kerjean tell you? We were married in the early fall of 1940, after . . . after the blitzkrieg had taken . . .'

'The child's mother,' said Kohler, watching her closely.

'Yes.' Was the look in his eyes always so empty? she wondered. Not cold or brutal – he was not like any other Gestapo agent Victor had ever come across – but Herr Kohler was to be watched all the same. 'Don't misgauge either of those two,' he had warned her only this afternoon. 'Keep your wits about you at all times. I'll do what I can.'

Poor Victor, he had so many, many worries not the least of which was herself.

'Inspectors,' she would give them a tight grin, 'I had best check the stew. Angélique does like to eat. Let us hope the trust I have in her good sense has not been misplaced.'

'*Mein Gott*, Louis, she's one hell of a woman,' said Kohler when she had left them alone. Nearly always restless, he got up to study the painting. No connoisseur of art, but of female flesh, he ran his eyes appreciatively over Adèle Charbonneau's slender figure. Then he took to studying the new wife. The artist had even captured the dark burnished copper hues in her hair. Her tummy was tucked in, her long legs were crossed. The hands were demurely clasped above the right knee. Slender . . . a glimpse of a nice, plump breast . . . a good back, lovely neck and ears . . . She was sitting on her towel with her back to the sun, this woman the Préfet said was being fucked against her will by the Captain.

Kohler breathed in deeply. The eyes were dark, the nose was prominent . . . It was all shit the Nazis spouted but one had to ask or else suffer the consequences. 'She's not Jewish is she, Louis?'

Hermann had spoken in German but hadn't turned from the painting. A sigh would be best. 'We're in Brittany, idiot. The Far Right, yes? The Church here calls the shots and if it doesn't, the people do. They would have got rid of her long ago.'

'I was only asking. Hey, your German's pretty good. I'm pleased you haven't lost it.'

'Nor have I, Inspector,' she said, causing poor Hermann to turn suddenly from the painting and self-consciously try to grin and shrug off his comment.

'You speak it well,' he said, giving her that same empty look.

'It was a part of my education. Adèle and I both spoke it and both of us visited Vienna and your country too, several times in the thirties when Victor was on tour.'

Touché, was that it? wondered St-Cyr. Had she really had sex with the Captain against her will or even with it?

'How's the stew?' asked Hermann and gave her such an unnervingly boyish grin, she had to grin in reply.

'Fine. Angélique is becoming a first-class chef. It's her stew, not mine. If you like, we could spare a little. Please, she wants you to join us. She insists. We don't often have visitors. It does get very lonely.'

'We haven't any ration tickets to leave you,' cautioned St-Cyr.

'That doesn't matter. The rabbit wasn't living in hopes of a ticket and neither were the two pigeons. They are sacrifices on her altar of necessity and it was she who decided to end their simple lives. There's bread as well and honey or jam for dessert. We'll not wait for her father. Please don't mention him just now. Maybe later you can ask her whatever it is you need to know.'

'And of yourself, madame,' he hazarded.

'Of course. Whatever you need I will give but later, yes? Let us try to make things as they were before this lousy war. She's always been with adults. Tell us about Paris and what it's like now. Tell us about your work. Angélique is secretly itching to ask. Please don't disappoint her but be truthful. Lies instantly put her off. One can never lie to her. She is like truth in crystal, captured in a treasured paperweight.'

The copper pots and pans were hanging above the old black iron stove among the ropes of onions and garlic. The dish-water was warm but there was no soap. Instead, there was fine sand for the difficult spots, sphagnum moss for the others. It had been the child's turn to do the washing-up but Angélique had let him wash since he would not know where things went and 'everything must be in its rightful place,' she had said. 'Place is so important.'

Had it been a warning of things to come?

Harsh words had obviously been spoken in the kitchen just before supper. Because of these words, the child had insisted Hermann and himself stay to eat. Intuitively she had known that if she could not convince them one way, she could try another.

She was clever, and she was playing a very dangerous, very adult game, but also she was betraying that very trust the stepmother had placed in her.

Merde, what were they to make of it? he wondered. 'When will your father return?' he asked. The supper had been quite pleasant. After an initial awkwardness, the daughter and the stepmother had become quite animated – oh for sure the one had accused the other of murder but there had been laughter, and it had been easy to see that they had once got on fabulously.

'Papa will come when he feels he can do no more. Sometimes, if the digging is good, he stays away for days. He digs *all* over, often in the most unsuspected of places.'

Ah *Nom de Dieu*, child, go carefully for your stepmother's sake, he begged her silently but she would have none of it.

'There is a map in his study. *That* is where he keeps his things, his discoveries. Well, some of them. Others are in the barn with the bicycles.'

And now, he thought, you are making me feel very guilty at questioning you because, my dear Angélique, you need your stepmother desperately.

St-Cyr squeezed the handful of sphagnum and let the water drain away before wiping the sink clean. 'It's perfect,' he said. 'It even imparts a mild soapiness.'

'It's my invention. *She* didn't want to use it at first but now she does. *She* even uses it as a sponge when she has her bath. *I* have to do her back!'

I'll hate myself if it was your father who killed that shopkeeper, he said to himself. Is it that you are so terrified of this, Angélique, you would blame the one person who loves you more than all others?

'Does your father no longer play the piano?' he asked quite pleasantly.

She shook her head. 'He's too busy. Besides, where are

84

the concert halls in a place like this? Who would come to listen? He *won't* play for the Boches. He refuses absolutely though the Captain has asked him many times.'

'The critics were very harsh with him after his last concert in Paris. I myself was there. He was magnificent.'

'*You* should hear him play Chopin then. *You* would see that he is not just magnificent but a genius!'

'He cuts his hands sometimes?'

'Who told you this?' she asked suspiciously. Her frown was fierce.

'Please just answer the question.'

She had told him. Therefore it would be wise to give him the shrug of indifference and then lead him like a dog to his breakfast. 'Sometimes, yes, but it is not so much, though once *she* had to perform the surgery and stitch his palm.'

Go easy, he warned himself as he dried his hands. 'And when was that?'

He was like a mush of wet clay in her fingers but she would not make it so greasy for him after all. 'I don't know. I can't remember. Maybe it was a long time ago. Yes. Yes, it was last summer. *She* cried. *She* held his hand as if it was made of ancient glass. She could hardly keep the needle still. *I* had to help her. It was an interesting operation. The result was good.'

'Why did she cry?'

We were getting near the breakfast now, *Monsieur le Détective*. '*She* said he was ruining his hands for the silliest of reasons and that he mustn't do it no matter the cost, that Adèle – my mother – would be greatly troubled if she knew.'

'And your father, Angélique,' he asked gently, 'what did he do?'

'Gazed at her with his wounded eyes and said, "I loved you."'

Oh-oh . . . 'It was only the other day, wasn't it? The day of the murder.'

'Yes. Now come and I will show you his study and his map so that you will have the proof of the location. Later we can examine her bicycle tyres. There is still some of the white clay caught among the treads.'

Hermann, he silently pleaded, why did you have to choose to interview the woman? Why could you not have chosen the child?

Hélène Charbonneau sat forward in her chair with arms resting on her knees and hands clasped before her as she stared at the fire. Etched into her face there was that look of deep intelligence but also a sensuality Kohler found disturbing. Kaestner must be in love with the woman but what of herself? he asked. She looked so sad.

He offered a cigarette but she absently shook her head, didn't even turn to notice the proffered package. 'It's something I never took up. Like too much of the sun, tobacco causes wrinkles. Adèle and I both agreed the sun was far more valuable and that, if we had to take our chances in life's little lotteries, we would choose it.'

The soft cream cashmere throw was wrapped loosely about her neck and worn over the left shoulder. The ribbed blue-grey cardigan suited, though it had been twice mended at the elbows and had mismatched buttons. The dark green skirt didn't match a thing, nor did the rose-coloured woollen knee socks. The low-heeled brown leather shoes had been mended with fishing line, he thought.

Hard times had cut into everything but then even the women in Paris were beginning not to care. Were they all giving up? he wondered. Everyone was tired of the Occupation, even some of the Occupiers.

'You must miss her terribly,' he said, betraying an unexpected sensitivity in one who looked so like a storm-trooper even in a shabby grey business suit. The duelling scar down the left cheek from eye to chin was at odds with the suit – how had he really got that thing? she wondered. Victor hadn't told her of it.

'I miss her, yes, of course,' she said, unsettled by his look, for it gave no hint as to where his comment might lead. But would it hurt to tell him how it really was? He ought to know. 'I held her in my arms on the road beside the car. The sun was very bright. It was such a beautifully clear day. Clothes, suitcases, wagons and baby carriages were all piled high with things. There were dead and wounded horses, smashed-up cars, yes, because we had money then but it didn't make a damn bit of difference. No one stood around. Oh *mon Dieu* no. Just the dead and us and the screams of those poor horses. Blood all over my hands and front. Her blood. She'd been hit in the chest. Those who still lived, hid along the roadside in the ditches or out in the fields if they could find a place, which wasn't likely. Your people didn't just machine-gun the road, Inspector.'

Was bitterness her first line of defence? he wondered. It very nearly got to him. He wanted to stand up and tell her he hadn't been there, that if it had been up to him, there wouldn't have been a war. He'd seen it all before, had seen far too much of it.

'The Messerschmitts came over again, a second pass. Yes, that's the way it was, Inspector. Like angry wasps. Adèle and I watched them. Yvon yelled at me to leave her but I couldn't. I didn't want to. Not then, not at any time. Bullets peppered the road and smashed into the car and things all round us. I screamed – I know I did. I cringed and tried to shield her and only when the fighters had left, did I realize she had already been dead for some time.'

'The child?' he asked.

'She still has nightmares.'

What else did you expect? – he could see this in the look she gave him.

'Does she have friends of her own age?' he asked.

Herr Kohler was a father with two sons at Stalingrad. Victor had said this might be used to distract him. He would want to know how the boys were, but she wouldn't ask. It would not be right of her to take advantage of another's worry.

'I teach her, Inspector. I won't have her going to the local school and coming home with head lice and whooping cough or some such thing. It's selfish of me, of course, but she's also far too intelligent for them. There is . . .' She paused to look again into the fire. '. . . the language barrier as well. Since the Occupation, the Bretons here in the Morbihan have been returning to their roots. It's something your people encourage so as to divide them from the rest of France and set them at our throats.'

She was really bitter but not without good reason. 'How is it you can entertain the Captain? We know you've been seeing him.'

Ah no. Had Victor told them or had Johann? 'The Captain . . .' She must try to flash a sad smile but do so to the fire since the Inspector Kohler was concentrating so hard on her. 'He comes here, yes, and we let him do so under duress. He's of the Occupier, isn't that so, Inspector? Oh *mon Dieu*, how could I ever forget what you . . . you people did to us, to me, to Adèle and, yes, to poor Yvon who is still so broken-hearted he cannot get her out of his mind and we have yet to make love?'

There, that ought to shut him up. She would shrug it off. She would say, 'A meal, a talk, a few hours about books, music, films we might have seen . . . What harm is there in that? So what if we speak German and it makes Herr Kaestner feel like he is at home? So what if it's a lie for me? I do so only because he asks. The Captain brings us food, Inspector. Food the child needs.'

'And the dolls?'

'You've seen them?'

Why was she alarmed? 'Yes. The one of your stepdaughter – the head. Louis has seen others in the shop.'

'Dolls,' she said hollowly and felt so helpless. How could she begin to tell anyone what it had really been like for her?

I mustn't, she said to herself, but Angélique will tell them. Angélique will make certain they know everything.

*

88

In the darkened study there were baby spiders in a clear glass fruit sealer and when the torch was pointed at them, they threw their tiny shadows on the map.

Forced to watch the game of *silhouettes terribles*, the detective took in short, sharp breaths of impatience and interest, ah yes.

'There,' she said, a sigh. 'I told you so. There are megaliths at the clay pits. The Ancients sometimes, but not always, cremated their dead in pits at the base of these standing stones, then buried the bones with pots and tools and occasionally bits of jewellery. My father was digging right near the clay pits on the day of the murder. *She* knew he would be working there.'

The bicycle tracks . . . the shed, the little bits of clay she had spoken of. Had the Captain been aware he wasn't alone? Had the watchman seen the father too?

'Does your father always let you and your stepmother know where he will be working?' he asked.

She could hear the hesitation in his voice. Were detectives always so cautious? 'This time he did. You see, the Captain sent us a message from Paris that he would be returning on New Year's Day and would drop in after he had been to the pits.'

'When was this message delivered?'

'On the 30th of December but you should ask first who delivered it, I think.'

She was making him feel completely out of his depth. 'Very well, who was it?'

'The Obersteuermann, Herr Baumann. Both my father and that . . . that woman he has married were present. Both read the note and thanked Herr Baumann. He had a cup of the acorn coffee and *two* of my biscuits, the flat ones with the sprinklings of crushed walnuts and watered honey on top.'

'They'd be very tasty.'

She nodded. 'Yes, they were. And now, if you like, I will switch on the overhead lights.'

He touched her arm. 'A moment, please, Mademoiselle Charbonneau. I wish to experience the study as you have first introduced me to it.'

The room, with heavy dark beams across its ceiling, occupied perhaps more than half the ground floor of the oldest part of the house. As in the living-room, there was a massive stone fireplace with granite mantelpiece, but no fire. On either side of this, and stretching into darkness, there were superbly carved Breton armoires and cabinets, tables and shelves – everywhere he looked there was both the ordered and disordered pilings of antiquity.

'It was once the billiards room,' she said, swinging the torch round. 'That is the table over there under all those things from the passage graves. The entrances are where the good finds are sometimes made. The Ancients blocked up the entrances to seal their dead in and stop them from coming out at night, I think, and in the blockages there are many things of value and broken things as well. A kind of garbage heap. A midden perhaps. Yes, it must have been like that,' she nodded severely. 'After working hard all day they would eat their supper and then throw the oyster shells and pig bones in too.'

There were shards of terracotta with simple decorations of dots in parallel lines or slanting dash strokes, zigzags occasionally and even on one reassembled piece, a swastika among its intricate designs.

Knives, spear-points and arrowheads of flint, copper and bronze lay with ceremonial axeheads of polished stone, all scattered in little collections among the shards – perhaps two thousand years of prehistory on the forgotten green baize of a late nineteenth-century billiard table.

'There are a few gold coins and some of silver,' she hazarded softly. 'Coins are very rare but those I like best all have the horse and chariot racing madly on the back, with the driver of course. The Armoricans fought naked, Chief Inspector, and were taken as slaves that way to Rome, or had the dagger plunged by themselves straight down into their hearts from the base of the throat. Then their heads were cut off.'

They did not always fight naked – this much he *did* know, but no matter. 'The Veneti,' he managed. 'The Celts and the last great battle in Julius Caesar's conquest of Gaul. A . . . a naval battle, I believe. Off the coast of the Morbihan in . . .'

'In 56 BC, in the Bay of Quiberon. Caesar is said to have watched from Port-Navalo but that's impossible. It simply does not agree with the geography of the times. The sea was not so close and only came in to flood the Gulf of Morbihan well after the event. At least, that is what the experts say. Perhaps careful readings of Caesar's *Gallic War* might bear this out, or the Greek historian and geographer Strabo's *Geography*. They are both in languages I cannot yet read, you understand, but my father has copies, as he has of most other things.'

'In any case, the battle was fought,' he murmured uncomfortably.

'Yes. The Veneti, the most powerful and brave of all the Armoricans, lost to the Romans and . . .'

He gave a sigh. 'And were then led into slavery.'

'With their women, their young girls, their virgins.'

Ah *merde*, why must she bait him like this? 'Please turn on the lights. I've experienced enough of your darkness.'

Bits of charred human bones in little heaps, all with carefully labelled cards giving the location and details of excavation, lay about among the artefacts. In all it was the work of a pack rat of antiquities. Prehistory, perhaps some two or even three thousand years of it up to 56 BC and a little more recently, yes, had been gathered in one room.

Skulls were among the treasures. Bronze cloak pins and belt buckles lay with linked cloak belts of exquisite design and glass bracelets of deep blue or soft pink, most of which had been broken long ago by age, by frost, or simply by ancient custom or carelessness.

Charbonneau had not been selective. 'Your father has been busy.'

She heaved a weary, much troubled sigh. 'Yes, but there are many sites he has yet to explore.'

'And that is his map of them.'

Herr Kohler was persistent. 'The Préfet . . . ?' she said. 'Victor is just a friend, Inspector. Oh for sure he's a little lonely now that his children are all grown up and his wife has turned to religion. What man of his age would not seek the cup of coffee or herbal tea with someone younger, especially if that someone herself was a little lonely and, yes, a little lost and perhaps even in need of help or just plain friendship? The people around here keep to themselves. Yvon's behaviour has . . . has, well, scared them off, I suppose.'

Ah *Nom de Dieu*, she demanded of herself. What had Victor said to them in that jail with Johann there and the others? Had he said something stupid?

'On the day of the murder, madame, did the Préfet pay you a visit?'

Again there was that empty look from the Bavarian. His big hands with the strong, blunt fingers of a peasant or a machinist, were seldom still but now rested on the arms of his chair, gripping them as if about to launch himself at her.

Gestapo . . . she said. Don't forget it for one moment. Never mind what Victor said about him to the contrary. Never mind what anyone says.

'He came to visit us, yes,' she said quietly. Would Herr Kohler notice how pale she had become? Had he seen her glancing apprehensively across the room to the door and the hall that led to the kitchen and Angélique? Were the child and St-Cyr still there or had they gone into Yvon's study or up to the attic?

'At what time did Préfet Kerjean get here, please?'

Could he always be so formal when needed? 'At about

one o'clock, I think. Yes, it was during lunch – we seldom eat dinner any more. He couldn't stay – urgent business, he said. I . . . I offered tea, I think, or a glass of the Muscadet – yes, I think there was still some left over, I . . .'

'Why not simply tell me?'

'He . . . he asked if I knew where Yvon was digging and I . . . said I didn't know. My husband seldom tells us, Inspector. Victor or his assistant, the Sous-Préfet le Troadec, bring him home if they think it necessary and they've been passing by one of his sites. Yvon really is not well. Though it is my constant hope that the three of us might obtain *laissez-passers* to leave the Forbidden Zone and return to Paris, I doubt very much if the Kommandant of this district would listen. He would only think we might tell others about the comings and goings of the submarines. Yvon won't have it either, of course, and in this patriarchal society Vichy has thrust upon us, the husband has the final say. Préfet Kerjean has been trying to help me. That is all there is and ever was to our relationship. He's a good man, and very kind. He wouldn't have killed that shopkeeper and neither would my husband.'

Kohler gave her a curt nod but didn't take his eyes from her. 'Then Kerjean was at the clay pits too, is that it?' he asked.

'I . . . I didn't say that! Now listen, you . . .'

'But you as much as did say it, madame. Was he there? You must answer truthfully.'

'Am I to be charged?' She felt her cheeks colouring rapidly and knew he would see this.

'Under French law the accused is guilty until proven innocent. The Kapitän zur See Kaestner is the one who has been charged.'

'But my turn will come?'

Verdammt! what was it with her? 'Perhaps. Now answer the question.'

Angélique will have told the other one everything, she sadly reminded herself. It was all so hopeless. A shopkeeper . . . Who would ever have thought that wretched little man could cause such pain?

'I don't know, Inspector. I wasn't there.'

'Then why did you say he couldn't have killed le Trocquer?'

She wrung her hands in despair and shrugged. 'I don't know why I said it. *There*, does that satisfy you?'

Anger made her very beautiful but it also heightened the aloofness of the *Parisienne*.

'Kerjean claims the Captain was having sex with you against your will.'

Ah no . . . 'He *what*?' She blanched and felt her eyes rapidly misting.

Kohler told her what had happened. Unable to look at him, she found the tiled floor no better, though she had always loved its warm and earthy colours and the small irregularities that gave character.

Her voice was harsh. 'Herr Kaestner would perhaps like to engage in such an activity with me, Inspector, but I have to tell you for me I could never contemplate it. I love my husband. I have always loved Yvon even when my dearest friend was alive, though nothing has ever yet happened between us or with anyone else. *Nothing*, do you understand? And you can tell *that* to the child! Please do,' she tossed a hand. 'You have my permission many times over!'

Was she lying? wondered Kohler. She appeared as if betrayed by things beyond her control – the child perhaps.

'I had best get Angélique to bed, Inspector. That girl, she would stay up all night if I let her. Usually she does anyway. Reading by candlelight or by one of those primitive lamps Yvon lets her have, though we really can't spare the oil. It's so scarce. She prowls about searching for answers to life's mysteries. The moon, the stars, her rabbit . . . she used to talk to it, the . . . the pigeons too. Ah damn! Damn this place! Damn those wretched stones!'

Unable now to stop herself, she buried her face in her hands and shut her eyes before the fire. He watched – she knew he did. He wouldn't say a thing. He wouldn't even sigh.

Sex . . . sex with Johann in that railway shed? She knew this was what he might be thinking.

'The lights . . . ?' he said suddenly.

Ah *grâce à Dieu*! 'The bombing. Every night now the Ger . . . they turn the electricity off so as to prevent fires and make certain no lights are seen.'

The sound of breaking waves was everywhere up here. The attic, high above the study, was crowded with things they could not see but only sense. For whatever reason of her own, the child had switched off the torch before their final entry from the staircase and was now depending on the night outside to light their way.

'It is over here, Monsieur the Chief Inspector. It is at the spyglass window. Give me your hand, please.'

Her fingers were cool and sure. His shoulders brushed against things – piled-high suitcases perhaps, or steamer trunks, an armoire whose doors were open – was there a mirror on the inside of one of the doors? A lamp, he said to himself, dark sheets or curtains draped over something as a sort of door perhaps, into another part of the attic, a rocking horse – was it really that?

He heard it.

The window was perhaps a half-metre in diameter and of very old glass with bubbles in some places, she told him. 'Big ones, little ones, some squished out, but still it is a good window and does not interfere too much. At night I open it anyway, or go outside to the sundial.'

They came at last to stand under the roof beams and she placed his hand on the cold brass tube. 'With my telescope you can see the craters that give the moon its face. You can see Mars and Jupiter and the rings around Saturn. You can see many things both far and near.'

'The beach?'

Ah, good. He had remembered the painting in the

living-room. 'Yes. The submarines too, of course, but only until they go below the surface which is much closer inshore now because the British aeroplanes always come to their Playground like hungry bumblebees.'

'They know when each submarine leaves or returns?'

'The time exactly! This I confide in you with the utmost secrecy. I've even watched them fight! I *have*.'

'What are you trying to tell me?' he sighed.

Was it so difficult for him? 'Only that sometimes when the *sardiniers* are gathered out there perhaps ten kilometres offshore where it is still too shallow to dive, the submarines slip among them to hide and you cannot see their conning towers among the faded burnt-red sails.'

He'd best be firm. 'You should not be watching such things, mademoiselle. It's dangerous. The Germans might come and . . .'

'And arrest us?'

Was she hopeful of it? 'Yes.'

'But *she's* the one who purchased the telescope for me when my mother was alive? *She's* the one who allowed the Préfet Kerjean to use it?'

Must God do this to him? Had the conscience of the patriot not been tried enough? 'When, please, did the Préfet use it?'

How cautious he was. She had him eating out of her hand but would the sparrow see that among the crumbs, illicit love had blossomed? 'First, in the early spring of last year, then again many times over the following months until he was certain of whatever it was he was looking for, and then again in October, from the 28th to the 3rd of November.'

'On each of those last days?' U-297 had returned on the 5th. The money had been missing for some time but the loss discovered only just before the submarine's return . . .

'It was risky, isn't that so?' said the child. 'She warned him of this, Inspector, but Préfet Kerjean has said he would come at different hours, though just before sunset was best, since the *sardiniers*, as has been their custom for centuries, always gathered then for the night. I heard the two of them whispering. I did.'

'What was he watching for?'

She heaved a disappointed sigh. 'It would be better if you were to ask . . .'

'*Angélique*! Darling, please come downstairs. The . . . the electricity has been turned off. It . . . it is time for us to go into the cellar.'

'I *won't*!'

Ah damn such interruptions. 'Please do as your step-mother says, mademoiselle. Bombs are no respecters of life or private property.'

The candle wavered in clasped hands, its pale light serving only to emphasize despair. Trapped by the light she held, the woman waited, caught among forgotten pieces of broken furniture too valuable to discard. A lamp whose dusty shade of pale silk was fringed with dark red tassels, a plain but beautifully carved chest of drawers, a blanket box without its hinges. Sheets draped over things . . .

Always there was the sound of waves, the nearness of the sea.

'Go,' he said quietly and, reaching out, plucked blindly at the child's sweater until he had a tight grip on her shoulder. 'Do as I say or I will get difficult.'

'Then stop pinching me!'

The child launched herself towards the stepmother but as she passed the rocking horse, Angélique pushed the head down hard to leave them with its sound as well. He would not see the dolls for they were hidden behind the sheets in their house. *She* would not dare to show them to him. Not her, the harlot!

'What did Angélique tell you?' asked the woman bleakly.

'Nothing. Only that she could see the rings around Saturn.'

'Please don't lie to me.'

'I'm not.'

The detectives were gone from the house and the child was asleep, or was she faking? Unable to stop herself, Hélène Charbonneau wearily climbed the stairs from the cellars to the attic, coming to stand at last beside the telescope. Angélique had been thrilled to receive it. They had had such wonderful times exploring the sites and other things, yes, of course. How could one have known this same instrument would be turned against oneself by that same child? The thing should have been packed away and hidden long ago. Why had she not insisted? They had taken one hell of a chance by leaving it out here especially.

'But I loved you,' she said, a whisper. 'I was your dearest friend and I could not see you robbed of joy when all else had been taken from you. Please don't do this to me, *chérie*. You really don't understand what's been happening or why.'

Not a light showed out to sea, and when she tilted the telescope down towards the shore, that same darkness appeared.

'You saw me down there with Victor – I know you did. You saw me with the Captain too, and no matter what I say to the contrary, your mind is made up. I've encouraged both of them and been unfaithful.'

When the sound of air-raid sirens came faintly, she instinctively stiffened – always it was the same. She simply could not get used to that sound, no matter how faint or how far it travelled.

When the bombing of Lorient started, she ignored the danger and went outside to watch – shivered without her overcoat and hugged her shoulders. Tried to find a solution to things.

Flak poured up from the anti-aircraft batteries making rapid little bursts of light among the clouds. The drone of the bombers seemed to come from high above her. Brilliant bomb-flashes hugged the low-ceilinged cloud some twenty kilometres to the north-west over the city and its harbour but came also through some trick of optics from far out to sea.

The Luftwaffe had no night-fighters stationed near Lorient. Even so, sometimes a plane would be shot down and sometimes its aircrew would be able to bale out. Sometimes these men were hidden; sometimes given up. It all depended on who found them first.

So far, none had come here and secretly she was glad of this for she had enough troubles of her own. 'Though it's cowardly of me,' she said, 'and I ought to do something. Everyone should.'

But I can't, she whispered inwardly. I dare not. The Germans would shoot us and Johann, no matter what he feels for me, would not be able to stop them, nor would Victor. Poor Victor.

When a bomber came in directly over the house, she ran indoors, throwing only a brief look up at the spyglass window.

'Angélique is there,' she said breathlessly. 'I know she is. She *can't* leave things alone. Not now. Never now.'

The bomb had not been fooling. Hung up in some bomb bay, it had finally dislodged itself and had sought a target of its own.

Now the bus lay on its back like a grilled crab with its stomach split open not far from the house.

St-Cyr could barely contain his anger. 'I told you we should have returned to Quiberon but oh no, you had to watch the fireworks from the beach.'

Kohler sighed heavily at the outburst. 'Look, I'm sorry, okay? Try to think on the positive side. If we hadn't left the bus, we would have had to pay for all those seats we burned up. Now everyone will just think we were damned lucky.'

St-Cyr threw questioning eyes up to God in exasperation. 'And the owner of that bus?' he demanded.

A shrug would be best as they humped it along the road. 'There's a war on. He'll just have to understand.'

'Well, so will you, my friend. It is *three* kilometres out to the main road and twenty-two more to Quiberon!'

He'd best distract Louis and get him working on things, though it was tempting to tell him it wasn't raining. 'That's about half-way to the clay pits but in the opposite direction, eh, Chief?' he sang out. 'That must tell you something, seeing as you're from Paris Central and the husband and the stepmother would both have had a long bicycle ride to get there.'

No one should have to listen to such things. 'These days long bicycle rides are an everyday thing, Inspector, or hadn't you noticed? Besides, they were common enough in the past and twenty-five kilometres is not so much, especially if you want to stop a murder.'

'Or commit one.'

'Ah yes, it could have been either way. It is also quite possible for a pretty woman on a bicycle to hitch a ride in a Wehrmacht lorry. You had best check this. As the senior detective of the partnership, I leave the task to you.'

Still bitchy? wondered Kohler. They were passing through moorland pasture, with clustered farm buildings and tiny, whitewashed houses whose dark slate roofs blended perfectly with the night sky. A dog barked. Another took up the challenge and soon he was able to tell exactly which farmers blamed their dogs for all their troubles. Most of them!

They'd best run through things again. 'On the 30th of December Baumann delivers a message the Captain sent from Paris, Louis. Both the pianist and his wife read it and have plenty of time to think about it. They *know* Kaestner will be at the clay pits and so does the child.'

The Sûreté's head was tossed in acknowledgement. 'The Obersteuermann carries the look of death perceived. 6,000,000 francs of their money are missing and presumably either stolen by this . . . this shopkeeper everyone seems to have hated or by his daughter. But . . .' He paused. '. . . the Captain does not appear to have been too concerned.'

'He's too busy making dolls and gathering clay,' snorted Kohler. 'If you ask me, Chief, Herr Baumann had every reason to slam that shopkeeper. Pay the son of a bitch back and get the Captain hauled in on a little charge of murder. From what we've seen of them, U-297's crew don't want to return to sea. They know damned well they won't be coming back and Baumann's look only reinforces this.'

'And the shopkeeper's daughter has the odds down pat.'

'Has she got the money? Is she just waiting for them to go to the bottom?'

'Or does she know who took it?'

Questions . . . there were always so many of them and so little time.

They had reached the main road, such as the traffic was at nearly midnight. 'Kerjean and the shopkeeper argue violently,' said St-Cyr. 'Le Trocquer then catches the noon bus to Lorient. That bus, as everyone knows, takes its time but not only does it pass by here, Hermann, it sometimes calls in at Kerouriec and would have done so on the 1st.'

'So, having delivered messages to the woman himself, he sat there in the bus waiting for it to carry on,' breathed Kohler.

'Did he spit towards her with hatred? Did he silently curse her for some reason – what, exactly, was his relationship with her? A woman who would not think of going into his shop even if down to her last centime?'

Kohler suggested they share one of the cigarettes from the shed and, once he had it going, continued. 'Ahead of le Trocquer, and in that little Renault of his, Kerjean drops in to see Madame Charbonneau long before the bus ever gets near the place. He warns her of trouble – what, exactly, we don't yet know, but then fragments of a doll are found and it's not one of the Captain's. It's from a Bru or a Steiner perhaps, but most likely a Jumeau, though we've only the Captain's word on this.'

'Cigarettes are left in the shed as is a woman's crumpled handkerchief and her bicycle – was it really sex under duress? She tells us Préfet Kerjean arrived at the house at 1 p.m. but he probably got there at noon or very close to it.'

'She denies knowing where the husband was,' went on Kohler.

'Yet the daughter contradicts this. While the woman says she was not at the clay pits, the child offers proof her stepmother was.'

'That kid has to be blaming the stepmother for what happened to her mother, Louis, but she must also believe her father killed the shopkeeper and that the only hope is to show us the woman did it.'

'Perhaps but then . . . ah *mais alors, alors*, it is very difficult, isn't that so? The child prowls about at all hours of the night. The father is often away for days on end and there cannot be any guarantee of when he will suddenly turn up. The Captain visits, the Préfet visits . . .'

Kohler handed the cigarette over with a nudge and a sigh that was so deep, exasperation was implied. 'She denies ever having had sex with Kaestner. She even told me to tell the child she hadn't been screwing around though she and the husband had yet to consummate their marriage.'

'But is it the truth?'

St-Cyr searched the darkness of the road for any other sign of life. He would have to go carefully now. 'There is a telescope with which a couple on the beach could easily be observed if in certain places.'

'Did the Préfet know of that telescope?' asked Kohler swiftly.

Hermann never missed such things! St-Cyr held the smoke in to warm the lungs and stall for time, deciding that, while the woman might not have used tobacco, she would quite willingly have accepted the cigarettes for her husband.

'Louis, I think I asked you something. I haven't kept anything from you, not this time and not on that last case either. Fair's fair.'

102

Must God do this to him? Surely Hermann could be counted on not to tell the SS and the Gestapo?'

'Louis . . .'

'All right, I'll trust you. Kerjean knew of the telescope. According to the child, he used it to watch the *sardiniers.*'

'And the U-boats? Christ, that's all we need. The fucking Resistance!'

'Now wait. Please do not be so hasty. Victor has a son. Just before the bombing raid, Angélique hinted that I should ask her how many *sardiniers* had been gathered. Unless I am very mistaken, that son left here for England aboard one of them. That still does not mean Victor didn't fall in love with the woman and become very jealous of the Captain's attentions to her. It simply means that he and Madame Charbonneau had to be very careful. This the child, in her own way, understands and yet she is not fully cognizant of the consequences nor of the hell the stepmother has been going through.'

'Your logic's perfect, Chief. There's only one thing you forgot. The money, eh? Money to pay some fart-headed little runt in tattered canvas for the ride.'

From far along the road to Plouharnel and Quiberon, a lorry sped towards them with unblinkered lights. Even from such a distance, Kohler knew it was the Freikorps racing to Lorient to help with the clean-up.

'Please don't say anything about it, Hermann. Yes, I'm begging you, and yes, I will owe you whatever you think is necessary. Victor's a good man. He has only one son among five daughters. Don't blame him for wanting the boy out of France, if that's how it was.'

Think of yourself advising your sons to emigrate to Argentina in 1938, eh? thought Kohler. Well, what about Kerjean's sending his son off to fight again?

Always things had to be laid on the line for them. If Boemelburg ever got word of it, Louis and he would be done for this time. Up against the wall or under the guillotine! 'Hey, what I want to know is was le Trocquer aware of the escape?'

'That is the question which troubles me the most.'

'*If* Kerjean was really watching the *sardiniers* for that reason, Louis. *If.* That's the question you'll have to settle first, and that, my fine patriot from the Sûreté, is an order. Even bumboats like one of their lousy *sardiniers* seldom sail with only one passenger.'

Ah *merde*, of course!

5

They had been fighting fires for hours and doing what they could. Lorient had been devastated. At dawn there was silence. It was as if those who remained took stock of things and held their breath lest a shattered wall collapse or a floor give way.

Everywhere there were bomb craters, everywhere the stench of burnt flesh and plaster dust, cordite and burning diesel fuel. Where the street ran downhill to the harbour, fog clung to railway lines whose torn-up tracks were bent and twisted. The tunny fleet was no more. Having been denied the fuel to put to sea, splintered masts and sunken blue hulls cluttered the quays.

The street was littered with granite blocks, broken glass and rag-doll bodies. Miraculously one woman still clung to her purse, another had given birth. A boy of seven would never ride his bicycle again. How had he lasted this long?

There was blood everywhere. Blood and plaster dust and stumps at the knees. And through the haze and the uneasy silence, the dock workers plodded downhill towards a twelve-hour shift in the bunkers, seemingly numb to the suffering that lay around them. Zombies in faded dungarees and black berets – black crudely stitched and tattered shoulder bags. Women too. Women in filthy grey coveralls with backsides the size of plough horses.

Kohler crouched over the boy. Louis said, 'Hermann, you will only think of your sons.' He would have to tell him.

'Kid, listen to me. Just try not to worry, eh? Everything is going to be all right. You'll see.'

'It's too late. He can't hear you. He's slipping away. Leave it.'

'Don't be stupid. He has what it takes.'

The boy could only watch the man with the big face who tried to tie tourniquets around his legs. Perhaps he noticed the scar down the left cheek. Perhaps that was what caught and held his attention.

'Louis . . . Louis, he's gone.'

'And he's left you thinking of your sons.'

'Yes.'

'They're gone too, Hermann. Look, I'm sorry. I knew I had to tell you sometime. Boemelburg left it to me. A telex from Army HQ Eastern Front just before we left Paris.'

'Missing in action and presumed dead?'

Hermann couldn't look up. He would deal with it in his own way. He was like that sometimes. 'What else can I say?'

'We'd best get to work. Try that, Chief. You sure can choose your times.'

'I'm sorry. I really am. I didn't want to have to tell you.'

They shook hands and held each other firmly that way, two shabby, dust-covered weary men from opposite sides of this war. 'It isn't right,' said St-Cyr, seeing the anguish in the Bavarian's eyes. 'None of it is. You could go home, Hermann. Compassionate leave? Surely they wouldn't deny you that.'

'I might never be allowed to come back. What would Oona and Giselle do, eh? What would you do without me, a patriot wanted by the Resistance in a land of the Gestapo?'

They had been through so much and Hermann did like to feel wanted and useful. 'Come on then, let's see if we can find ourselves a ride back to Quiberon.'

'The bunkers first, and then Doenitz's former command post at Kernével. It's time the Kapitän zur See Freisen coughed up a little information. I want a look at Dollmaker's report on the morale of U-297's crew. I want a lot more. I want answers, Louis. Answers.'

Kohler pulled up the collar of his greatcoat and tucked his head down further against the cold and the fog. *Mein Gott* he needed a cigarette, would have to latch on to some soon.

A catwalk had been laid across a bomb crater full of filthy water where the tracks had been torn up, and the long line of shuffling dockworkers had to cross this in single file to get to the checkpoint. Damage crews were everywhere – picks, shovels, cars, lorries, ambulances and pumper trucks – yet through the chaos and the fog, the Keroman bunkers rose like megaliths of their own. Long, grim, tall and menacing with huge black armour-plated doors for each of the forty or so bays and grey, rust-stained concrete. Concrete that had resisted even the 2,000-pound bombs. There wasn't a scratch. Seven metres of ferro-concrete on the roof and walls – concrete with iron filings in it *plus* reinforcing rods – had allowed work to go on non-stop inside. 'The bloody things will still be here a thousand years from now,' he snorted lustily to no one but himself.

So savage was the Admiral's penchant for dealing with spies, the warning signs had been among the first things to be replaced or straightened. One stark poster near the guardpost showed a goitred little dockworker hanging by the neck. His sobbing wife and children knelt in prayer under the steel-grey Schmeissers of jackbooted heroes who, everyone knew, were just about to pull the triggers.

The SS had put that one up. The Sturmscharführer with the snappy cap and snazzy uniform reminded him of Klaus Barbie and Lyon, a recent case of arson and a naked woman on her hands and knees under torture. 'I spit on you,' breathed Kohler, standing back to take it all in. 'My sons are gone because of types like you.'

No letter writer, he would have to write to Gerda – she'd be crying her eyes out and remembering. Like Louis had said, he ought to go home for a visit but after nearly two and a half years, he wasn't Bavarian any more or French but something in between, a pebble that had been thrown into a pond to make its own ripples.

'I even forget myself and swear in French half the time.' *Merde*, what was he to do?

'Get on with it,' he said grimly. 'Admit that deep down inside, you've known for some time the boys weren't coming back.'

Verdammt! but it was a piss-assed life. 'I really have had it,' he said, trying to probe the fog to find the end of the bunkers. No tears yet. 'Concrete coffins to hold the iron ones,' he snorted. 'Like Baumann, death is with me all the time. I see it in Oona's eyes sometimes and in Giselle's too, and I worry about them both because when this war turns sour, it's going to do so with a vengeance.' Both would be classed as collaborators.

Louis would be thinking of him and worrying too. He would have seen the Admiral's signs and automatically understood that for him the bunkers were off limits. He would find the Sous-Préfet and then head back out to the clay pits for another look.

Louis seldom missed things. They had both been lucky to be assigned each other. Boemelburg had known of Louis from before the war. A Gestapo watcher had been needed for the Frenchman, someone to take care of the guns and hand one over when the shooting started.

He had wanted detectives and that's what he had got.

It would be best to use the badge and shield. 'Kohler, Gestapo Central, here on the orders of Gestapo Mueller.'

Kohler . . . Kohler of the Kripo, that most insignificant arm of Herr Himmler's police force, Common Crime. The whip scar was there, the graze of a bullet wound on the forehead, the shrapnel scars from that other war. '*Ja*, it is him, Heinz.' The Feldwebel with the bulbous nose, the warts and the blackheads thumbed the ID and shrugged, then plucked a notice from a clipboard on the wall and proceeded to read it slowly.

'Good *Gott im Himmel, Dummkopf*, I'm on a murder

investigation! Let me through or Gestapo Mueller will have your ass.'

The puffy blue eyes blandly surveyed him. The nose, with all its curly black hairs, was pinched in thought, the fleshy chin grasped. 'Herr Mueller's in Berlin. We're here, or hadn't you noticed?'

'Nom de Jésus-Christ! I only want to have a look at the place, eh? A bit of background to flesh the thing out and get the Dollmaker off.'

'Heinz, our detective even swears in French and is both judge and tribunal. It was the woman's husband who did it, Herr Kohler, or the Captain. At the moment we're undecided and the odds are about fifty-fifty. You can, if you like, put your money where your mouth is.'

'How much?'

Herr Kohler had understood only too well the price of admission. '250 Reichskassenscheine, 5,000 francs.'

'Now look . . .'

'Take it or leave it. The Captain had his eel into the bone-digger's wife. The shopkeeper found out there wasn't enough grease and tried to put the squeeze on him. The husband was jealous. Money was missing, a lot of money, so it's all quite simple, yes? The Dollmaker should have left that cunt alone and gone for the less sophisticated but some men, they need a challenge. They need to climb the highest mountains, those with the peaks that are always cloaked in snow and ice.'

A poet! 'You're full of news but what if neither of them did it?'

The fleshy lips widened in a grin to betray broken teeth. 'Then you put your money on that and take your chances.'

The son of a bitch had been fishing for news on the Préfet's involvement. 'Okay, I will. I'll mess up the odds and cause you all a tumble, eh?' He dragged out a wad of bills that would have choked a horse and peeled off the necessary. 'Oh, by the way, who's the bookmaker?'

The Feldwebel took his time. 'Death's-head Schultz.

Siegfried to his mother and father, if he had one. U-297's cook.'

The acorn-and-barley coffee was full of saccharine and plaster dust but at least an attempt had been made. Suddenly overcome by exhaustion, St-Cyr slumped into a chair and fought to keep his eyes open.

The windows of the Café of the Golden Handshake were gone. The glass had been swept up but he was still the only customer. Across the square, the ruins of the Préfecture revealed the impossibility of fighting crime under such conditions. Requisitioned in the fall of 1940 as a barracks for the U-boat crews, it had been abandoned to the police who had moved back in when the bombing had become too much and Quiberon and the other places in the countryside had seemed better for the Germans.

Of course the Organization Todt had built a bomb shelter in the cellars. Of course it should have been sufficient – how were they to have anticipated that a 1,000-pound bomb would skip and jump and deflect itself right into the cellar? – but now a warped bicycle frame, its spokes fanned out like the spines of a poisonous sea urchin, seemed all that was left of the Sous-Préfet le Troadec.

Yes, the situation was not good. He had counted on le Troadec to tell him things the Préfet would never reveal.

The eyelids were too heavy. The mind drifted off. Sadly he drew in a breath and from deep in a pocket, uncovered a vial Hermann had left on a woman's night table in Lyon. Exhaustion then, too. A week . . . had it been as much since then? A case of arson. So constant was the blitzkrieg of Boemelburg's demands and those of common crime – they had only been on this present case for thirty-six hours, a century it seemed and no sleep! – Hermann had succumbed to the pep-up. 'He's addicted,' swore St-Cyr under his breath. 'He's been taking small handfuls and trying to hide the fact from me.'

The pills made the heart race and when a man is fifty-five or fifty-six years of age and inclined to lie a little about it, and is big like Hermann and never wanting to slow down, why a constant harassment. 'He could drop dead when most needed. I'm going to have to get his heart checked.'

Shaking two of the tablets out, St-Cyr added a third, crushed them up with a spoon and, grimacing, downed them with the coffee. At fifty-two years of age and still a little overweight in spite of the shortages and all the exercise, the pills were chancy. It would take awhile for them to work. He would concentrate on the shopkeeper no one should have chosen as a business partner let alone the Kapitän Kaestner. He would consider the victim's wife and daughter and the freedom the money might bring to either of them.

When Sous-Préfet Gaetan le Troadec found him, he was fast asleep. The coffee had been tipped across the table – a sudden, instinctive jerking of the left hand perhaps. Everyone hated having to drink that stuff.

A vial of pills had been scattered, the pipe and tobacco pouch forgotten beneath hands whose fists were those of a pugilist. Indeed, the Chief Inspector St-Cyr had won several medals at the Police Academy in his early days and had most recently flattened the Préfet of Paris, an arch enemy. The left hand was still swollen. The fight had not been in the ring, ah no, but on a case just finished, that of a missing teenaged girl, a neighbour, Préfet Kerjean had said. There'd been a robbery too. Eighteen millions, one for every year of her life.

Quietly le Troadec found another chair and sat opposite him. Exhausted, he took off his gloves and hat and signalled to the *patron* to bring him a coffee.

St-Cyr still wore a gold wedding band. He would understand why the wife and kids had had to be moved out into the countryside, thus saving the life of the Préfet's assistant. He would understand a lot of things but he would not let them interfere with his pursuit of the truth. Not him.

The coffee was hot, payment signalled on to the account with a cautionary wave. Let this one sleep. I want to take my time with him.

Both the Chief Inspector and his Gestapo partner meant business. Préfet Kerjean had made a point of warning him to be careful of what he said. There had been a bus – Madame Charbonneau had thought the two detectives might have been killed. Préfet Kerjean had driven all the way to Lorient and the hospital and then to the temporary morgue just to find out if they had.

He'd been disappointed at the news but had quickly recovered. He hadn't stayed and, though he had avoided saying where he was going, it was evident he had gone right back to tell her the news.

Everyone quietly said they were having an affair. Would the woman have wrung her hands in despair at not finding the detectives' bodies in the wreckage of that bus? Would Préfet Kerjean have put an arm about her shoulders and tried to comfort her?

Were they in it together, harsh though that thought might be? Who, really, had killed that shopkeeper? The Captain? The woman – could it be possible? Had her husband been at the site of the murder too?

With a sinking feeling, le Troadec had to admit the husband could well have been there but why, then, would he have killed the shopkeeper? A mistake perhaps?

Everyone knew the Captain had also taken a decided interest in the woman. Yvon Charbonneau was a jealous man but had chosen to take himself away to search for the past rather than confront the couple – he, himself, had seen enough evidence of that, oh for sure.

Préfet Kerjean had deliberately not mentioned seeing things he would normally never have missed.

Then why protect the husband by arresting the Captain, if not to protect the woman from Herr Kaestner's advances and keep him away from her?

The deep brown ox-eyes of the Sûreté opened. Suddenly

there was a grin of welcome and relief, the explosion of, 'Ah, *grâce à Dieu*, I am glad to find you alive!'

Such an outburst could only mean trouble.

The eyes swiftly narrowed. 'Tell me about the Préfet's son.'

'The son . . . ? But . . . but what has Henri-Paul to do with things? He's in Paris. He was wounded twice and discharged. He works in advertising, I think, or is it insurance?'

And you are going madly back over the case to find the reason for my question, thought St-Cyr. They were quite alone. The *patron* was behind the zinc tidying things. Still, it would be best to keep the voice down. 'The *sardiniers*, Sous-Préfet. Was one of them reported missing on the 3rd of November?'

'The *sardiniers* . . . ?'

Was the question such a calamity? Feeling suddenly sick, le Troadec clumsily searched his pockets for cigarettes but found none.

'Please answer the question and then tell me what the cost is of sending not just one person but several to England?'

The Chief Inspector could not possibly see the zinc from where he was sitting, not without turning. Frantically le Troadec swept his eyes over the all but empty café before settling them on the owner.

'I know of no such things, Chief Inspector. It's preposterous. The Germans maintain a very tight control. Ah, what do you think you are saying?'

The Sous-Préfet's shrug was massive in rebuke, a hand was tossed in dismissal at such idiocy.

'Just answer me.'

The Chief Inspector hadn't seen the *patron* take up his broom and come closer. 'I don't kn . . .'

A hand shot out to grip him by the wrist. '*Do I have to tell you how it was?*' hissed St-Cyr. 'Don't be so loyal to your boss. It's admirable. Oh for sure it is, but not when murder is being discussed.'

113

Le Troadec looked coldly at the hand that held him. 'I tell you I know nothing of such things. *Nothing*, do you understand? Isn't that correct, Monsieur le Cudenec?'

Ah *merde*, thought St-Cyr, have I given him away?

'Now if we are finished, Chief Inspector, I must attend to my duties. There are still the dead who must be identified and whose families must be notified.'

From the square, the streets ran outwards in all directions, some miraculously spared, others a shambles.

Half-way up a ruined street, they stopped beside the shell of what had once been a school. Desperately le Troadec searched the street for possible witnesses. 'They'll kill me if I tell you.'

'No one will know of it.'

'So long as the Nazis don't question you, Chief Inspector.'

This was true of course. Under torture one never quite knew what one might reveal until that moment but . . . 'Please don't force me to ask around, eh? It would not be wise.'

'Then yes, a boat went missing. You could have found that out from anyone. The Germans made a great fuss – they always do. Twenty-six boats went out from Quiberon, Port Kerné, Port Quibello and other places in the last week of October. Twenty-five returned on the 3rd of November.'

'Good. Now please, the fee per passenger? You can trust me.'

'I've a wife and three small children, two others as well.'

'That is understood.'

'Is it that you think the money was stolen for this purpose, Chief Inspector, and by Préfet Kerjean?'

'I am merely asking because I must examine all aspects of the case.'

As he had suggested, St-Cyr could well ask others who might then inform the Germans of his interest. 'The fee is high because the risks are high. The Germans have minesweepers and patrol boats out there all the time. They board and search the *sardiniers* and other fishing boats whenever they feel so inclined. If there is anything at all suspicious, the captain and crew are arrested on the spot and their boat is confiscated.'

'But it doesn't stop there, does it?' acknowledged St-Cyr quietly.

'If guilty, they are shot and their families deported.'

He'd give the Sous-Préfet a grim nod. 'There is also the risk of being spotted by the Luftwaffe's long-range patrol planes which go out from here to search for Allied convoys.'

'And the risk of being strafed by the fighter planes that are based along the north coast.'

'Yes, those too,' said the Sûreté with that same nod.

'450,000 francs per man. There are some who say the British drop money and arms to the Resistance at night but of this I know nothing. How could I when I am forced to work with the Germans all the time? The Resistance wouldn't trust me for a moment.'

A man with several children . . . A man in a very favourable position of authority and certainly most useful to them. *Sacré nom de nom*, why must God do this to them? 'Of course not but, please, there will have been rumours perhaps. How many went with the Préfet's son?'

'Préfet Kerjean didn't steal the money from Monsieur le Trocquer, Chief Inspector. He didn't kill him either. He was nowhere near the clay pits. He was in Quiberon on New Year's Day. He rang me up to wish us well and to tell me I was to take the afternoon off.'

So as to be out of the way? 'How many went with the son?'

Again there was the searching of the street, again that look of desperation. Could he really trust St-Cyr to say nothing of it?

He would only pursue the matter elsewhere if not told.

'I honestly don't know. I have my informants – all of us

do. Some say five others. Three from Paris, two from Brest. Don't ask me how they got here.'

Six in all, for a total of 2,700,000 francs. It was a lot. 'I won't, but if anyone should ask you about me, please tell them I am not a collaborator as some hotheads in Paris believe, but a patriot and staunch supporter in spite of what happened to my wife and little son.'

Le Troadec surveyed this man who had so easily made an offering of himself in return. Now he held the Chief Inspector in the palm of his hand if needed. Death from the Resistance if necessary for betraying a trust, or from the Occupier for withholding information.

'Now take me to the morgue and let us go over the autopsy report since all the other evidence you have gathered will have been destroyed in the bombing.'

The plaster casts of the bicycle tracks, the bits of leather from a pair of gloves . . . 'Look, the Préfet is seeing Madame Charbonneau. Of course I know of this but . . .'

'But there is nothing to it. They're just friends.'

Kohler shuddered inwardly and walked as a Neolithic farmer might have done at midnight to some horrific ritual among the standing stones. The Keroman U-boat bunkers were huge but until that moment of stepping into the acrid haze and metallic din, he had not realized the full extent of the Nazi menace. Oh *mein Gott*, the place tore the guts out of one. More than forty 'boats', some floating, others in dry dock and three to a bay, were being swarmed over by at least eight hundred grey-clad dockworkers and dark blue-clad German technicians. Arc welders flashed. Acetylene cutting torches sprayed sparks and droplets of molten metal while giving off dense clouds of pungent smoke. Riveting hammers went at it day and night. Rusty red-lead undercoating paint was being scraped and banged from hollow hulls, new sea-grey outer paint being applied else-where. Brush, brush, hurry, hurry. Torpedoes were being loaded. Anti-aircraft and cannon rounds were disappearing into another hull, hams, sides of bacon and big round loaves of black bread into yet another as if swallowed up by the ravenous tin fish of the thousand-year Reich before they went out to kill.

And in the far bay whose ceiling, like all the others, went up and up a good thirty metres of heavy, corrugated iron plates, a crew of fifty-two moth-eaten, stinking men had assembled on the deck of their boat in their 'leathers', grey-wrinkled and stiffened, stained and rancid.

Unshaven and unsmiling, they waited. Their bug-eyes were the size of ping-pong balls. Their faces were bleached of all colour, so much so, many would refuse to go home with the first half of the crew simply because their families would see them this way and not understand what forty-five or sixty days inside the hull of one of these things could do.

They were all so very young. Eighteen, nineteen, twenty-two, maybe twenty-four at the most. Not for them, or for any others now these days, the pomp and ceremony of the heroes' welcome in the Rade de Lorient. Now the slinking inshore underwater as far as possible and then the tug, the RAF at any moment perhaps, and finally home. Right inside the womb.

Silently they waited, these heroes of the deep. One by one and from out of the gloom, the band of the local garrison assembled. Tubas, trombones, euphoniums, trumpets, flutes and clarinets and a big bass drum . . .

Still everyone waited, the band above on the concrete edge of the bay, the crew a couple of metres below them so that they looked up from the submarine with their bug-eyes, and the band in field-grey, and all the bulges of slack-assed troops and fat cats, looked down. The water around the boat reeked of dead fish, diesel oil and sewage.

At a signal, instruments were lifted, lips moistened. Freisen had arrived in his dress uniform, all spit and polish, to deliver the gongs. A Ritterkreuz for the captain, one for his first officer, North Atlantic Campaign badges and so forth.

The band began with '*Deutschland über Alles*' – everyone to attention, *ja, ja* and Heil Hitler. Then they hit the '*Horst Wessel Lied*' and finally, having warmed up, blew their guts out in the '*Western Wald*' as the crew and even Freisen shoutingly sang, '*"Eins, zwei, drei, vier, Erika."*' Boom, boom. '*"Erika!"*' and grinned and laughed or smiled.

It was deafening but it didn't even stir a glimmer of interest among an all-female crew in filthy dungarees who simply slammed home their rivets vindictively into a nearby sub and looked as if they would gladly throw handfuls of Carborundum into the gearboxes.

Freisen saluted the boat's captain and shook hands before pinning to the salt-stiffened sheepskin jacket, the coveted Knight's Cross with Oak Leaves.

Then the Senior Officer U-boats Kernével went down the line. Every man got something, if only a handshake of congratulations and welcome.

'He's not the Lion, is he?' spat a guttural voice into his ear. 'The men don't really warm to him as they did to Doenitz. Herr Freisen is like a cold woman not quite knowing what to do with a hot, stiff pecker before it loses interest. They say he should be forced to go back to sea and maybe he will if you and that French dog of yours fuck about with our Dollmaker.'

Oh-oh . . . 'And who might you be?' Kohler didn't look up or down but straight into the laughing dark eyes that held the lark's trace of insanity.

'Schultz, Herr Kohler. Without me and my little stove, the Freikorps's most decorated crew would not be able to shit so well in the only head we use aboard because the other one is my special larder.'

Fifty-two men were being fed by this . . . this giant with mitts like hams. The galley couldn't be any more than a metre wide and deep. No one would complain about the food. No one.

Like Baumann, the eyes were deeply sunk beneath thick, dark bushy brows but here all similarity ended. The head was a blunt battering ram that had often been used ashore in the bars and brothels. The hair was thick and meticulously trimmed to two centimetres on top – shaved closely on the sides. In front, it receded well back towards the temples but came forward in a broad triangle to point directly down and over the massive brow to a fleshy, broad, well-picked nose and a thick, wide soup-strainer of a Kaiser's moustache.

A fastidious man, one of many tastes, ah yes. A man straight out of fifty or one hundred years ago and some West African safari for diamonds and naked slaves of the female kind, the younger the better.

Kohler understood him only too well. Men like Schultz had made good corporals in the artillery but one had had to watch them all the time, lest they lose a couple of fingers while slamming a shell home to earn an honourable discharge and extra pension.

'Got any pipe tobacco and cigarettes?' he asked blithely.

'Maybe,' said the cook cautiously.

The Bavarian grinned. 'Fifty-fifty. I feed you all the inside dope on the investigation, you lay off the bets and we make ourselves a bundle. Right?'

The lark's glimmer never died but it didn't brighten either. 'A bundle . . . ? I thought you wanted tobacco?'

'That's extra. That's to help my partner think. Without it, he's useless.'

'Don't you "think"?' asked Death's-head.

'Not often. I'm too busy hustling supplies for us. We need some rubbers too. Maybe a hundred, and none of your "used" crap.'

A cool one. Even here in the Freikorps Doenitz they washed their condoms sometimes, was that it? 'Okay, let's see what we can do. Insider information in exchange for thirty per cent and a little tobacco. We'll throw in the rubbers free of charge.'

'Forty per cent.'

'Hey, let's think about it. Our First Officer is supervising the loading of the eels today. Tomorrow it's the ammo and on Wednesday, it's my turn to stuff her. Everyone helps. Then on Thursday we put to sea, Dollmaker or no Dollmaker, Freisen or no Freisen, it's up to you and your "partner".'

'And you don't want to sail with Freisen?'

'On a Thursday? That's too close to Friday, and it's bad luck to go then, since we might be delayed and no one, I mean no one, goes out on a Friday unless forced to. Besides, bullets get flattened, dollmakers come home and if we have to go, we'd sooner Kaestner took us.'

Doenitz must have laid it on the line to Freisen. 'Where are you from?'

'And here I thought you were a big-shot detective from Munich and Berlin?'

'Mainz or Koblenz and nowhere near Essen and the sea. That accent's like cold cod liver oil and broken glass.'

The grin widened appreciatively. A tooth was sucked. 'Rüdesheim, and yourself?'

'I think you already know.'

They understood each other and that was good, yes good. They'd make a deal. 'Come and lay a hand on one of our eels for good luck, Herr Kohler, then follow me to the Quartermaster's stores, our Ali Baba's Cave.'

Did everyone in the Freikorps have a nickname? It seemed so. The laying on of hands was simply a crude little test of guts from a man who was far too swift for such things. A puzzle unless someone less intelligent had ordered him to do it. An officer perhaps.

U-297 was a Type IXB Atlantikboot. Wider and larger than the Type VIIs, she was a little slower on the crash dive and cruising speeds but a lot steadier in bad weather and with substantially longer range. Hence the tours of duty on the east coast of America.

There was no number on her conning tower – none of the

boats carried those for security reasons – only the insignia flag of a blue-eyed doll with blonde braids and a pretty green skirt with white apron and crossover ties above a red, long-sleeved blouse. White shoes and white stockings and nothing suggestive about her. Just a child's love, the smiling face of innocence, a fringe that came all but to her eyebrows and a ribbon of lace across the top of her head to keep the hair tidy in the wind. Pink cheeks too, and red lips.

'She even has pantaloons,' quipped Kohler, grinning.

The cook lost the lark's glimmer so fast, the eyes became dead in rebuke. 'No one jokes about her, Herr Kohler. No one.'

'Sorry. Does she have a name?'

Was Kohler really such a *Dummkopf*? 'She has as many names as there are men aboard her. None speak those names. That, too, is considered back luck. The flag is cherished, yes? and taken down each time we put to sea.'

The heavily greased eels had to be handled like babies at birth, but they were going into the doll, not coming out. The guidance systems were tricky and could easily be knocked off kilter. The crews seemed to know what they were doing.

'1,600 kilos a piece, Herr Kohler. 500 of torpex – do you know what that is, Herr *Detektiv*?'

'High explosive. TNT and Cyclonite with, I think, aluminium flakes. If I could I'd like to see the detonators.'

'Spoken like a former demolitions man, but you can't. Top secret, yes? There's no wake with the G7s. They've electric motors, not compressed air so they can't give us away and the Captain refuses to load any other. What he says goes. Even the High Command in Berlin are tolerant of our Dollmaker. Four tubes forward, two in the stern and fifteen of these babies. It's impressive, is it not?'

Schultz pushed the visitor's hand down into the grease and held it there. Again Kohler took in the lark's glimmer of madness. The cook was either looking for praise or sadistically impressed with what they could do. Their power, their stealth . . . the rape of the seas. 'What happens to them when a depth charge hits you?' he asked, just to put the bastard off. One had to do things like that sometimes.

The glimmer vanished. 'They don't usually explode, if that is what you are wondering. Sometimes they simply fall out of their cradles and crush a few torpedo hands.'

Borne on railway trucks of their own, the eels were hoisted up and tilted front end down so as to slide in the torpedo hatches. Each torpedo bore a label from the Trials Command along the shores of the Baltic, giving its idiosyncrasies of deviation on test firing.

'The Dollmaker likes to get in close, Herr Kohler. No more than 500 metres for that one. The Bullet shoots from the maximum range of 5,000 metres and that, my friend from the Gestapo, is why the Lion prefers our Dollmaker.'

'Let's find Ali Baba's Cave and work us out a deal. There are at least three others who might have killed that shopkeeper. Your boy wasn't the only one.'

'Then wipe your hands and smile sweetly at the Herr Oberleutnant, the Baron von Stadler, our First Officer. He's the one who likes to see that uninvited detectives get dirty.'

'What's his nickname?'

'Shit to some, when behind his back, Jesus at all other times because of his beard and piercing blue eyes, and because of his godly manner, especially after eight weeks at sea.'

'He doesn't like your cooking?'

Was it so puzzling? 'No, he doesn't. Now stop trying to have the last word. That always belongs to the cook. Even you should know a thing like that!'

Death's-head's laughter turned several female eyes and brought their smiles and catcalls, a popular man.

A dealer in the black market, swore Kohler inwardly. The son of a bitch has been selling stores on the side and getting all the ass he wants.

The city's morgue was overcrowded. Draped with bloodied, bomb-ravaged white sheeting, old bits of sail canvas, plum-purple curtains, a woman's red dress – whatever had come to hand – casualties from the raid all but covered the cold concrete floor.

Alone, at the back beside the ice storage vaults, the body of le Trocquer lay on its upraised pallet beneath a clean white sheet that had been drawn away to expose his battered head.

He was naked, of course, and the crude stitching of the coroner's incision would not be pleasant.

A cinematographer at heart, St-Cyr let a breath escape slowly as he waited for the Sous-Préfet to bring the autopsy report. 'Hermann couldn't have stood this,' he murmured to himself but aloud since no one else would hear. 'He'd have thought of his sons and of all the dead he had ever witnessed.'

The smell always took a bit of getting used to. For one who prided himself on his sense of smell, it was not offensive, ah no. Merely unpleasant.

The paltry contents of le Trocquer's pockets lay in a cardboard tray that had seen years of use and was stained with blood and other things.

'One dirty handkerchief,' he muttered softly. 'One black comb with six teeth missing – did he try to use them as toothpicks?' Identity papers and ration tickets – one wallet containing fifty-seven fanned out francs and twenty-five sous in change. A deer-horn pocket-knife, not very good, two elastic bands, an eraser . . . a lipstick, a compact and a small vial of cheap perfume . . .

A door opened, and the noise of it, crashing through the tomblike silence, startled him so that he looked up suddenly and only just stopped himself from saying anything.

Looking very tragic in a black-and-white polka dot cloche that was worn well down over her left brow, Paulette le

Trocquer paused. Large silver ear-rings dangled. The thick blonde hair was brushed out into masses of soft curls. The black turtle-neck sweater, whose silver-and-rhinestone choker could just be seen beneath the black overcoat with the upturned collar, would cling to her.

There would be a broad belt with a large bright buckle of some sort and a tightly fitting, dangerously short skirt. Silk stockings too – ah, they were so scarce these days one hardly ever saw them any more – and, yes, black high-heeled leather shoes with criss-crosses and anklets of rhinestones and leather.

She swallowed tightly and lost the blush of colour in her fair cheeks. The red lips quivered, her chest filled. 'Is . . . is this the right place? Is . . . is that him?'

A nod would suffice and he gave it curtly. Then he watched as she picked her way delicately towards him and he thought . . . Ah *Nom de Dieu*, what did he think? Only the Germans could have coined a word for it. The Germans . . . She is like a *Leichengaengerin*, a woman who walks over the corpses of her own making.

So many of them were there and she so tightly skirted, her progress was difficult. She looked down at each shrouded figure. She hesitated several times as if puzzled as to who the victim really was. Then, at last, she stood beside him at the foot of the pallet, now green beneath the dusky eyeshadow and the soft brush of beautiful eyebrows.

'Mademoiselle, did Préfet Kerjean order you to come here to identify your father's body?'

Perhaps she did not hear him, perhaps she was thinking back to childhood days and those bright moments that hung like ornaments on the tree of one's life.

Unbidden, the china-blue eyes dropped to the cardboard tray. 'Can I take those?' she asked, a whisper. 'They're mine. He can keep the perfume. I won't be needing it any more. I'll have far better.'

Fastidiously her black-gloved hand found the lipstick and

124

the compact. He hated to tell her she couldn't have them just yet, though he found a vindictive pleasure in doing so.

'It doesn't matter,' she said and gazed fully at him. 'Mother couldn't come, could she, so I had to. Someone had to. It might just as well be me. It's always me.'

Kerjean should have accompanied her. Had the Préfet made her do it as a warning, a way of forcing her to keep silent?

It was a thought most troubling to him.

Hesitantly the girl ran her eyes over the shroud and only at the last forced herself to study her father's head and the terrible wound that, because he lay face up, was only partly exposed.

'Why is his mouth open like that? Why are the eyes? He had bad teeth. Even garlic couldn't hide the stink of his halitosis.'

'Tell me something, mademoiselle,' he said quietly and, tossing a look the Sous-Préfet's way, cautioned that one to stay put for a moment. 'Where was your father on the day before his death?'

The 31st of December, last Thursday . . . 'At the shop. It's a busy time, isn't it, the last day of the year? The Germans always buy things they've forgotten to send home. Maybe it's guilt that causes them to remember their loved ones.'

'Did he sell any of the dolls?'

Ah, the dolls, was that it? 'One doll in particular, Inspector? A doll whose head was then broken?'

'Please just answer the question.'

'Ten of the dolls were sold. Ten! *There*, does that help you? All to Germans from the army and the U-boats and other things. All had to be parcelled up for the postmistress, yes? I ought to know. *He* made me do it. They donated the paper.'

'And he didn't pay you, did he?'

'He didn't even give me pocket money. I'd only waste it on things like those.'

She indicated the lipstick and the perfume the father had obviously confiscated.

'What else did the men buy?'

'China ashtrays – one had a dog mounting another. Does that tell you anything?'

'Please, we need your help. Don't ever taunt a police officer, not if you plan a life on the streets.'

'I don't. I'm too good for that. I've better things in mind but it's interesting you should think me suitable.'

St-Cyr sighed sadly. 'I don't, mademoiselle. For myself, I think you worthy of far more, especially now as you are so close to freedom.'

'Monsieur Charbonneau and his daughter came to the shop. I saw them looking in the window.'

'What did they buy?'

A doll – was this what he thought? Hah! she'd make him beg for it.

'Mademoiselle . . . ?'

That look of his was not cruel, but so searching it would uncover secrets she could not let him have. 'Some green glass candlesticks the child wanted. A gift for her stepmother.'

His interest intensified. She could see the nostrils of that robust nose pinch themselves, and noted that the hairs were a little darker than those of his moustache.

'Did you serve them?' he asked, and she knew he was trouble and vehemently shook her head.

'I came downstairs to see my father tucking the candlesticks into Monsieur Charbonneau's rucksack.'

'But . . . but you have just said you saw them looking in the window?'

'Mother had to be seen to. *He*,' she indicated the corpse, 'wanted me out of the way so,' she shrugged, 'I went up to her even though it wasn't time.'

But you did not stay, he said to himself as he studied her and asked, What was going through that mind of hers? What infamy had she really been up to if any? 'And the child?' he asked suddenly.

Her smile was brief. 'She was watching my father do so, that's all, Inspector. She was very cautious and silent as most girls are of that age, isn't that so?'

Nom de Jésus-Christ, what was she hiding? 'I think there is more to it, mademoiselle. Angélique Charbonneau would have seen Herr Kaestner's dolls on display. Had she a doll of her own?'

So it was back to the dolls, was it? She'd be serious with him and would frown. Yes . . . yes, that would be best! 'I . . . I don't know. I don't think so. She's a little too old for dolls, isn't she?'

'Too intelligent perhaps but then . . . ah then, mademoiselle, age and intelligence do not always coincide and one can still welcome the comfort of friends.'

'And that child has none of them?'

'None.'

'Does she play with her dolls – is this what you are thinking? Dolls the Kapitän Kaestner had made for her? Dolls of her mother, her stepmother and her father, perhaps? The Dollmaker could have used photographs of the dead mother, couldn't he?'

The attempt had been desperate, the truth still hidden. 'The doll I want was neither of those but something the Captain did not make.'

'Then I can't help you, can I?'

There was nothing he could do to ensure caution. With some it was useless to try. They had to discover everything for themselves. 'Take care of yourself mademoiselle. I may want to talk to you again.'

She would give him a moment more to see if he remembered the briefcase and wanted to ask her about it. She would study him as he had studied her, stripping away not the layers of clothing but those of the mind. She would smile briefly and extend the hand of friendship just in case. '*Au revoir*, Inspector. *Auf Wiedersehen.*'

The Sous-Préfet's comment was terse as they watched her pick her way among the corpses. 'That girl is trouble. I

127

would not be at all surprised if she not only knew where the money was but counted it before bed.'

'Don't tar the child with the sins of the father – this is something I am presently telling myself. No child can be totally blamed for the loss of innocence, yet all lose it, some far sooner than others.'

Unsettled by the all too evident sadness in the Chief Inspector's voice, le Troadec handed him the report.

He handed it right back. 'You tell me, please. For the moment my eyes are not what they should be and I am too lazy to find my glasses.'

Understandingly the Sous-Préfet nodded. 'Chocolate in the stomach. Candied cherries too, and cognac or brandy – enough alcohol in the blood to make him more belligerent than usual, which is saying something.'

'Anything else?'

'Yes. Black bread and smoked sausage. Pork most probably. No sawdust, and whole peppercorns, both white and black.'

'U-boat food.'

It was not a question but a statement of fact, the Chief Inspector gazing off towards the door through which the girl had disappeared. 'Someone from the crew must have visited him,' said the Sous-Préfet. 'The cook perhaps.'

'Good! I'll be in touch. Excuse me, you've been most helpful.'

He ran. Nimbly, as the soccer forward he had once been, the Chief Inspector reached the door and darted after the girl.

She was waiting for the bus amid the ruins where dazed and grief-stricken stragglers till wandered and the firemen were coiling their hoses. She was not happy to see him coming towards her with such determination . . .

'The customers that came to the shop before your father left to take the bus, mademoiselle?'

She would hunch her shoulders forward and draw her neck in a little deeper so that her collar would push her hair up a bit. It had been most wise to listen to her intuition – she must always remember to do so and never deny it. She was glad she had decided to head home instead of going to see someone. Yes, she had listened to the warnings of her innermost self.

'Mademoiselle . . . ?'

The line-up for the bus was long and doubled. Several were taking notice and the detective had realized he should not have spoken out but he had had to know.

So she would tell him *and* tell them. Yes she would! 'Don't you remember, Inspector? My father had locked me in my little cage in the cellar so as to punish me. He *liked* to think of me in there as his prisoner.'

Ah damn her! 'For *what*, please, were you being punished? For playing around with the enemy?'

A slip of the tongue, was it, Inspector? Beware the snake who listens then, beware the gossips in a little place like Quiberon. 'The Germans may be your enemy, Chief Inspector St-Cyr from the Paris Sûreté, but they are not mine. Now, please, the *autobus* is negotiating the destruction given us by Mr Winston Churchill and the bombers of the British Royal Air Force. Unless you wish to stand in its way, I . . . why, I think you had better leave.'

'For what reason did he lock you up, mademoiselle?'

Was it so important to him? 'For things both he and my mother imagined.'

The smoked sausage had been good, the beer perfect and the black bread and Edam cheese added treats. Ali Baba's Cave had turned out to be a brand-new concrete bunker some five kilometres to the west of Lorient on the outskirts of a small village. There had been tonnes of stores. Far more than enough for a little criminal to indulge himself.

But the warehouse had had another advantage. It was but a nice little walk to the clay pits and Schultz had logged himself into the warehouse on the morning of the murder: 1000 hours bang on and ready.

Kohler drew on his cigarette, one of many he had so recently acquired. He leaned the newly requisitioned Freikorps bicycle against the stone wall beside the road, and took time out to enjoy the day.

Death's-head Schultz had been in his element. Surrounded by ramparts of tinned ham, pickled beef, peas, beans, chicken stew, tomatoes, plum jam, et cetera, et cetera, with whole smoked hams and sides of bacon hanging above among the rounds and coils of sausage, the son of a bitch had held court over a keg of fresh eggs that in Paris would have brought 200 francs a piece.

Four tins of Dutch pipe tobacco resided in a rucksack, along with six hundred cigarettes, eighteen bars of Swiss chocolate, thirty of soap, four towels, two face cloths, six handkerchiefs, eight pairs of socks and two litres of Russian vodka just to remind him of his sons, Hans and Jurgen Kohler.

'But have I been had?' he asked himself. 'Ah *Gott im Himmel*, Louis, your partner who prides himself in getting the best of every deal is not so sure this time.'

Louis was still in Lorient, for all he knew, so the confession was safe from prying ears that would remember and recall it six months from now if necessary.

Schultz had played the usual game of distraction. 'Flash' cards of pretty Breton girls had been turned over as in a game of poker, some naked and in unusual and awkward poses, others half-naked and doing things no girl should let herself be photographed doing, others chaste and clothed and caught with sudden uncertainty in their eyes.

But none of them had been the shopkeeper's daughter yet the clay pits were so near.

He wished he could see the autopsy report on the father; he had a feeling it would turn up something.

The deal had been set at a split of 33 to 67. Schultz had not been forthcoming about the Dollmaker, Baumann or any of the others of the crew. Indeed, his only derogatory comment had been about their First Officer, and even on the Baron von Stadler he had clammed up.

'They're special,' he had said with that grin of his. 'What one does for another, all do. We stick together because we must. We let the mould grow over us at sea and we brush it off our bread until the loaf is too soggy and the mould too deep to eat.'

When the sun came out, Kohler lifted his face to it and thought briefly of home and of the boys. He smelled the pinewoods, the perfume of new sawdust and that of wood-smoke at night. He heard the cows in the barn at milking, the horses as the plough broke the heavy clay. He felt the earth and squeezed a handful so hard, it was as if he was really there.

Then he got on the bicycle and headed down the long arm of the estuary to Kernével and Doenitz's former command post in the requisitioned villa of a sardine merchant.

When he found her, Elizabeth Krüger was hard at work typing a report into one of two Siemens Geheimschreiber T-52 teleprinters.

To Befehlshaber der Unterseeboot Doenitz, 18 avenue du Maréchal Maunoury, Paris . . .

How nice. Looking right over the Bois de Boulogne.

'Herr Kohler, you . . . you should not be here. It is top secret, yes? No one without the proper authority is to be allowed in this room.'

She smelled nicely, of soap, hot water and clean woman. 'Not even if he's from the Gestapo and on a special mission for Herr Mueller in Berlin?'

'*Get out!* Please go to my office. The Kapitän zur See Freisen has not yet returned from the Keroman bunkers. There is . . . is coffee. Please ask Herr Gruber, the orderly, to provide you with some.'

She was really a very attractive young woman, this *Blitzmädel* who secretly had the hots for the Dollmaker. The blue eyes moistened nervously under scrutiny, the soft pink cheeks began to darken as the blush of embarrassment flooded across them. 'Please,' she said. 'I could lose my job.'

'Who else is around?'

Must he do this to her? 'The other officers are all in the Tracking Room downstairs and *that* really is off limits even to a member of the *Geheime Stattspolizei*.'

'Okay. Finish your telex, then let's have a little chat in your office. We'll even close the door so as to be totally private.'

He left her then and she shut her eyes and tried to still the panic. Herr Kohler could not know what she had done. No one could or would except for the Captain, the Dollmaker.

Delays in transmission only caused trouble. Forcing herself to do so, she completed the telex then sat a moment trying to collect her thoughts. What could Herr Kohler possibly want with her?

Unbuttoning her jacket, she slid a hand in under her tie to pluck the buttons of her shirt-blouse. When she found the tiny, folded scrap of paper, she took it out and read again, as she had so many times since deciding to do this thing, the details gleaned from the two detectives' dossiers. Things she thought might be useful to the Kapitän Kaestner. It had taken courage to sign the note *Elizabeth*.

Kohler could hear her coming along the corridor. He had just time to scan the psychiatric report on the Dollmaker Doenitz had had done in Paris on the Captain's last visit and never mind getting a bunch of ladies there to dress up a bunch of dolls. Over two years of constant duty had cut into the Captain's psyche. During U-297's last cruise, Kaestner had been on *Luminalette*. A case of nerves, nervous exhaustion and far too little uninterrupted sleep.

Oh for sure he had brought them home and had taken them through hell – that's why Doenitz still had faith in him. But there'd been the nightmares of corpses rotting on the bottom of the sea all tinned up in their little fish with the eels lying dormant and waiting for the barnacles. Few of

132

the crew knew of these nightmares – Baumann and the other officers had somehow clamped a lid on things – but the boy Erich Fromm had once found the Captain staring at him after one of these episodes of fitful sleep and had never forgotten it. Hence the constant guard and the boy's desire not to return to sea.

The Dollmaker insists he is fit for duty and will not listen to your allowing the Kapitän Freisen to take over command of U-297. Subconsciously he is terrified of returning to sea. The dolls are a way of shutting it all out and of giving himself and the crew that sense of having something they are all going home to. A business for him, an investment for the others. But he knows it will be the last time for him if he does go back to sea and he thinks he can keep on hiding this from his officers and crew because to them he is their saviour.

Luminalette was a phenobarbital, a sedative and hypnotic. The usual prescription was three times a day but the dosage had been increased to six times when necessary. The assessment had not been done in a clinic but at the Hotel Claridge on the Champs-Élysées where generals and holders of the Knight's Cross often stayed.

When she caught him reading the report, Elizabeth Krüger had to sit down and could not look up at him.

'So, okay,' breathed Kohler, softly closing the door. 'I'm going to ask you only two things.'

She waited. He felt sorry for her but could not let that interfere. 'Yesterday, during the interrogation break, we gave you a cigarette. Presumably it came from the American freighter the Captain boarded last summer.'

Again she waited, gripped her knitted hands so hard the knuckles were white.

'With tobacco in such short supply, even with that hoard in the warehouse, how could an almost full packet of those cigarettes still be hanging around? We found it in a railway shed. A woman's crumpled handkerchief was deep down in the straw.'

Her blonde head fell to her knitted hands and she

began to rock herself gently back and forth. Kohler hated himself for having to do it to her but they had to have answers.

'I . . . I don't know. How could I?' she blurted. In tears, she tried to face him. He was standing over her. He wouldn't stop! 'The . . . the Dollmaker and . . . and who, please?' she asked bitterly. 'Madame Charbonneau? Was it her? Was it that . . .'

'That bitch?'

Again he waited. At last she nodded. 'Then just answer my question truthfully, Fräulein Krüger. No one else will hear what you tell me.'

'Oh?' she demanded hotly, flinging her head up to look at him.

'Kaestner's a fool,' he said and meant it too.

'He . . . he asked me to keep cigarettes for him. A few packets . . . a carton. He . . . he made a little joke about the . . . the pianist needing a steady supply which unfortunately would have to be interrupted by their long absences at sea.'

Kohler gave his thoughts aloud. 'Then the Charbonneau woman met the Captain in that shed.'

'For love? For sex? Then why, *please*, did she *not* take the cigarettes?'

'Maybe she forgot. Maybe she was in too much of a hurry. Maybe someone came along to interrupt the . . .'

'The fucking, the fornication?' Angrily she wiped her eyes and cheeks with her fingertips.

'The husband was there among the standing stones . . .'

'The husband?' she blurted tearfully and buried her face in a hand.

'The cigarettes,' he said so gently it was like a caress.

Kohler laid a hand on her head then crouched and tilted up her chin. 'Hey, I think you can smile. I don't think I need your answer to my other question. Be good. Get yourself tidied up and say nothing to anyone. I'll see you later and we'll pretend we never met here.'

He left her then and for a time she could not move from the chair but blew her nose and wiped her eyes.

Then she took out the little piece of paper she would press into the Dollmaker's hand, and wrote, *Kohler believes the pianist did it.*

In her haste to put it back, the note got tangled with her neckchain and the spare key to that prison cell. Guiltily she brought both things up to her lips, then tucked them away and tidied her blouse and jacket.

The key had lain unattended on the edge of a desk in the front office of that wretched little *gendarmerie* and when Préfet Kerjean had returned for it, she had told him he must have left it elsewhere.

6

West from Lorient, the railway line passed among grimy warehouses which had miraculously been spared the bombing. Alone, St-Cyr worked the lever of the handcar. Now easily up, now a push down hard, the sound of its iron wheels on iron rails the only sound in all this wilderness of shock and stunned disbelief. It was as if the RAF had unleashed on Lorient a reign of terror that had only paused. The silence made him uneasy. The clickety-clack of the wheels drove the uneasiness home.

He came to a bend but there was still no sign of open fields or houses. He worried about approaching trains, for he'd had no schedules to guide him and had simply found this thing on a siding and had pushed it on to the main line.

'Ah *merde* . . .' he said and let the lever drift up of its own accord at the sight of splashed white paint on walls where giant letters still ran: the V-for-Victory . . . the Croix de Lorraine, the symbol the Resistance had adopted . . . and then . . . then the shrill slogans of bitterness: *LAVAL AU POTEAU!* (Laval up against the wall!); *LA GUILLOTINE POUR PÉTAIN!*; *VICTOIRE! LIBERTÉ!*

NOUS SOMMES DES TRAVAILLEURS INVOLON-TAIRES POUR L'ALLEMAGNE! (We are involuntary work-ers for Germany!) This slogan stretched on and on around a broad bend. The handcar speeded up. Suddenly he had to be away from the place. Suddenly he was terrified of a lonely meeting here with those who would still accuse him of gladly working for the Germans, those who did not *want* to understand that he had had no choice just like them . . . *NOUS LES AURONS!* (We'll get them!) was splashed on both sides of the tracks.

With a sigh of relief, he reached the last of the ware-houses and was soon passing through farmland, which like almost everywhere else in Brittany was a patchwork of tiny fields. Low stone walls or hedgerows of stunted hawthorn and bracken separated them, the landscape bleak, its whitewashed cottages with their pink or blue-grey slate roofs stark and tiny on a treeless plain.

He was glad Hermann hadn't seen the slogans. When it came, as surely as it would some day, the war's end would bring a vendetta equal to or surpassing the one the Germans had initiated in June 1940. Right against Left, Fascist against Communist, businessman against competitor, shopper against shopkeeper, neighbour against neighbour, husband against wife. The anonymous letters the Germans encouraged were still far too much in use, the public denunciations too, and the secret ones, those whispered into the ears of the SS and the Gestapo. 'Hatred only breeds hatred,' he muttered sadly. 'They have turned us into a nation which betrays itself only too willingly.'

The news from Stalingrad was a disaster for the Germans. One hundred thousand men – the whole of the Sixth Army – were surrounded and about to be annihilated. The news from North Africa, where massive Allied landings had raised such hopes, was little better for them. It was only a matter of time until the invasion came and slogans like those appeared everywhere.

Now he was in open moorland too poor for farming. Finally he reached the spur that serviced the clay pits. With all the delays – things no one in a hurry who knew the way would experience – it had taken just under forty minutes to run that gauntlet and cover the six or so kilometres.

He was rhythmically pushing the hand lever down and letting it effortlessly rise of its own momentum, when he noticed white leaflets blowing across the tracks. Like tiny flocks of Bonaparte gulls, they lifted and settled only to rush on again. Momentarily some were caught against a rail or among the tall grass and bracken but were soon plucked away.

Dropped off target by the RAF during the bombing raid, they gave in German and then in French the rates required to insure the lives of U-boat crews. 5,000 marks per man – 100,000 francs; 260,000 marks for a crew of fifty-two. In francs, some 5,200,000 (£26,000), all at the official rate of exchange which one simply did not use because it was impossible to do so and no one would be fool enough.

Per tour of duty . . . ' "If they should last so long," ' he read aloud. ' "Similar notices are being delivered to all families and loved ones of the German U-boat personnel, Keroman Base Lorient. We have their names and home addresses in the Reich. No doubt these same loved ones will soon be writing to demand of these same young men why their Führer and their Admiral have placed their lives at such terrible risk." '

War took many forms and the leaflets were but another of them. More subtle, yes, than guns and bombs but, like the denunciations, effective in their own way.

Scrap paper was, however, always useful for notes if blank on one side, as these were, if not, then suitable for the stove and a faint suggestion of warmth and light. Foraging, he gathered several, stuffing them into his overcoat pockets, sometimes in wads as thick as bundles of 1,000-franc notes. Yawning hugely, he blinked to clear his eyes of sleepiness, and said, 'I mustn't take any more of those damned pills,' and wondered if he, too, wasn't becoming addicted.

When he reached the shed, he could hardly keep his eyes open – it was all this fresh air and exercise, the sun . . .

There was a man's bicycle leaning against the inside wall next to the door, black and much muddied and with a metal seat that was naked of all padding and polished smooth by wear.

The bicycle was padlocked twice. Woven through both

the front and rear spokes and the pedal-sprocket, a sturdy chain not only made theft difficult by its added weight, but ensured much inconvenience to the would-be thief.

It had not been requisitioned by the Occupier because its tyres no longer had inner tubes but were ingeniously stuffed with strips of old leather. Short lengths of rusty baling wire bound the tyres to their rims. Much-used wicker baskets were mounted front and back, and there were two shabby saddlebags as well.

'The pianist . . .' he said, yawning hugely and so suddenly he was caught off guard and had to pause. His heart was racing. 'Easy, *mon ami*. Go easy, eh?' he said to himself and shunned the pills.

Lifting the bicycle over to the far wall, he moved the hay aside and buried the thing. A few places needed tidying. He stood back and stretched as he looked it over – yawned again. On first sight, the shed would appear quite empty, the bicycle gone.

Only after a moment or two of consternation and panic would Charbonneau realize what had happened. 'And by then I will have him right where his wife lay on the straw with the Dollmaker.'

Or had it been like that on the day of the murder?

He didn't think so. The woman had been warned by Préfet Kerjean that there might be trouble. Both of them knew the husband and the Captain would be at the clay pits. The Préfet and the shopkeeper had argued violently.

Between the time the Captain was seen leaving the clay pits and the time of the murder there could not have been time for lovemaking.

A doll's head had been broken, a hand had been cut.

Otto Baumann had delivered the Captain's message to the Charbonneaus two days before the murder. Paulette le Trocquer knew far more than she was willing to let on. A packet of American cigarettes had been left on a timber over there. The tightly crumpled ball of a woman's handkerchief had been pressed down into the hay. The smell of its perfume had been good and definitely not cheap and not that girl's, not yet.

Softly closing the door, St-Cyr put the latch on and started out.

Why had the pianist returned to the scene of the murder? Was Charbonneau so desperate or such a fool he thought he could get away with it unnoticed?

Or was he so obsessed with the findings of his labours, he could not leave them?

Alone beneath the sun and drifting cloud, the grey and lichen-encrusted pillars of the megaliths stood well beyond the site of the murder and their alignment on high, overlooking everything. Tall, and weighing several tonnes – feats of engineering would have been required to raise them – they appeared omnipotent, inducing doubt and fear.

Wind played among the bunched grasses at their feet. The iodine and salt-fish smell of the sea was everywhere and when he stood directly opposite them, he saw that none were out of line and that the tallest of the seven stones was nearest the tracks yet still some forty metres from them.

Already their shadows were long. They did not fall upon each other. There wasn't a sign of anyone, only the sounds of picks and shovels in the clay pits just to the north and west. Denied diesel fuel, gasoline and dynamite, the miners had had to reverse a good seventy-five years of history and return to digging by hand.

Retracing his steps to the site of the murder, St-Cyr left the tracks for the irregularities of the moor and began to make a wide detour so as to come upon the standing stones yet cast no tell-tale shadow of his own.

When he found him on the far side of the sixth megalith and digging at its foot, Yvon Charbonneau, whom he had only seen in a black bow tie and tails in concert, was on his hands and knees and buried up to his shoulders. The laceless, shabby leather boots were smeared with sand and

140

whitish clay, the dark brown corduroy trousers were patched and filthy and worn through in the crotch where his underwear showed whitely.

A grey and crumpled handkerchief trailed from a bulging pocket. Mounds of earth containing bits of charcoal and charred bone were heaped on either side of him. To the left, there was an earth-encrusted shabby brown briefcase. A short-handled pick rested near the briefcase along with a short-handled shovel and stonemason's hammer – tools that could more easily be carried on the bicycle.

Laid out in a fan-shaped array on a mud-caked towel were three beautifully carved and polished deep green axeheads, some pale creamy brown flints – scrapers probably, or knives – several potsherds and a few broken bracelets of dark blue glass.

Charbonneau withdrew from the excavation. He did not yet sense company or that the Sûreté now knew beyond doubt that he had hidden the shopkeeper's briefcase on the day of the murder and had returned to recover it but had found his obsession too great for prudence to overcome.

The blade of flint he carefully cleaned off was half the length of a callused, grimy left palm whose ham had been crudely stitched and was still red and swollen. Delicately, as if caressing the notes of Rachmaninoff, Schubert or Brahms, he ran the fingers of his right hand over the long oval blade. Each conchoidal hollow and cusp left by the pressure flaking was felt and judged perfect, the point too.

Then he turned to reverently set it among the other pieces only to see that he was not alone.

'Monsieur . . .' began the Sûreté.

The flint was dropped, the hammer seized. Charbonneau lunged at him. They grappled. The hammer was raised . . . *His wrist, damn it!* shouted St-Cyr, grabbing it. *Must stop him. Must force him to . . .*

He was carried back in a rush and slammed hard into the last stone. Air . . . he needed air . . . *Can't breathe*, he cried. *My chest . . .*

His head hit the stone again and again. A last sight gave the pianist, whose thick and tousled black hair was flecked with iron-grey and whose dark ripe olive eyes soon lost their wild hatred and grew slowly sad.

Ah nom de Dieu, de Dieu, he is about to kill me, thought St-Cyr. There was a sharp crease between the eyes. Well down from them, a mottled grey-black, thatched roof of a moustache extended right into side whiskers that ran across the cheeks but did not climb to the ears . . .

A last image was of Paulette de Trocquer flicking a smile coyly at him as she stepped fastidiously over the corpses of her own making.

Collapsing, he hit his head against the stone again but did not feel a thing.

The hammer was raised. They were all alone. The hammer came down.

Kohler awoke with a start to find himself on the back seat of a car, looking up into the eyes of Elizabeth Krüger. The girl was leaning well over the front seat. Cautiously she released his lapel and watched as he wet his throat.

'Louis,' he croaked. 'Where the hell is he? Come on, damn you. He should be with us. I . . . I heard him cry out my name.'

In spite of the noise from the canneries, Herr Kohler did not realize where they were or what had happened. 'Please, you have been asleep, Inspector. Such a sleep. The Kapitän Freisen and I found you in the car when we came out of the Kernével villa to drive here to Quiberon.'

'Quiberon . . . ?'

She smiled faintly. 'The interrogation, yes? Have you forgotten? You did not even hear us get into the car.'

Oh-oh. Two hours, three . . . He recognized the stench of boiled sardines in oil. 'I was tired. Where's Freisen?'

It had been good that Herr Kohler had been asleep. It had made things so easy for her. Johann had been pleased with her help. 'Inside the prisoner's cell. We have waited for you such a long time. It is almost dark, yes? Do you wish to cancel the interrogation for today or to carry on?'

Again he asked for his partner. He sat up and flexed his arms. He discovered the rucksack he had used as a pillow and pulled it possessively towards him.

'Your . . . your friend is not at the Hotel Mégalithe. Indeed, he may still be in Lorient or . . . or with Frau Charbonneau and her husband.'

'Is the Préfet here?' he asked sharply.

She withdrew and now knelt not touching the back of the seat. 'No. No, he hasn't shown up either.'

Gott im Himmel, was it trouble?

That faint, hesitant smile crept over her. 'Please, they will come, yes? The Kapitän Freisen is most anxious to get the investigation over so as to clear the Captain's name. The Kapitän zur See Kaestner is . . . is willing to talk.'

Kneeling like that, she took him back to lonely roads, hot afternoons and cars parked among the fir trees. 'But is he willing to tell us what really went on,' he asked, 'or is it going to be more of the same thing?'

'The . . . the Admiral Doenitz has ordered the Kapitän Kaestner to be truthful and frank and to give you all the help he can.'

'And the Captain Freisen?'

'He . . . he cannot possibly have had anything to do with the . . . the murder.'

'But the two of them are playing a tight little game of their own, fräulein. The Admiral is unaware of this. You are.'

'I . . . I don't know what you mean?'

Blushing made her even prettier. 'I think you do. I think you would like to see Herr Freisen take over command of U-297. But what you want doesn't matter to them. Point is, Fräulein Krüger, though he wishes he could avoid it, Herr Freisen will go to sea if ordered but the Dollmaker is a stubborn man. Only he can bring that boat back but in his heart of hearts he knows he won't be able to and so do

143

Baumann and that boy they've got in there. Now only being convicted of murder can settle it. Murder.'

'You . . . you . . . Why did you have to come here?' she blurted. 'He's ill. He needs help. He . . .' She choked back a sob.

It would be best to be gentle but to tell her where things really stood. 'He won't let Freisen take command even if Doenitz, against his better judgement, orders it. He won't, Fräulein Krüger. He's too damned clever to allow it to happen, too cool, too arrogant, too proud and yes, too damned good. Hey, he's Lorient's top ace, a survivor. Though the men might make book on it and lay off their bets on the outcome of our little investigation, they're still counting on him. And who's to say they won't try to take him with them if necessary? Ah yes, fräulein, there's that to consider.'

She brushed her tears away. 'Then you had better talk to him.'

The din from the canneries was unbelievable, the stench horrendous yet both were totally ignored as in a submarine after weeks at sea.

'Vati, it is the Inspector Kohler.'

The boy, Erich Fromm, stood aside in the narrow corridor to let them squeeze past. Kohler took in the faded blond hair and furtive blue eyes, the broad jaw, cleanly shaven cheeks and the bad case of acne that had erupted over-night.

Fear made the boy dart his eyes away from him; embarrassment from those of the Fräulein Krüger. Nerves made him pick at a pustule. Some were bleeding.

'I'm going to want to have a private little chat with you, my friend,' breathed Kohler. 'Death's-head tells me you put all your money on the Captain. Right?'

There was no answer, only a rapid moistening of the eyes. No constriction of the swarthy throat yet but it would come.

The telegraphist stood uncertainly in the doorway waiting for him. 'Well?' asked Kohler.

Like a ramrod, the kid snapped to attention. '*Jawohl*, Herr Haupsturmführer Kohler.'

'Good. Now save us both time by telling me why you think he killed that shopkeeper.'

A desperate look for help was thrown at Fräulein Krüger; a wary and uncertain glance down the corridor to where Baumann and the Second Engineer were both bored to death rereading the Christmas issue of the *Völkischer Beobachter* on whose front page the Führer had splashed a map of the Atlantic that was peppered with red dots.

'. . . *like drops of blood*, the text had read. *Each one marks the position of the sinking of an enemy merchant ship . . . January to 17 December 1942*. Clang, clang and up periscope!

'Well . . . ?' asked Kohler.

'The . . . the Kapitän has . . . has ordered me to do so, Herr Hauptsturmführer.'

'Kaestner told you to bet against his getting off?'

'Yes, sir.'

'When did he do so?'

'As . . . as soon as he heard Death's-head was making book on the outcome.'

Verdammt! the bastard. If he really was guilty, Kaestner was making damn sure the kid would double his money, if not, he was slanting the odds so as to make a bundle himself. Half the crew had money on his head. A great joke if it wasn't true and he got off scot-free.

He was also creating yet another smokescreen from behind which he could slip away. Who else would so blatantly admit to murder in such a fashion? He had to be protecting someone and he had known instantly when ordering the boy to bet against his getting off, that this detective and his Sûreté partner would try to see beyond the smoke to Madame Charbonneau.

He's too sharp for us, grumbled Kohler testily. Louis . . . where the hell was he when needed most? Probably sawing

145

it off or sipping pastis while poring over his bits and pieces of a broken doll.

Kaestner was grinning broadly; Freisen was frowning impatiently and rhythmically striking a pencil against the edge of the table as he rocked back and forth in his chair.

Unlike the previous meeting, the Captain sat alone with his back to the wall in which a tiny, barred window of meshed and frosted glass let in the last of the day.

Freisen sat opposite the telegraphist – the seating had all been worked out in advance. The C.-in-C. U-boats Kernével could better signal the telegraphist from there to pause if things got rough.

Another visit to the toilet? wondered Kohler.

Drawing out the only other chair, he sat down across from the Dollmaker and only then realized the chairs for Louis and the Préfet had been removed.

'So, we begin it again,' he said. 'Start by telling me about your relationship with the pianist.'

Elizabeth Krüger could not hold back a faint smile. Flushed with elation, she did not dare to look up from her pad but waited for them to continue.

Kaestner rested his forearms companionably on the table and grinned good-naturedly. 'All right, you win. Yes, he was there earlier. When I arrived at the clay pits, I found Yvon digging at the foot of one of the standing stones. We spoke briefly.'

Merde, he was being too co-operative. Ah damn, thought Kohler and asked cautiously, 'How was he? In what state of mind did you find him?'

The shrewd grey-green eyes sought him out as they would a distant tanker. 'Vague as usual and reticent – he is a very lonely man. Many creative types are really very shy and withdrawn. You will have found this out in your work, I expect?'

'Just answer. Never mind playing around with my career.'

'Of course. Sorry, but I wasn't "playing around", Inspector. Yvon Charbonneau spoke of the passage he was working on in his symphony – a major interlude, I gather. One needs always patience with people like that. I was in a hurry. I hope I didn't upset him.'

The hypocrite.

Friesen handed cigarettes around to interrupt things and head off trouble. All but Elizabeth Krüger took one. 'U-boat rations,' grinned Kohler. 'I always knew you fellows were being treated as well if not better than Goering's fly-boys. The symphony?' he asked, giving Kaestner a nod.

' "The main theme had to be broken", he said, "so as to give structure and attain greatness. The druids had not yet gathered among the standing stones." '

'The druids?'

'Yes. Look, I can't explain it any better. The symphony is Celtic, druidic, very brooding and like Wagner's *Tannhauser*, I should think. Very of the Morbihan and the megaliths. Very bleak, uncomfortable, and unfriendly, if you ask me. Joyless because, poor fellow that he is, he is taking life far too seriously at the moment. The passage graves and dolmens are a daily thing with him, the alignments and even the single standing stones, the menhirs.'

Kohler set his cigarette aside and studied the smoke curling up from it as a chief druid might when about to explore a virgin's womb or stab her in the heart. 'Has he got a name for this "symphony" of his?'

Kaestner grinned inwardly as he sat back to survey this Gestapo gumshoe from Paris. 'Veneti, what else? The last great tribe, yes? The one Caesar defeated in 56 BC and led into slavery.'

Louis hadn't been the only one to hear the child's tale. 'But the stones are thousands of years older?'

'As are most of the artefacts and bits of charred bone he finds but the Veneti worshipped at those stones as well, and if not, at least held them in awe and were respectful of them.'

The Dollmaker and the child must have talked it over several times. 'And when you left the clay pits?' he asked.

'Did I see him then?' countered Kaestner. 'No. Of course not. He . . .'

'He *what*, Captain?'

Kaestner drew on his cigarette and took his time, then tried to make apologies for accusing someone perhaps unjustly. 'Look, Yvon, he . . . ah, he could have been out on the moor. Yes, of course. Hidden among the stones of that alignment. There are seven of them and they are all quite tall and big around. I didn't see him when I came back along the tracks. I thought he had left but . . .'

Freisen noted the Captain's shrug but said nothing and kept a weather eye on the Fräulein Krüger. Was he upset with her for telling the Captain something? wondered Kohler. She would definitely not have told her boss a certain detective had been reading a certain psychiatric analysis. 'Would the pianist have had any reason to kill that shopkeeper?'

The thin lips were tightly parted in a grimace of thought. 'He hardly knew him. Hélène . . . Madame Charbonneau never went into that shop. Yvon is . . . well the husband isn't wealthy. In fact they're very hard up these days. It's a tremendous strain on him of course. He's also very secretive and fanatically possessive of his finds until he has completed excavating them.'

'And has finished listening to the music they give him?'

'Yes, of course, if you want to put it that way.' Why wouldn't Kohler accept that the pianist had done it?

'He has a map of the locations,' muttered the Gestapo, lost in thought. 'My partner saw it in his study. I gather it's quite like the Führer's map in that newspaper out there. "Hits".'

'But not all of them,' came the wary answer.

And the pianist didn't object to your 'intruding' on his find? thought Kohler. Well, we'll see, shall we? 'So you saw and heard no one. Is that right?'

Freisen was trying to signal the woman to get her to ask for a break, but she was having none of it. Too worried to even look up.

148

'I heard shouting, Inspector, as you well know from our previous session. An altercation in French. Then the sound of iron hitting iron – yes, the switch-bar. Now I remember it. The bar must have been flung aside in disgust at what he had done.'

'The pianist?'

'Who else?'

Kohler looked at each of them in turn. 'Who else? Yes, of course. The person who was either sitting on the railway bed between the rails or standing. The person who dropped the doll, perhaps just as that switch-bar came down, Captain. The person who must have been between you and the victim if what you say is true. The person who then stepped on the shopkeeper's glasses.'

'Please, I . . . I must go to the toilet, yes? A moment.'

Kohler threw out a hand and gripped her by the wrist. 'Sit down. Hold on. I'm not quite finished.'

'This meeting is concluded,' snapped Freisen, getting to his feet. 'We're late as it is, Fräulein Krüger. The reception, yes? and then the party for the Kapitän Hahn and his crew or had you forgotten?'

The submarine that had returned to base this morning.

'No one leaves,' said Kohler. 'Not yet. If you do, Herr Freisen, I will ask your secretary here to telex my objections to Gestapo Mueller in Berlin.'

Freisen didn't like it. 'Very well. Elizabeth, you may leave us. I'll take over the notes.'

'It . . . it is all right. I can wait.'

Knees pressed together now, was that it? snorted Kohler inwardly. Well, prepare yourself, *Liebchen*. Hang on.

He dragged out the small black notebook he liked to use on such occasions and flipped it open. 'Apparently early on the afternoon in question, the Unteroffizier Jacob Dorst and the Feldwebel Helmut Ruediger gave a lift to Lorient and well beyond it out of courtesy to a pretty French-woman in her late thirties with dark brown almost black hair underneath her kerchief and dark hazel eyes. She had a bicycle with Wehrmacht issue tyres and she was in a hurry.'

Involuntarily Elizabeth Krüger gripped her stomach. Freisen remained in the background silently watching the Dollmaker who hadn't moved a hair and hadn't liked that little bit about the free tyres with, no doubt, the healthy inner tubes.

'There was a packet of American cigarettes in that railway shed, Captain. A woman's crumpled handkerchief had been shoved well down in the straw. You and Yvon Charbonneau's wife are, to put it discreetly, on very intimate terms. On more than one occasion the pianist's daughter saw you with her stepmother on the beach.'

'Walking. Just talking. There is no harm in that.'

Was Kaestner so cool he could treat it all as if waiting for a convoy to pass on either side of him before opening fire? 'Yes, but you also came to stay the night, Captain, when Angélique Charbonneau's father was away' – it was just a shot in the dark. 'The child apparently wanders but not in her sleep. From what my partner could gather, the kid is a regular one hundred per cent night owl and we both know kids of that age have ears.'

Anger flared so suddenly, Kohler was taken aback. 'Kerjean is crazy. He has put this . . . this idiocy into your heads! Did she see us making love?' The Dollmaker slammed a hand down hard on the table. 'Of course she didn't because it never happened! We'd have been speaking *Deutsch* anyway and *that*, my fine imbecile from the Gestapo, Angélique does not understand. Not yet anyway. Christ, the interfering bastard! And he calls himself a Préfet!'

Calmness would be best. 'Then why the cigarettes and the handkerchief in that shed?'

'Why indeed? Yvon left his bicycle there and yes, I might have left a package of cigarettes or some tobacco for him now and then as a gesture of kindness, but not there, Inspector. Never there. Hélène and I never used that shed or any other. Never once. The child is lying and so is Préfet Kerjean.'

A shoe tipped over and Kohler felt it do so as a tender reassuring foot was stretched out to touch the Captain's leg. She'd stay in this . . . this pigeon-hole with him all night if she could. The constant racket and the stench of sardines wouldn't matter a damn to her. Nothing would. Not even the presence of Baumann and the others or their relief.

'So, okay you weren't having an affair but she still came to see you that afternoon or to . . .'

Kaestner didn't smile. Every particle of him was focused on the target. 'Or to stop her husband from killing the shopkeeper, Herr Kohler? Is that how it was?'

Ach! The bastard had him by the balls. 'The doll?' bleated Kohler. 'Where would it have come from?'

'The shop. Someone must have either left it in trade or simply forgotten it. Le Trocquer never buys – at least, he never did if he could avoid it.'

'In trade for what?'

'Some of his rubbish. A sweet dish, an ashtray – who's to say, Inspector? It was . . .'

'The morning of the murder or the day before it, Captain?'

'I really wouldn't know. How could I? I was in Paris, or on my way back and then out to the clay pits.'

A Steiner or a Bru doll but most probably a Jumeau. Louis might have something more on what had gone on in that shop but Louis had yet to show up. *Verdammt!* Where is he? wondered Kohler. 'Why did you choose le Trocquer as a partner?'

'Our cook found him for me. The men went there to buy things to send home to their girlfriends and families. The dolls do sell but only at certain times of the year.'

'And at other times?'

Kohler was like a heavily laden ship that simply would not go down. Not yet. 'A few here and there. Surprisingly le

Trocquer did have good contacts – people he hadn't yet tried to cheat. An uncle, due soon to retire, is part owner of the faience works we use and want to purchase and improve. There are also his wife's sister and brother. One has a shop in Quimper and the other in Quimperle. That wife of his comes from a long line of shopkeepers. Little people but effective when one needs them. Most of the dolls stay in Paris at the Galeries Lafayette, two very exclusive shops on the rue du Faubourg Saint-Honoré and another on the Place Vendôme, near the Ritz. I didn't trust everything to him, Inspector. I'm not so foolish.'

'And the money you left with him?'

'He said he needed time and I gave it to him. I had every reason to believe and still do, as did he himself, that his daughter Paulette had either stolen it or had had a hand in its stealing but that the money would soon be recovered in total.'

An optimist to say the least! 'And you know of no reason why the pianist might have wanted to kill him?'

'Only that Yvon feels very threatened when one of his discoveries appears to be intruded upon by others before he has finished excavating the thing.'

But not by you yourself, eh? thought Kohler. Is that how it was? 'And the Préfet?' he asked, closing the notebook.

There was a brief smile of admission. 'No reason whatsoever. My God, a Chief of Police? Don't be an idiot.'

You bastard, thought Kohler, sizing him up. You've already accused Kerjean once. You get me to think it was the pianist, then you throw the blame right back on to the Préfet by telling me you had no reason to accuse him even though Kerjean obviously thought you had.

'This session is concluded. I'll want a copy of your telex to the Admiral, Fräulein Krüger. See that it is delivered to my hotel along with the first one and make goddamned sure both are in a sealed envelope. I don't want Madame Quévillon having a read. I don't want her steaming the envelope open either.'

The fish stew – or was it the soup? – was cold and not very good. The dining-room at the Hotel Mégalithe was lighted only by one parsimonious candle stub. Every sound was magnified – the creaking of the damned floorboards, the sighing of timbers, a clogged drain that sucked hollowly at its fuzzy plug and gulped to the building of a sou'wester. Christ! were they now to have four days of solid rain?

Kohler shoved the soup plate forward until it lay like a sick moon just before the fanned-out, biliously chartreuse ration tickets the Préfet had left for them. Louis hadn't shown up here. He hadn't been with Kerjean either. Ah damn, where the hell was he? In trouble . . . was that it?

Reaching down to the floor, he caught up the Lebel Model 1873 six-shooter the Sûreté carried when needed. Guns were this Gestapo's responsibility when not in use, a stupid rule of Boemelburg's that ought to have been done away with long ago.

Breaking the gun open, he squinted down the barrel at the candle flame. Clean as a whistle and ready to go as always. A careful man. Louis could knock the head off a pigeon at thirty paces but was a lover of nature, a tree-planter on occasion even when investigating a murder! He seldom used a gun, preferring his precious bracelets and leaving the guillotine to do its work. 'The basket always catches them,' he'd say.

He had come here with Marianne on his second honeymoon. She had been a very pretty thing. Blonde, blue-eyed and quite innocent at first, no doubt. But in the buff, she had had an absolutely gorgeous figure, not only awakening to the joys of sex but eager for them, so eager. The poor Frog. The Hauptmann Steiner had made damned good use of her for far too long and Gestapo Paris's The Watchers had photographed the couple at play on several occasions, none of which had been cluttered up by bedcovers or clothing. Half the boys at the rue des Saussaies had seen the films. They were still holding regular showings when they thought it funny and Louis, who had yet to see the films and never would, wasn't around.

But now the cuckold was missing and the pretty wife was dead. And oh for sure, someone else had come along and Gabrielle Arcuri, the chanteuse, was superb both in voice and looks, et cetera, et cetera, but that romance had yet to be consummated. Kohler was certain of this. 'He's too shy. He's still feeling the loss, still loyal to the wife in spite of everything and unwilling to commit himself a third time.'

Idly he wondered what Louis's first wife had been like. She had run off with a truck driver, or had it been a door-to-door salesman? He never said much about her, out of deference to the second wife. Truth was, the Sûreté was seldom home. Truth was that even when awakening to a naked woman in his bed, a gift from his partner and friend, he had remained steadfastly faithful. Politely muttering excuses, he had always been kind to these nocturnal visitors and afterwards would say, 'Hermann, you must always remember that girl was someone's daughter. I would not wish to offend the mother, not to mention the father, of course, or the husband or the lover.'

Closing the revolver's cylinder, he slid his right arm through the straps and buckled up. Then he checked the Walther P38 on the other side of his chest, popping the clip, banging it back in and shucking cartridges rapidly before reloading and making certain there was one up the spout.

Satisfied, he put the safety on and slid the pistol away.

'Madame Quévillon,' he sang out – at least it sounded as if he did. His voice crashed from the walls and fled among the fully dressed tables that waited in the all but darkness as schoolgirls wait to dance a first dance when no one asks them and the boys haven't come.

'Monsieur?'

Still mesmerized by the artillery probably, that formidable giant in black sackcloth and boots stood watch from just inside a far doorway. Arms were folded defiantly across her chest. The headgear towered above her.

'Madame, the *cotriade* is among the finest I've tasted but until I find my partner, I'm . . .' He shrugged and threw her a lame look. 'I'm afraid I simply have no stomach for it.'

'Perhaps he is already with the others.'

With the dead? 'At the party?' he bleated.

'Or at the shop of Madame le Trocquer. The shop will, of course, be closed and that girl, that Paulette will be at the . . .'

'The party?'

'You might call it that, Inspector. For myself, I would call it the work of the Devil. Such drunkenness and goings on are shameful. Debauchery, licentiousness . . .' She crossed herself. '. . . and now murder. It is only to be expected. That girl . . .' The lips compressed themselves tightly. 'Paulette le Trocquer is trouble. Some are saying she knows where the Captain's money is hidden, others that she helped the thief to steal it and now waits for him to return. Hah, there's fat chance of that! You'll see. She'll go to the party now that her father's dead and never mind the required days of mourning. *Those* she will spend on her back, the silly thing. Please stop her. Her mother needs her.'

Ah *merde*, the giant had reduced herself to tears in front of the enemy, something she would never have done otherwise. 'Hey, it's going to be all right, madame. The U-boat crews may be rough – hell, they don't have easy lives or long ones, but they're not criminals. They wouldn't harm a pretty girl.'

'Even if she had stolen their money or knew who had taken it and where it was?'

Verdammt, she had sucked him right in with those tears! 'If you've got any thoughts on the matter, you'd best let me have them,' he said warily.

She would tell him now. It would be for the best, a free conscience and a pure heart. 'The Côte Sauvage, Inspector, and the caves no one sees from atop the cliffs. I am worried someone will take that girl to a place no one else knows of. Then they will force her to tell them what they want to know and then they will kill her.'

The rain came suddenly to the standing stones. The darkness was everywhere as the wind shrieked across the moor. Dazed and aching badly, St-Cyr clawed himself to his feet to lean against the stone and try to still the agony in the back of his head.

'This way,' he gasped and lurched from the stone to stumble and fall into the grass and lie there letting the rain wash over him. 'Hermann . . . Hermann, where are you?'

A memory came of their first meeting, 13 September 1940, each warily regarding the other with open hostility and doubt. Then Hermann had grinned and extended that big hand of his. 'Ah what the hell, eh, Monsieur Jean-Louis? Let's work together and show them all it's possible. I like your car.'

Hermann had been living at the Hotel Boccador then with others of the Gestapo. Girls in, girls out, the traffic jams in the rooms and corridors had been heavy.

When the gale struck him, he was pushed along to teeter madly, to slip and let out a piercing cry. Then the clay pits took him. Down and down he went, banging into the rocks, shooting over muddy, rain-washed slopes until, with a sound he did not hear, he was swallowed up. Clay to the left, clay to the right. It sucked at his arms and pinned his legs. It threatened to drown him.

For a while he tasted the chalky milk of it that poured down the cliff face behind him as he squeezed its unctuousness between clenched and useless fists.

Only by easing a foot around did he find rock solid enough to stand on and by sheer force of will pry himself upright. '*H . . . ermann!*' he cried out into the beating rain. 'H . . . ermann!' It was no use. 'Where am I?' he asked. 'My head . . .'

The clay was so greasy. It took all his strength to pull

himself out of the hollow. He began to climb rocks that crumbled at the least touch or simply rushed away in torrents of gravelly mud that struck him in the face. 'I must,' he said.

Hermann had immediately taken possession of his car, that big black beautiful Citroën four-door sedan all the boys on the rue Laurence-Savart in Belleville had admired so much. Now he drove it nearly always and his little Sûreté Frog sat as a passenger – a *passenger* in his *own* vehicle!

Half-way up the cliff, he had to stop. 'I can't do it,' he said. 'I haven't the strength. *Hermann, damn you, help me!*'

A pair of green-glass candlesticks appeared before him in colour, the shattered face of a doll.

The Parian head of Angélique Charbonneau loomed suddenly and he saw it with a clarity that shocked because the head was so perfect, so exquisitely sculpted. 'But there are no arms or legs?' he said, now greatly troubled. 'There is no torso?'

The child knew more than anyone. The child held secrets of her own.

Her hand stretched out to him. Desperately its fingers tried to grasp his own as he strained to reach them and only then wondered how this could possibly be.

'Inspector, it's Hélène Charbonneau. Have you seen my husband?'

'My father.'

'Not since he tried to kill me.'

'You'd be dead then,' swore the child. 'He'd have *smashed* your head open like a buttered egg but he didn't, did he?'

'No . . . ah, no, I guess he didn't.'

'But he could have if he had wanted to.'

'Just help me up. We can discuss it later.'

157

7

Sparks danced up from the driftwood logs in the fireplace, and when she turned to stand beside where the Chief Inspector St-Cyr lay asleep on the old brown leather sofa in her father's study, Angélique Charbonneau's shadow fell over him. And she wondered at the casting of shadows among all the things her father had collected, and she raised both arms and stretched up on tiptoes in her night-dress like a spectre.

The Chief Inspector snored sometimes, but not too loudly. She nudged his shoulder more sharply this time, more bravely.

'Asleep and dead to the world,' she whispered. 'I don't need to worry about him any more tonight.'

Passing by the cluttered billiard table, she saw that shadows from the fire flickered hauntingly over the skulls and bones. 'Father's out there somewhere,' she whispered sadly to a skull whose clenched teeth and hollow eyes grinned and stared back at her. Light . . . it was so amazingly light without its flesh. 'Musty too,' she said, sniffing delicately at it. 'And porous but not like the feel of broken bisque. Much coarser.'

Raising the skull high above her as a druid would, she turned so that its shadow was thrown with her own across all the bones and things and finally on to the wall.

'My father is hiding the briefcase he found on the railway tracks,' she whispered to the skull. 'Having buried it once, he has taken it to a place where no one will ever find it.'

Late in the day, Préfet Kerjean had come to the house

looking for the Chief Inspector, wanting to talk to him in private, to explain perhaps and to plead for help, who's to say? Together, he and the stepmother and herself had driven to the aerodrome near the clay pits and had left the car on a lonely road. With the Préfet in the lead, they had walked across the moor and along the railway tracks past a shed the murderess had refused to look at, past the place of the killing which had made the murderess cringe.

'By accident or by some trick of the standing stones, we heard the Chief Inspector crying out to his partner and friend. Brought back to the house and given brandy and soup, he has had the huge bath in the kitchen and afterwards, though very sleepy, has washed his clothes in that same bathwater and hung them up above the stove to dry. His shoes also, and his overcoat, but not his fedora, alas, for this has been irretrievably lost.

'Offered a bedroom, he has refused and has chosen instead, this study.'

She killed the skull's fleshless cheek and set it soundlessly among its fellows. 'The Chief Inspector is waiting for my father to return. He is going to confront him with assaulting a police officer and with attempted murder. *She* is beside herself with worry and despair and cannot forgive herself but can only wring her hands and pace the floor or lie weeping the cold tears of remorse in her cold bed.'

Préfet Kerjean had not stayed to talk to the Chief Inspector after all. Indeed, he had left in such a hurry. But had he gone, as he had said he would, in search of her father? The alignments at Kerzerho crossed the main road not five kilometres from the house. The Dolmen of Crucuno, said to be the finest in the Morbihan, was nearer Plouharnel and the Quiberon Peninsula. The alignments at Saint-Barbé were even a little closer than this.

At each of these prehistoric sites the briefcase could be hidden.

But had Préfet Kerjean really gone in search of her father,

or had he gone to Quiberon itself and the shop of Monsieur le Trocquer, the shop of the daughter and her mother?

Yes, he had been very worried and not without good reason, for he had been seen through the telescope of truth, seen talking on the beach last summer to Madame Charbonneau, and many times since then. Talking very seriously about things only they thought they knew.

The *sardiniers* and a son who, with his comrades, would at last escape to England if not first discovered and killed. Their families too.

When she had reached the top of the stairs and, without the aid of a light, had crossed the attic, Angélique touched the cold brass tube of the telescope and remembered another warm day last summer in early August, not a stormy night like this. The Captain had returned.

She had been half hidden by the marram grass and pine needles, and by the edge of the bluff and some rocks so that only her chest and middle had shown while the Kapitän zur See Kaestner had stood facing her.

He had laughed. He had said something and had smiled. He had reached out to her and . . . and had touched her pure white blouse, had plucked at a button.

She hadn't moved. She hadn't even objected and when her breasts had spilled into the sunlight, she had let him kiss them.

'You shouldn't have let him do that to you,' whispered Angélique spitefully. 'You should have stopped him long before this. Did you really think my father wouldn't discover your treachery? I didn't *need* to tell him, madame. He saw it in your eyes, in the way you could not look at him. He saw it, too, from up here – oh yes he did on other occasions. There were many of these *liaisons sexuelles* weren't there?

'I found him watching you. I heard him crying but even then I did not go to him. Poor father, poor rejected pianist, poor symphony.'

Raindrops were being killed against the spyglass window.

Now a sudden gust, a blast of gunfire from the rain-Messerschmitts, now a pause while the raindrop-blood ran down the glass and cannon-breakers pounded the beach where *she* and the Captain had lain together.

Only their bare feet had been seen and watched from up here that time. Her feet had been spread widely. The heels had dug deeply into the soft, clean sand, digging deeper and deeper and deeper, the toes stiff and upright, his toes dug into the sand . . . the sand . . .

'I mustn't tell the Chief Inspector what I did on the day before the murder. I mustn't!' she blurted.

When St-Cyr found the child in the attic, Angélique was quietly playing with her dolls. Dolls that Kaestner had made but others as well. Lots of them.

The Bar of the Mermaid's Three Sisters was packed. The telegraphist's silk-stockinged knees were really very nice, and when she sat primly subdued and worried on her bar stool facing him, Kohler was tempted.

'Another beer?' he asked.

She shook her head. 'I'll drown if I do.' Longingly she looked across the crowded dance floor towards the stage and the Dollmaker's wind-up Victrola with its lovely stack of records. Everyone took a turn; everyone got a chance.

Teutonic, bare-breasted, blue-eyed and blonde-haired mermaids in a turquoise sea of their own formed a backdrop to this icon of heroism and daring. Neptune blew on a conch among the jade-green, trailing weeds while wrapping an arm about a slender waist. Was he calling others to supper? Giant clams, still in their closed shells, were being held aloft to the gods of gluttony by the mermaids. Fish tails and dolphins swam about or wiggled from the prongs of Herr Neptune's fork. His muscles bulged.

No art critic, Kohler grinned and tried to make conversation. 'Whoever painted that backdrop did a damned good job.'

'He's dead. The Fähnrich zur See Johannsen was a

volunteer from Oslo, Herr Kohler. A draughtsman in his father's firm. Midshipman Paintbrush went down with U-356 on the 30th December, just two days before the murder of that lousy shopkeeper who has caused us all so much trouble. Fourteen of the enemy's convoy were sunk using a *Rudeltaktik* of eleven boats, fanned out in an arc to the south-west of Iceland and well beyond the range of the enemy's air patrols but not, apparently, of their destroyers. He was a nice boy, full of fun and we shall sadly miss him. His photograph has not yet been hung on the wall but as you can see, space is so hard to find, we are now covering the opposite wall.'

Glenn Miller was playing 'Moonlight Serenade'. The deep and mellow sounds of that fantastic trombone filled the place. Pretty, pink-cheeked Breton girls danced with pasty-faced U-boat ratings in dark blue sailor suits that did nothing to hide their jaundiced looks or overly large eyes. Close . . . close . . . cling, cling . . .

The *Blitzmädels* from home, apart from the one sitting beside him, were determined to have a good time. All ranks and branches of the services mingled, the boys from the band, the boys from the garrison. All ages from sixteen to fifty-six at least, this one included.

Due to the severity of the storm, Lorient would most likely be spared a visit from the RAF, so everyone who could possibly get leave had got here early. Men outnumbered girls by at least twenty to one. Starvation either drove the boys to hunger after the girls or to cluster in little groups round the tables and try to out-talk and outboast each other over beer, wine and cigarettes with brandy chasers. Slosh time was coming up.

There was still no sign of Louis. *Verdammt*, where was he?

'Let's dance. Come on, it won't hurt you. It'll help to keep the bees from swarming and you might even enjoy it.'

'I can't. I won't. He . . . he isn't coming.'

'He's in jail. Even Baumann wouldn't take it upon himself to let the Captain out just for this.'

'But it is a party, yes? Both for the homecoming boat and for . . . for U-297's departure on Thursday.'

Ah *merde*, more tears. Kohler took her by the wrist and pulled her from the bar stool. Barging through the crowd, he swept her into his arms. 'Relax. It's only a dance. Hey, there's a war on and even detectives get lonely.'

'You've two women in Paris and a wife back home.'

When he didn't say a thing, she gave up and let him hold her. Already he was caught up in the music. Already he was making her feel that if she shut her eyes and let her mind go, it could just as easily be the Captain. For a big man, with big shoes, Herr Kohler was very light on his feet, deceptively smooth and, though sensitive to her every move, very strong. Yes, strong. 'Your wife must miss you,' she said, finding her cheek pressed against his own.

'She doesn't. Not any more.'

'Pennsylvania 6-5000' was next and it was fast and really quite a lot of fun but suddenly the music stopped, suddenly there was cheering, such cheering . . .

Kohler felt her leave him. He felt her hesitate.

A space was cleared ahead of the Dollmaker and his entourage of Baumann, the boy Erich Fromm and the Second Engineer.

Préfet Kerjean, looking dismayed and unhappy, brought up the rear.

Men stepped back, their girls too. Kaestner acknowledged the homage with head held high. Grinning he clicked his heels lightly together as he bowed and brought her hand to his lips.

'Fräulein Krüger, may I have the honour of this dance? Herr Hauptsturmführer, you will not mind, yes? The Préfet Kerjean wishes a quiet word, I think.'

Already the command had gone ahead to the stack of records and a selection had been made. Already the trumpet of Harry James was playing 'You Made Me Love You'.

'He's just too damned smooth,' swore Kohler. 'Now he's

going to mine that woman for all she's worth and she'll do anything he wants.'

'Inspector, please. I . . . I had no choice but to give in to their request that the Captain be allowed to attend. My job, it is not always easy. The Admiral . . .'

'You're sweating, Préfet. Where's Louis?'

'Where is the pianist, that is what I want to know.'

Deep in the attic's clutter, and far from the spyglass window, the child had made a place for her dolls, a house of last retreat. Black sheeting closed in the light from two megalithic stone lamps on the floor. A large and very floppy, red-rosed *chapeau* rested on her head as she sat quietly in her nightgown on a cream silk *chaise-longue* that was draped with intricately fine, antique black Breton lace. And all around her and behind and into the distance among the gathered mirrors of her imagination, the dolls stood or sat on ramparts of covered trunks, old suitcases, boxes, chairs and commodes.

Wire and bamboo birdcages had even been used – were the dolls inside them being incarcerated for minor misdemeanours or crimes like murder? he wondered.

Not one doll looked her way. All looked at him through the flickering light from the past as if with breath held, waiting to see what he would do. Blue eyes, brown eyes, large eyes . . . their pink cheeks stiff with stillness. Dolls with big hats and red roses like her own. Dolls in frilly bonnets, lace nightcaps and kerchiefs. Dolls without anything to hide their masses of blonde curls or waves of lustrous brown or black or blonde hair. Some wore nightgowns but these were far better than her own. Most wore extravagantly elaborate gowns of silk brocade, taffeta, lace, velvet or satin in shades of sapphire blue, soft pink, citrine yellow – even a bright orange, a burgundy, a crimson, a black – yes black silk. Draped necklaces of pearls were much in evidence, of amber too, and agate and coloured glass. Diamonds also.

There were about forty dolls. Some were obviously quite old, others much more recent but still perhaps turn of the century.

Directly behind her in the distance, on a bare wooden box before an oblong mirror, there was a row of heads with piled curls in waves and rosy cheeks. These dollheads were of Parian and among them the child had placed the head the Captain had modelled after herself.

'Oh, it's all right,' she said at last. 'I suppose you had better come in but *don't* trip. *Don't* touch anything. It wasn't fair of you to cheat like that. I thought you were asleep.'

'I apologize.'

'It's perfect, is it not? They are all waiting for you to tell them who killed the shopkeeper since you do not believe it was *her*.'

The doll that Kaestner had made of Hélène Charbonneau stood enclosed in gilded wire. The gown was of a deep brown velvet that glowed softly in the lamplight of lamps that could well be more than four thousand years old.

There was a diamond at her throat. A saucer of water lay behind her.

'Well?' said Angélique sharply. 'Aren't you coming in? You had better not keep them waiting.'

'A moment, please, mademoiselle. The cameras of my mind refuse to rest.'

The dolls were exquisite, yet the more he searched among them, the more he realized they stood or sat not waiting for his verdict but in judgement of Hélène Charbonneau.

The lamplight was disturbing for it gave to the dolls and the child the aura of some mystic rite.

Ah, at last! he said to himself. One is missing. There is a space next to the sailor doll on the floor beside where she has forgotten to pick up her scissors.

'What is it?' she asked, and the shrillness of her voice seemed to startle the dolls.

He found himself reflected in the mirrors and this was also disturbing. 'May I?' he asked, indicating the *chaise-longue*.

'No. There is a chair. *You* are to sit before us.'

The large hazel eyes of the stepmother peered through the bars at him. Forehead, nose and chin, the ears and the throat, the long almost dark black hair with its coppery hues and the fine brush of the eyebrows, all were of Hélène Charbonneau. The Dollmaker had spared no effort. She was perfect.

'This is Adèle, my mother,' said the child, watching him closely.

'Which one?' he was forced to ask.

'*There*, I told you so. All of you. *He* calls himself a detective, a Chief Inspector!'

The gown was of sky-blue satin. The deep blue sapphire pendant was very real.

'Hélène should be with her dearest friend,' he said uncomfortably.

He was making her so angry. 'She's going to the guillotine,' she hissed. 'I *won't* even put her head with the others.'

The detective longed for his pipe and tobacco but these had unfortunately been soaked through at the clay pits, though he felt the pockets of the robe for them. Rain thrashed the roof above. The wind cried out.

'There are so many of them,' he said. 'They are so very beautiful.'

'*She* and my mother used to collect them for me when they were with my father on his concert tours.'

'Ah!' He tossed his head in acknowledgement. 'Vienna, Berlin, Thuringia perhaps and Waltershausen or Erfurt – a side trip, a little holiday. The Parian heads. The Captain didn't make all of those. They were picked up in second-hand shops. Shops of fine antiques and beautiful little curios.'

A Bru, a Steiner or a Jumeau, Kaestner had said of the

166

fragments of bisque, but of these only the Steiner was German.

'What makes of doll have you?' he asked, again wishing for his pipe. He would now be very difficult for her to deal with. Even the flames of antiquity would not disturb him any more.

'Steiner,' she said hollowly. 'Jumeau – there are several with the Jumeau *Médaille d'or de Paris* incised on the body and only sometimes on the back of the head and hidden by the hair. The Bru dolls have the letters BRU in a vertical row on the left shoulder. The Captain has told me this. He has identified the makers of all of my dolls and has even done so first with his eyes closed. He made a bet with me and he won it. He knows each one simply by touching the bisque, by touching their cheeks, their skin like this.'

She shut her eyes and felt the softness of her cheek and chin and then her throat.

'There are some Armand Marseilles – he was a German but had a French name. It's curious, is it not? The A.M. is incised on the back of the neck. Simon and Halbig made others. H.H. stands for Heinrich Handewerck. I've three of those and like them very much but then, I like all of my dolls. Well, almost all of them.'

The child was holding something back. She didn't like him asking about the makers of the dolls, nor did she like him looking at her scissors on the floor and that empty space. 'The Royal Kaestners?' he asked.

'They are the finest, can't you tell?'

'Please, I am more interested in their trademarks at the moment.'

She fidgeted. She looked away. 'A king's crown, of course, with two streaming ribbons. The left ribbon has the initials J.D.K.; the right ribbon, Germany.'

'Good. Any others?' he asked suddenly and got up to reach out to take a doll down from its perch.

'*You're not to touch them!*' she hissed, alarmed.

'I will if I must,' he countered.

'It's a Bru, so there! Can't you tell by its face? Don't you know anything? The face is always heavier. It's more highly coloured than the Jumeau that is nearby. Jumeaus have the largest, most beautiful, soulful eyes and the best clothes, though the Captain says this is not so. The clothes, that is.'

The Royal Kaestners were better.

'You have lost a doll, Angélique. Please tell me what happened when you and your father went into the shop of Monsieur le Trocquer. It was the day before his murder. You purchased a pair of green-glass candlesticks for your step-mother.'

They had turned on her in the mirrors. Now all the dolls were watching her and it was as if she herself was on trial and it wasn't fair.

'Well?' he asked. He would not leave it now. He even picked up one of the lamps and held it out before him so as to see her better.

'Then, yes,' she spat. 'I purchased candlesticks for her.'

'What did you pay for them?' The stonework of the lamp was so very beautiful, the design so very simple, the shape, the long half of a small butternut squash. 'Well?' he said.

Why must he ask? 'Twenty-five francs each. It . . . it was a lot. Candles can't be bought except on the black market and that's illegal. He knew this, yet he insisted on the price.'

'But you made the sacrifice anyway.'

'Yes,' she muttered spitefully and wished he would put the lamp down.

'Did your stepmother like the candlesticks?'

Anger flared. 'Of course not. That is *why* I bought them!'

He set the lamp down carefully on the floor. 'What happened to the doll that is missing?'

She could not tell him. She mustn't. 'I . . . I don't know. Someone stole it, I suppose.'

'Was there anyone else in the shop besides your father and Monsieur le Trocquer?'

'Paulette . . . Paulette was there. Of course! It was she who stole my doll. It was, Inspector. It must have been.'

'Paulette?'

'*Yes!*'

'But . . . but Paulette has told me she went up to see to her mother? Please don't lie, Angélique. Not now. Lives are at risk. A murderer hides and though you say it was your stepmother, this may not be so.'

'Paulette le Trocquer stole my doll. I . . . I set it on something. I can't remember. I had thought to sell it to Monsieur le Trocquer or at least to exchange it for the candlesticks but . . . but he didn't want to. He said the doll did not interest him.'

'Yet he must have taken it in his briefcase when he went to find the Captain Kaestner on the following day. The Préfet had come to the shop. They had had an argument. Things were broken. Paulette and her mother each swear they heard them cry out a name. I think you know whose name that was and I think you should tell me what really happened to that doll and why you took it to the shop in the first place.'

'*I can't. I mustn't! She killed him and she'll kill me too if you're not careful!*'

He could not leave it. He got up again from his chair and, seizing the scissors, threatened to strip all the dolls if necessary to examine the marks of their makers.

In tears, the girl blurted, 'It was a K and R, so there. Kämmer and Reinhardt, does that make you feel better? A dark green velvet gown with a *décolletage* and appliqués of frilly white lace at its cuffs and down its front and real jade buttons. They were really real.'

'K and R . . . ?'

The letters meant nothing to the Chief Inspector, and when she saw this, Angélique wiped her tears away and shuddered involuntarily. Paulette would know all about it. Paulette would tell him.

*

169

Kohler listened intently as Préfet Kerjean told him of his search for the pianist, and only occasionally did he catch a glimpse of the shopkeeper's daughter. The girl was dancing with one of the junior officers from Kernével. She was having the time of her life and getting lots of hungry looks from the boys.

'That girl should know better,' grumbled Kerjean testily. 'No respect for the dead. None either for convention and morality.'

The stump of a grimy forefinger stabbed at the map he had spread between them on the zinc. 'I went first to the alignments nearest Yvon's house but without success. As I expanded the search towards Plouharnel, I began to see more and more that Yvon must go to one of his special places. Locations where I had often found him in the past.'

The girl's tight black leather skirt was far too short. Her legs . . . silk stockings . . . there was only one way she could have got them, thought Kerjean. 'He had hurt your friend quite badly. Indeed, he might well believe he had killed him.'

'What was in the briefcase?'

'That I do not know. Papers of agreement for the Captain to sign, perhaps a portion of the missing money – a show of good faith.'

'But le Trocquer definitely went to the clay pits to see the Captain?'

'Yes. Yes, of course. Why do you ask? Is there something I have missed?'

'No. No, I just wondered. *Verdammt*, I wish Louis was here. No partner and I need to talk.' And you're still sweating, said Kohler to himself. 'Another *fine à l'eau*?' he asked, indicating the empty glass. Another house brandy with water.

'One for the road and then I must go. Yvon . . . Yvon Charbonneau is a very difficult man to fathom, Inspector. Please appreciate that he is not in his right mind. He is also a demon on that bicycle of his. Eighty, ninety kilometres. Nothing stops him, especially not the weather.'

'Get to the point, Préfet. You're making it sound like you're building yourself an alibi.'

Kohler was of the Gestapo and whether he was one of their 'best' or 'worst' members would not matter. 'I did not kill le Trocquer, Inspector. I had no reason to. I am a police officer.'

'Since when did belonging to the law stop anyone?'

Nom du ciel, must he be so difficult? 'As I was just saying, increasingly I came to believe – and still do – that Yvon, in fear and great anxiety, would retreat to one of his very special places. Of those nearest Carnac, the tumulus of Saint-Michel, which is on the north-eastern edge of the town, seemed the most promising. Yvon could have hitched a ride part way in a lorry – there were plenty of them heading here, isn't that so?'

'And?'

'It is a place in which I have found him many times. There are two entrances and he has ways of getting in there no one else knows. A hill some twelve metres high and one hundred and twenty long beneath which there are the passages which are lined with large upright stones and massive cap rocks, and the graves, of course, the firepits. The entrances to the tumulus are at the base of the hill. Long passages go to the right and left. There are rooms and other, lesser passages – turnings. One has to have a light – ah, it is so dark in there. One also has to duck the head and crouch or crawl. It is not easy particularly if you are dealing with someone who is deranged.'

'But he wasn't there?'

It would be best to shrug. 'What can I say? I was only one man looking for another. He has no fear of such places. Indeed, he is so steeped in them, he is of them and knows them far better than anyone else. My trousers, the palms of my hands – you can see for yourself the state I am in. Soaked to the skin from the clay pits, worn to a frazzle.'

'And you're certain he tried to kill Louis?'

'No, I did not say that. I said he might well *think* he had. This might . . .'

'Might make him do something foolish?'

'Yes.'

'Such as?'

There was much sadness in Kerjean's dark blue eyes and for a moment the Préfet found he could say nothing. 'He might kill himself, Inspector. Hélène . . . Madame Charbonneau would never forgive me, so you see, I must find him not just so that we can settle this matter but that another tragedy will not happen.'

Kohler reached over the zinc to find the brandy bottle. Refilling the Préfet's glass, he nodded curtly at it and waited while it was downed. 'Now another and that's an order. You've done what you can for tonight. Go home, get some sleep. We'll pick up the pieces tomorrow.'

Did he really believe such a delay was possible? 'Then do us all a favour and watch that girl. Paulette may well be enjoying herself but freedom always has its price. I am certain she either knows where the money is or who stole it. They,' he indicated the men and particularly the table where Kaestner sat with Baumann and the others, 'may not be so patient with her as we would wish.'

As Kerjean reached for his cap and gloves, Kohler asked if he had seen the autopsy report on the shopkeeper and saw him shake his head. 'My assistant will have done so. I am sorry, but I had no time.'

'Didn't Louis say anything about it?'

There was that shrug. 'He was freezing, wet to the skin and had received several terrible blows to the back of the head. He was dazed and in a great deal of pain. We must get him to a doctor. Another of the pieces we must pick up, Inspector. Stubborn like our peasants and refusing absolutely to let me take him straight to the hospital here, but the concussion all the same, I think.'

Kohler watched him leave then looked the place over.

172

There was now no sign of the Captain or of Baumann and the boy or the Second Engineer. They had somehow left the party unnoticed and quickly. Even Death's-head Schultz had vacated the table and others now crowded round it.

When Paulette le Trocquer, breathless and radiant, came towards him, he had to grin and take her by the hand. Someone called Kay Kyser was singing something called 'Playmates'. Then there was 'Marie' and then there was 'I'm Getting Sentimental Over You'.

But still there was no further sign of the Dollmaker and the others. None at all.

It was now nearly 1 a.m. Berlin Time, Tuesday the 5th of January and some fifty-two hours since they had arrived in the area to begin the investigation. Parting the heavy green brocade drapes in Yvon Charbonneau's study, St-Cyr looked out into darkness and rain. The clay pits would be awash. Another hour and where would he have been? Drowned by swallowing that thick, creamy milk of clay? Buried in it perhaps for ever. Yet it was not easy to be released from one trouble only to fall into another.

'K and R,' he muttered grimly. 'Kämmer and Reinhardt.'

He turned away but stood looking across the cluttered refuse, the hints at former lives so distant from his own. 'The bits and pieces of lost millennia,' he murmured, 'and those of a doll.'

In need of tobacco, he found a tin Charbonneau had used as a makeshift ashtray, and dumping it out, toasted the remaining contents of the Obersteuermann Baumann's tobacco pouch over the fire. That everything should boil down to a doll was frightening. Emotionally exhausted by her fear that he would discover what she had done, the child had dropped off to sleep. The *chaise-longue* with its black lace and cream silk had become her bier. The finely chiselled face, with its large eyes closed, had become the face of innocence, but behind that innocence lay a hardness that deeply troubled.

He stood a moment more trying to fathom exactly what she had done. The dolls up there in the attic had waited too, with breath seemingly held. All of them had watched her from the mirrors. Image after image had been repeated. Some had even overlapped themselves.

They had watched him too, so much so that for a moment there he had been afraid to move for fear of frightening them. They were so lifelike.

The Dollmaker, who could identify each maker's bisque with his eyes closed, must have been all too aware that the fragments were not from a Jumeau, a Steiner or a Bru. He had given up the pieces readily enough during the inter-rogation which could only mean he had been satisfied they no longer posed a threat.

'Then he must have known the doll would not be discovered.'

In turn, this could only mean he had known Yvon Charbonneau had buried the briefcase and the pianist would make damned certain the doll was never found.

'And Kerjean knows it too,' he said, a whispered sigh. 'He was so anxious to go after the pianist tonight. The doll is the key to everything. Its absence is crucial to the Captain but does Kerjean want it found so as to prove Herr Kaestner killed the shopkeeper, or does Victor want to be absolutely certain it is never seen again?

'And what of Paulette?' he asked. 'Paulette either saw her father pick up the doll Angélique left in that shop or she brought it to his attention.

'The Captain was to return from Paris on the following day. He would go straight to the clay pits. What better place to confront him, especially as he would then pay the house by the sea a visit?'

Kaestner had waited a full twelve hours before reporting the murder, a long enough delay to clearly indicate he was protecting someone.

Madame Charbonneau had been there at the time of the murder, as had her husband.

When Hélène Charbonneau found him, the Chief Inspector was lost in thought and tobacco smoke, poring over the pages of her husband's scrapbooks. There were news photographs of Adèle and herself with Yvon, and others of just the two of them sightseeing, shopping, buying dolls. She had not been able to destroy the clippings. Angélique had needed all the records of her mother and father she could accumulate. And myself? she asked. I could not bring myself to burn them even though Yvon wanted me to, but left the task to me as a reminder.

'Vienna in the autumn of 1938,' said the detective. 'I wonder what it must be like there now. It was the city that, next to Paris, I loved and admired the most.'

She waited, not knowing what to do or say. The long dark hair fell loosely over the shoulders of the heavy white flannel nightgown. The lovely hazel eyes were full of despair.

'Salzburg,' he went on, 'the 24th and 28th of October. Then Munich on the 30th, Köln on the 3rd November and Berlin, ah Berlin, on the 9th.'

She clutched the throat of her nightgown and held it close. She must say something to him. She could not go down in defeat so easily. 'Yvon would not travel without us. Like many artistic people, he was often insecure. He always needed the reassurance only the two of us could bring.'

Several pages were turned. 'Yet he went back to the Reich the following spring but only with Adèle, madame? Three concerts. One at the Opera House in Köln, another in Berlin and then Frankfurt.'

'Things were very tense. Visas were so hard to get. I was ill. I had my shop to look after. I had to earn a living and make my own way in life. I could not go with them. If you will read the reviews, you will note that they were less than favourable. Yvon needed me as much as he needed Adèle.'

'But you were never sexually intimate with him.'

The crooked smile was brief, embarrassed and sad – ah, so many things.

'I'm not denying he tried, nor am I denying I didn't want it to happen. But Adèle – you had to have known her, Inspector. She and I were the dearest of friends. Inseparable, yes? Ah *mon Dieu*, men are such imbeciles sometimes. We had shared everything for so long, had been schoolgirls together. She was like a sister to me, the sister I had lost so tragically I can still remember how it was the day she drowned. Yvette . . . her name was Yvette and she was only ten years old at the time. Ten, the same age as Angélique.'

Hélène Charbonneau tossed her head to indicate the attic roost. 'I had my troubles, Inspector – a failed marriage, the shop that was always facing such terrible competition and needing something always. Fabric design is very demanding. Clients seem always to be needing reassurance and new and exciting things – at least they used to when I had the shop, but I left all that in Paris of course. We shared so much. I could go to her at any time with my troubles and she to me. I always put her between Yvon and myself and that is all there was to it.'

'Until the blitzkrieg.'

'Yes. Yvon fell completely to pieces. Somehow – God only knows how I managed it – I got the three of us here but he had sunk into such a deep depression. Ah, you've no idea what it was like. He would not touch the piano but spoke increasingly of a symphony only he could hear among the standing stones and tumuli. My God how I hate those things. They've got to me too.'

'You were married.'

'Yes, in the fall of 1940. Yvon wanted it that way. I was quite willing to simply look after him and Angélique for the . . . the Duration of this lousy war the Nazis have thrust upon us. He wouldn't go back to Paris. He blamed himself for having panicked like everyone else. He blamed himself for having taken the road and caused her death.'

The reviewers had been unkind. A last concert had not gone well.

St-Cyr closed the scrapbook and ran smoothing hands over its cover. She asked how his head was and offered two aspirins from her emergency supplies. 'They are impossible to get now but . . .'

She placed them between his hands. 'I will make us some tea. Camomile, I think. I can't sleep. I am so worried Yvon will . . . will do something stupid out there or catch pneumonia. I've taken a couple of blankets up to Angélique. She'll be warm enough. You needn't worry.'

'You've always been very kind to her.'

'It's what a mother does, isn't that so? Besides, every time I see her, Angélique reminds me of Adèle and of my sister.'

Her eyes pleaded with him for compassion, and to tell her what the girl had said but he could not yield. She hadn't liked his going through the scrapbooks. No, of course not. When one hides, one must be so careful.

'The palm of your left hand, madame? A moment, please.' He got up quickly and turned towards her. 'It has been recently hurt?'

'It . . . it was only a scratch. A few simple stitches – didn't Angélique tell you about them?'

He shook his head. 'She told me about the ones you had sewn in your husband's hand on the evening of the day of the murder. The palm . . . the ham of the thumb and a deep puncture. One much bigger than your own and still quite swollen.'

'Yes . . . why, yes. I'm getting rather good at mending people. It's what I do best these days, isn't that so? At least it is what I try to do best.'

If tapped, he felt she would shatter. Moisture had collected in her eyes. She fought to stop herself from breaking down and only succeeded through a supreme effort of will he had to admire.

'I'll make the tea, shall I?' she said.

He could not punish her by asking any more. 'Please go into the kitchen, madame. I will join you in a moment.'

On the night of 9th/10th November 1938, black-shirted and brown-shirted Nazi hoodlums had ransacked property throughout the Reich. Burning, looting, raping and arresting. Smashing so many windows, the sound of breaking glass could still be heard by all those of conscience.

For a visitor such as herself it must have been an especially terrifying experience. Some said over twenty thousand had been arrested without cause on that one night alone. Innocent people taken from their homes and beaten in the streets. Looting, arson and murder. It had gone on for a week.

All border crossings had been sealed. Her passport and visa would have been left with the hotel's management. She, like so many, would not have known what was about to happen. They might even have had to drive through the streets.

When St-Cyr rejoined her, Hélène Charbonneau was standing in front of the stove with the kettle still in her hand. She could not speak or even turn to look at him. She could only bow her head and let the tears fall freely knowing that they, too, would betray her.

On the 16th of July 1942 in Paris alone, twelve thousand Jews had been rounded up. Others had quickly followed. They had poured in from all over the Occupied Zone. Now perhaps as many as forty thousand had been arrested. It was a number one could not yet put a finger on or completely comprehend the tragedy. Most didn't want to think about it. Subsequently they had all been deported, even the youngest of children and separated from the parents. He had had no part in it. He had been out of touch on a case with Hermann, though he could not have done much except resign and go with them, yet he still felt guilty at not having done a thing. He had since taken steps to gather evidence against the perpetrators, particularly the Préfet of Paris, a dangerous thing especially as Talbotte now knew of it. A last case, a left fist that had exploded under the Préfet of Paris's jaw when it should have minded its own business. A case of missing persons, of fourteen girls whose only crime had been a desire to become mannequins.

The blitzkrieg, the isolation of the Breton coast and marriage to Yvon Charbonneau had saved her but only for the moment. She would have lived each day never knowing if and when she would be discovered. Never knowing when they would come for her.

'Madame, please. Your secret is safe with me. I will do everything I can to keep it hidden, no matter the outcome of this investigation.'

'It won't be enough. Not after what Angélique did to me. Not after what has happened.'

'Please tell me before it is too late.'

She slammed the kettle down. 'I can't! I won't! I mustn't! *You're* the detective. *You* figure out what happened.'

Ah *merde*, she had burned both her hands. She still had one of them on the stove.

'Paulette . . . Paulette . . .' she cried. 'Dear God, why did she have to do it to us? Why could she not have seen that Angélique was so unhappy?'

There was still no sign of the Captain and his keepers. A vocalist named Bonnie Baker was belting out a song called 'Oh Johnny', and the Bar of the Mermaid's Three Sisters was jumping. It was slosh time.

Kohler found another cigarette and lit up. He'd take four more of the Benzedrine and that was it. They didn't mix too well with alcohol.

Still ravishing in her tight black skirt and turtle-neck sweater, Paulette le Trocquer was dancing with one of the boys from U-297. Though a little tipsy, she wasn't so far gone her eyes didn't seek him out at the bar for reassurance.

'She's wary and that's good,' he grunted and tossed down the pills.

Bleary-eyed ratings, their middy-collars stained and rumpled, thought of home, slept sprawled over their tables or wantonly ogled the girls and threw lewd asides to their pals.

Several fights had broken out. When there were so few girls to go around, what else was there to do? No one had been seriously hurt but sailors were sailors. Beer flowed and was spilled. Brandy and wine, the rougher the better, were downed as well with no thought of the day to come. The rush to the heads was constant. There were line-ups, distractions in there, much ribald laughter and encouragement. Ah what the hell.

He felt like a grandfather on duty.

One torpedoman, caught in the clasp of his girlfriend, had hiked her skirt and slip up her backside to show his pals that the painted stockings on her legs stopped at generously firm thighs. No secret now. She was too drunk to notice the whistles and catcalls until, entangled in her underpants, she took a swing at her boyfriend and hit the floor. Puke all over the place and wallowing in it, she got up slowly, teetered and dashed for the toilets.

They gave her the run and they crowded in after her. Everyone heard the cheers.

'*Anblasten!*' (Blow tanks!)

'*Boot steht!*' (Boat steady!)

'*Boot steight langsam!*' (Boat slowly rising!)

And then, as the song came to an end and couples looked towards the heads, '*Folgen!*' (Track!) '*Feuerlaubnis!*' (Permission to fire!)

'*Rhor Los!*' (Launch!) There was a huge cry from the men in there and then, in chorus, '*Eins! Zwei! Drei!*' (One! Two! Three!)

Pale and shaken, the shopkeeper's daughter took the bar stool next to him and sipped his beer. 'They are pigs,' she swore. 'Oh *mon Dieu*, what am I to do?'

'Stick with me, I think.'

One by one the Captain's keepers began to filter back

into the party. They came via the front entrance and there were six of them. Baumann . . . the boy, Erich Fromm . . . the Second Engineer . . . and three others. Tough . . . *Verdammt!* were they the flotilla's champions? They did not sit together but lost themselves among the tables.

The cook was the last to arrive and he stayed nearest the entrance, leaning against the wall in darkness like a petulant shadow.

'Wait here,' said Kohler. 'A friend has just arrived.'

Taller and bigger than most, the detective headed straight across the dance floor and she watched with dismay as he dodged fluidly among the couples until, at last, he had reached the cook.

'Death's-head,' she whispered distastefully, 'you are not the reason I am here, idiot! The Leutnant zur See Huber has left me to take the telegraphist Elizabeth Krüger back to base, the Ensign Becker is sick. You can have your stockings back. I don't want them.'

Gone were the promises of better things. When Herr Kohler's beer was done, she asked for brandy and kept it near, for it would sting the eyes and she wasn't going to give them what they wanted.

8

It was now perhaps three in the morning. The Chief Inspector was very worried. As he carefully spread antiseptic cream over the strips of gauze for her burns, Hélène Charbonneau could see that his mind, though concentrating on the task, was rapidly fitting the pieces of the murder together and leaping ahead to their inevitable conclusion.

At a sound – a loose shutter upstairs – he stopped so suddenly she felt the instant of alarm. He relaxed. He said, 'I had best go and close it, madame. A moment, please.' It would only shatter the window-panes if left – she knew this was why he hurried away.

'He thinks I will remember *Kristallnacht*. He is conscious of my feelings and afraid I might panic.'

A roll of gauze, a pair of scissors, a lighted candle on the kitchen table between them, and one already bandaged hand later, she had told him nothing further. He had not pushed. He had only been kind and was therefore a very difficult adversary. 'He will uncover the truth,' she said sadly, and reaching out, held her bandaged hand just above the candle flame. 'Yahweh, I was never yours. As a family, my grandparents and parents had put You from us. I really didn't think much about it – I was away at school so much and just like the others. But now You have come to reclaim us. It isn't fair. Angélique never suspected it of me before Adèle was killed because the matter never came up. My maiden name wasn't even Jewish because my grandfather had changed it. But of course it was all there in the records and of course I had to have help in hiding.'

She took the hand away from the flame and examined the gauze for scorch marks. Finding none, she said more loudly, for she knew he had come back, 'Victor helped us with the records and the marriage certificates. He's a good man, Inspector. Oh for sure his son came to place impossible demands on him but, please, Victor did not mean to do what he did and you must spare him so that he can continue to help others.'

Sacré nom de nom, was she accusing Kerjean of the murder or only of the theft?

The Chief Inspector went over to the sink to wash his hands and dry them. Without a word, he sat down and began to dress her other hand. So great was his concentration, he did not meet the look in her eyes until the job was done. 'Three weeks, perhaps four,' he said. 'The dressings should be changed . . . ah, let's say twice each day. More if you get them wet or dirty. Angélique will have to help you. She's really very capable.'

There wouldn't be time and he knew it too, but would go on as if there would be out of kindness. 'I should have told her the truth about myself, Inspector. That might have helped. I . . . I really don't know. These days everything is so uncertain, so tenuous. Children can be made to tell others. The Captain and she were often alone discussing things. He was teaching her everything he knew about dollmaking, he was teaching her to identify the various types of bisque. He . . .'

'Did Herr Kaestner ever suspect it?'

'Never. I took steps to see that he didn't. I had to, isn't that so? When Johann first became interested in me, I kept my distance for as long as I dared but he was too persistent and would not take no for an answer. A man like that never does. Yvon had left me completely alone and it was obvious I was worried about my husband and not knowing what to do about it.'

'Please, I know it must have been very difficult for you.'

'Oh? Do you really understand how it was, how I felt

when he kissed me, when he put his hands on my body – my nakedness, Inspector? I could not cringe. I could not in any way let him know how I really felt. I learned to cry inside.'

Ah *nom de Jésus-Christ*! 'How long has the affair been going on?'

Her eyes leapt. 'The affair – is that what you would call it?'

Rebuked, he waited. He did not answer. 'For over a year and a half I and my little family of two have had to live with it, myself hiding always in the arms of the enemy. There, does that make you feel any better?'

'Of course not. Is Kaestner a Nazi?'

'What do you think?'

She would have to be told how serious things were. 'I believe he must have been a good Nazi at first – even one of the hardliners – but now he has become very disillusioned. Like so many of our German friends, the Reich's mounting losses are causing them to have second thoughts. This does not mean, madame, that honour if slighted cannot be reclaimed. Herr Kaestner is much revered by his men. In their eyes their chances of survival without him are zero; with him, but a little better perhaps, or as Herr Baumann feels, not at all, since nothing for that one can now prevent the inevitable.'

'Johann is tormented by nightmares of failure, of dying encased in steel at the bottom of the sea, but when awake, he is the most totally alert man I have ever met. I some-times used to wonder if he ever slept. Then when he did, I found out and had to stop him from screaming.'

Angélique would have seen them in bed together, perhaps even naked. 'Did he take a snapshot of you with him?'

'To pin up in that cubicle he calls his "cabin"?'

'You know that is what I mean and why I must ask it.'

There was no place to pin up anything in a submarine but he would have taken it out now and then. The men would

184

all have seen it and commented amongst themselves. 'He had snapshots of myself and Angélique with him always, and yes, I think he was very much in love with me if ever such a man can truly love anyone. He wanted me to leave Yvon. He used to plan what it would be like for us after the war and I had to listen to it. Sometimes naked on the beach and with only the sun above us and the gentle sound of lapping waves; sometimes in bed with the softness of a breeze blowing among the curtains and the sound of gulls crying. He wasn't going to go home right away, Inspector. We would live here for a time and in Paris while he built up the business. We would have everything just like it had been for his grandfather in the old days. It was a fantasy that terrified because if it ever came true, I could never have lived it, and because I knew increasingly that he was using it to hide his very worst of fears.'

'But then the money went missing and then there was the murder.'

'Yes, but first there was the telescope and Victor paying us so many visits even the gossips got wind of it, and then there was Angélique and Yvon spying on things best left unseen. Oh, I finally awoke to the fact that each of the two people I loved more than anything else had, in their separate ways, watched me with my Nazi lover. I was certain of it – can you imagine how this has been for me, but,' she shrugged, 'what could I have done? Things had already gone too far by then. I was in too deeply with Victor, Préfet of the Morbihan.'

She was still a very strong person because she had had to be. With luck perhaps they might survive. It didn't bear thinking about. Luck was far too fickle. 'Kaestner will come for you, madame. For the moment he may still be content to stall, hoping that his men will not find out. But once they do, there will be no turning back for him. Honour will have to be saved. Honour.'

There was fatalism to the look she gave that troubled deeply.

'Paulette will tell them,' she said quite simply.

'And Kerjean?' he asked gently. 'What of the Préfet, madame?'

The sadness in her eyes only deepened. 'Poor Victor, he tried so hard to help us and oh for sure, when he needed help for his son and the others, I had to help him in return. Risk piled upon risk,' she shrugged. 'That's the way life is these days. The times, they are not normal but have they ever been? Isn't it that life for most of us simply wavers from catastrophe to catastrophe with little pauses in between to make us think things are "normal"?'

He found himself liking her immensely, a dangerous thing. 'Your secret will be safe with my partner but if he does find out, madame, I will not be the one who tells him. Even I who know him far better than most, would not place that burden on him.'

'Paulette will do that. Paulette.'

'Did Kerjean steal the money?'

She had known all along that it must come to this and that she would have to tell him. Friends could not always remain friends; helpers sometimes had to help themselves.

'He borrowed it.'

St-Cyr sat back and drew in a breath before pinching his moustache in thought. 'If they ever find out, they will shoot him.'

'They will shoot his family also,' she said quite simply, 'and then they will come here for Angélique and Yvon and myself, though I will be the last to get it and they will make me watch the others die.'

'How was he going to pay the money back?'

6,000,000 francs. She would have to say it plainly. Betrayal must not come with trappings. 'There were things Victor could not tell me but I think he was expecting an airdrop – was praying for it to happen before it was too late. He was desperate.'

'From the British?'

Was it so impossible that Victor was up to his ears working with the Resistance? 'The British, yes, of course.'

Then it had not been the Sous-Préfet after all who had been working with the Resistance, but the Préfet.

Nothing more could be said about it. The implications were far too desperate.

'Monsieur le Trocquer, the shopkeeper, was not a nice man, Inspector. He always gave me to understand that he knew far more about me than he was willing to let on. He was envious of our fine house by the sea and scornful of our having come from Paris to live like recluses with a few rabbits and pigeons. He was even more scornful of what had happened to Yvon. But Johann was always there if only in the shopkeeper's mind. Monsieur le Trocquer was very afraid of him. Afraid that if he should make a mistake with the dolls, the Captain would have him arrested.'

'It is what he knew about the Préfet that interests me, madame.'

'Was he aware that Victor had "borrowed" the money? Is this what you mean?'

'You know it is. You know I must uncover exactly what was said between them in that shop before Monsieur le Trocquer left it for the clay pits.'

And a confrontation with the Captain that Préfet Kerjean had warned her about, ah yes. She knew this was what he meant and could only look steadily at him.

'Angélique and your husband visited the shop the day before the murder, madame. A pair of candlesticks.'

Her smile must be faint and whimsical. 'She has far better taste, Inspector. I ought to know. I helped to raise her.'

Merde, why would she not tell him? 'The doll, madame. Kämmer and Reinhardt were the manufacturers.'

The sadness only deepened the lovely hazel of her eyes and he was at a loss as to how to make her tell him before it was too late.

Again there was that smile and then a tiny shrug. 'The

Star of David, Inspector. The K is within the left-hand point, the R within the right and that is why she chose it and kept the doll of me a prisoner for later. Johann must have told her that the firm had been Jewish and since it was the only one among her dolls that bore that particular trademark, Angélique used it but . . .'

'But *what*, madame?' he asked gently.

'But cut from yellow velvet a much larger star and, having pinned that to its breast, added the word step-mother.'

Jésus, merde alors, how could the child have done such a terrible thing?

'I . . .' began Hélène Charbonneau only to suddenly stop herself.

Had they both heard it, he wondered? The scrunch of tyres on gravel in the drive?

For a second they looked at each other and held their breath. A sudden gust drew the flame of the candle out, but then it retreated to flutter normally.

Both of them looked towards the front hall. St-Cyr swept his eyes around the kitchen. His clothes were hanging above the stove, his shoes by their laces . . . 'Madame,' he whispered.

She could not move. Fear tightened her cheeks and darkened the look in her eyes. Like himself, she waited for some other sign that they were no longer alone.

When nothing further came, St-Cyr pinched out the candle. 'Say nothing,' he croaked. 'Stay right by me. If it is Herr Kaestner, he will go upstairs to your bedroom first. Let me find my clothes and get dressed. Put something on – anything dark so as to hide the whiteness of your night-gown. Boots . . . try to find some. We may have to go outside. He won't harm the child.'

'The child,' she said. 'The child . . .'

Hermann . . . where the hell was Hermann when needed most?

*

188

Through the haze of tobacco smoke, and from across the crowded dance floor, Kohler and the cook could see Paulette le Trocquer sitting pensively at the flotilla's bar. She was very pretty and of course there should have been intense pressure on her to dance, but now it was as if she had best be left alone. Her knees were together. The high heels with their studded rhinestone straps were spread so as to hook themselves into the lower rung of the stool. The glass of brandy to her right was still untouched, the stool next to her on the left was empty. Though the clamour for sustenance went on all around her, there were no offers.

She was spoken for.

The cook's laughing dark eyes with their trace of insanity flicked over her and then returned as Kohler asked him if the Captain was back in the lock-up.

The bushy dark brows furrowed, the Kaiser moustache was wiped with the back of a beery knuckle. 'I just left him. No problem. Vati has had his bit of fun and will now sleep like a baby.' Schultz hoisted the borrowed stein in salute.

'Sleep? And not have any nightmares?'

Was Herr Kohler so naïve as not to notice he was surrounded? 'You've been reading things you shouldn't, Inspector.'

'*Luminalette*, eh?' snorted Kohler, digging a hole for himself. 'Six times a day if necessary? Your Captain's so high-strung he could well have done something he might now regret. Why not help us? The odds against him are still too high but another possibility has entered the race.'

Oh-oh, was that it?

Kohler tapped the iron-bound drum of the giant's chest. 'You were at the warehouse on the morning of the murder, my friend. It's only a pleasant little stroll across the moors to the clay pits.'

Schultz removed the finger from his chest but did not break it. 'So, I had stores to check and this makes me a suspect? Maybe you should have noticed when I clocked out, Inspector. By 1330 hours I was in Lorient and back at the bunker.'

'A man like yourself? A man who has a vested interest in things? Come off it. You were in that shop on the day before the murder. It wouldn't surprise me if the autopsy shows our shopkeeper had pickled pork hocks, sausage and a whole lot of other goodies inside him. Working the black market is against the law, my friend. *Our* laws, never mind the French ones.'

Ali Baba's Cave had a logbook and detectives were always minding other people's business and noticing that those who entered always wrote down their times of leaving. Glenn Miller's band was playing something called 'String of Pearls'. All around them the racket and the comings and goings went on and still the girl sat alone. 'Okay, I forgot to write down when I left. I was in a hurry.'

'I'll bet you were, and now I'm going to lean on you,' said Kohler. 'Something went on in that shop before the murder. That girl over there has finally realized you are aware of it. Either you were there or you saw someone going into the shop. Whatever it was, it made you put yourself in position well before the murder. Sure you've been plying her with silk stockings. A sweet little piece of ass like that. Did you think I wouldn't notice that cologne she's wearing isn't the bilge water you boys like to take to sea so that your iron coffins won't always stink of farts and sweat and urine but smell like a brothel? You've had your eye on her for some time.'

Schultz indicated the thugs from the torpedo and engine rooms. Baumann was there and so, too, were the Second Engineer and the boy.

'She's terrified,' said Kohler levelly. 'You leave her alone. You touch her and I'll have you up on suspicion of murder.'

'All right, I went into the shop on the day before the murder. What does that prove? A few things in trade for a few bits of sausage and candied fruit. Some silver-plated spoons to send home to my mother.'

'With six millions missing? Good *Gott im Himmel*, don't be a *Dummkopf.*'

'As I left the shop, the pianist and his daughter went in. I hung around and watched them through the window. The kid had a doll but when she came out, the doll wasn't with her.'

'A doll?'

Was it so surprising? The detective looked away across the room and said, 'Ah, Christ, you bastards . . .' One minute the girl had been there at the bar, the next, she was gone and her glass of brandy was still waiting for her to come back.

In desperation the Bavarian's gaze sifted the crowded dance floor. He heard the ribald laughter, the singing and then the shouting from the toilets.

A girl was being helped into a chair at one of the tables. She had lost her purse but was too fuzzy-minded to remember where she had left it. Another girl was chugalugging a pitcher of beer to cheers from the men around her. Yet another was sprawled asleep with her mouth wide open and her head thrown back.

Swiftly Kohler's eyes returned to that empty stool, then he ran. Barging his way through, he hit the door to the toilets and stopped cold as couples lay entangled on the wet-tiled floor or stood against a wall or leaned over the sink. No stockings, no underwear, skirts and dresses hiked out of the way, blouses open and burst-buttons scattered. Trousers dropped. Couples going at it while others watched and gave encouragement and the boys took turns.

No sign of Paulette. *Not here. Not here*, he shouted at himself and ran outside into the rain, the wind and darkness.

The club was not far from the cliffs of the Côte Sauvage. The sound of waves exploding against the rocks came to him. '*Paulette!*' he shouted. '*Paulette!*'

Gott im Himmel, what had become of her?

Schultz and Baumann and the others were nowhere to be seen. She must have made a run for it and they had gone after her.

When Kohler found the girl's scattered shoes on the walk that led to the lorries and staff cars, he realized she had done just that. She had waited, knowing what they wanted of her, and then had chosen her moment because they weren't about to leave her alone and she had seen he could not stop them.

'She knows too much,' he said, and dragging on his overcoat, stuffed her shoes into the pockets and headed out along the coast road with the words of Madame Quévillon ringing in his ears. '*The Côte Sauvage, Inspector. Caves that no one sees from atop the cliffs.*'

Caves that could be used to hide contraband and to store goods for the black market. Caves that no one else would ever find.

'The child,' said Hélène Charbonneau – St-Cyr heard all of a mother's yearning in her voice. 'I must go to her. Please, you must let me. I have to tell her how it really was. I have to make her understand.'

'*Madame, please do not be so foolish!*' he hissed. They were in the study now and it was better here, for there was none of the flickering light from the stove. Here there were only a few hot embers in the grate. 'If it is Herr Kaestner, he will be armed, madame. I have no gun. My partner . . .'

He left unsaid that Hermann kept the gun until needed. A tremor passed through her. Fleetingly he felt the coarse, homespun wool of the overcoat she had put on to cover her nightgown. Subconsciously he plucked at it as memories of the railway bed and the places where her heels had dug in came rushing at him. The fragments of bisque, the droplets and stains of blood.

'Please don't think of leaving me, madame. He will only kill you, and if he does, the child will never believe the truth I will have to tell her.'

'You're cruel. You are heartless. She's up there and we are down here, and he is . . .'

'In between perhaps. If it is Herr Kaestner, we will never know until he is so close we can but do what instinct demands.'

'And if it is the Préfet?' she asked, a harsh whisper.

'Victor will have to kill you too. He cannot afford to let you live. Not now. Not after what has happened. Myself also, I am afraid. The Resistance will demand it, and he will be only too well aware of this.'

Perhaps it was some sound foreign to all those of the house and the storm that stopped them from breathing, perhaps it was only fear. Hélène Charbonneau reached out to him and he felt the trembling of gauze-wrapped fingers. 'If it is Victor, he will have to kill Angélique also, Inspector. I can't let it happen. I owe her mother that.'

Ah *merde* . . .

Try as he did to sort out all the sounds of the house – a shutter that was wanting to break loose, a slate . . . the hissing of raindrops in the fireplace, the distant pounding of the waves – St-Cyr could not pin down what had caused them to hesitate. 'Victor won't kill the child until he is certain he has you too, and even then that will not be enough, for there is myself he has to contend with.'

'And Paulette,' her words came sadly. 'And Madame le Trocquer and . . .'

'And your husband, madame, since he must now know far too much.'

'Yvon will try to shield the child. She's all he has.'

'And if he is now up there with her, madame, what will your husband do to you?'

'He will hand me over to the Germans. He will have no other choice.'

'Then he will be turning in the Préfet too, and Kerjean must at all costs prevent that.'

It was a dilemma. It was not fair. A *shopkeeper*, for heaven's sake. A man everyone wanted dead anyway and now there were hearts to be broken, his own entirely because he knew without a shadow of doubt that even if she was innocent and he saved her, the single suitcase and the closed railway truck awaited her at the end.

It was a tragedy so in keeping with the bleakness of the moors and the standing stones.

He felt for something to use. A skull, a rack of charred and broken bones and a few flint scrapers came to hand. Then they both heard one word. '*Maman* . . . ?'

The child raced up the stairs, the woman broke away from him and followed . . . He tried to stop her. He hit the foot of the stairs and tripped – tripped and went down hard . . . hard . . . Then he, too, raced up the stairs until . . .

Breath would not come fast enough. His chest was aching like hell. A shutter broke free. It swung in with a bang, then went out only to come in with a crash that startled him.

Back and forth it went until finally, at a sudden, fierce gust, the window shattered. Glass flew across the hall. The musical rain of it was everywhere and he thought of her in a street of broken glass, and he wondered what she was feeling and thinking now.

Caught on the stairs to the attic, she heard the rain of glass behind her and could not make her legs and arms respond. The street was dark, the torches bright. Adèle and she stood back to back, ringed by laughing, brutal men in brown shirts, black ties and swastika armbands. The torch-light touched the black and glossy peaks of their caps. Now up, now down, now tilted this way and that, some taller, many shorter, some swarthy, some thin . . . They jeered. They chanted. They made threatening gestures, then suddenly at a sharp command, they all shut up and the ring of torches came closer . . . closer . . . Jackboots . . . jackboots . . .

Berlin, the night of 9–10th November 1938.

St-Cyr found her at last but when he took her by the

194

arms, the scream she gave was ripped right out of her to fill the house. *'NICHT JUDISCH! NICHT JUDISCH!'*

Another window broke and she cowered on the stairs at his feet, weeping, 'Please don't hurt me. Please don't tear my clothes off. Please don't teach me a lesson. I'm not a Jew. Lots of people have hair and eyes like mine. We are visitors from France.'

'Madame, it's me, St-Cyr. Please . . . Here, let me help you up. Did they rape you in that street?'

She would not answer. Brutally she shrugged him off and continued on up the stairs and into the attic until, at last, the light from the stone lamps on the floor found her, and the dolls all waited.

There was no sign of the child. The blankets had been removed. Black antique lace lay smoothed over the cream silk cover of the *chaise-longue* and on top of this, the child had placed the birdcage in which the doll of her step-mother was held a prisoner.

Frantically St-Cyr tried to see if the child and Kaestner – it had to be the Dollmaker – were waiting to find out what they would do, but the black sheeting closed every-thing in and the mirrors only threw back the faces of the dolls.

In defeat, Hélène Charbonneau stepped over to the *chaise-longue* and when he saw her look down sharply, St-Cyr leapt to pull her back.

'Ah, no,' he said. 'No, madame. I cannot allow it.'

'Bâtard!' she shrieked and tried to fight him off. He ducked. He reached down and snatched up the tiny white pill the Dollmaker had left for her in the saucer of a child's tea set.

They heard his car start up.

'He's taken her with them,' she wept. 'He has left me the only honourable way out.'

'But I have a murder to solve, madame, and until that is settled, no one takes potassium cyanide. Now, please, you must try to pull yourself together.'

'For *what*? For the lesson he would teach me? What *lesson*, please?'

Even as he took her downstairs to her room, the cinematographer within him saw her standing on a railway platform with her small suitcase, waiting for a train to nowhere, and he knew he could not let it happen. 'My partner will help us, madame. Please, you must find it in your heart to understand that Hermann, he is not like so many of the others. He's different. He's also a very good detective and very resourceful. He will help us. I know he will. He always has in the past.'

'But this is not the past,' she said bitterly. 'This is the present.'

The sea was boiling, and when he reached the last rung in a railing that led down the cliffs, Kohler realized a good portion of it had been torn away. The path ahead simply no longer existed. He tried to see if there was a way directly across the face of the cliffside but the rain was too hard, the wind too strong. It's too damned dark, he said. Too dark. '*Paulette!*' he cried out. '*Paulette, it's me, Kohler.*'

The wind tore the tops off the waves and flung spray far on ahead of them so that he was momentarily blinded and then totally drenched as they exploded.

He gave it up. It was no use. And when, after perhaps an hour of being away, he got back to the Mermaid's Three Sisters, he borrowed a tarpaulined Wehrmacht lorry, pausing first to rip the black-out tape from the headlamps. Paulette le Trocquer would not have an easy time of it. Baumann and the others could well do things in anger they might not do otherwise. Death's-head was among them.

Long after curfew, the streets of Quiberon were empty even of their hourly patrols. Water ran in rivers. Sewers overflowed. Hunched grimly over the steering wheel, Kohler peered ahead into the hammered ink. Pine branches skidded across the boulevard Chanard. A tattered poster from some cinema tumbled drunkenly away to hit the edge of the pavement and leap into oblivion. The engine faltered. He cursed himself and gave it the throttle. Away from the sea, rubbish swept by and he had to put the lorry into low-low and grind uphill until the flood was behind him.

When he reached the shop, it had long since lost its wreath. The door was ajar. 'Ah *merde*,' he said. 'Why can't things be easy for once?'

Not liking it one bit, Kohler tried to wipe the water from the Walther P38, then gave the door a little nudge. Old door sills were always warping and jamming their doors, especially in France and in places like this.

Softly closing it behind him, he forced the lock on and waited until he drew in the musty smell of things not so old and old and unwanted.

He took a step and then another. The floor was littered with broken crockery and glassware. Cabinets and shelves had been toppled over – the cash counter was strewn with debris. A doll . . . another doll . . . a broken doll. He felt their faces, felt the jagged edges and knew they had all been slammed head first down on the counter. But why? he asked. It made no sense unless, so enraged at the loss of their money, the crew had destroyed the one thing that had offered hope and a future.

Have I missed something? he asked. Something everyone else knows but me?

It was not a happy thought, but he had to agree it could well be true. Louis might now know of it. Louis . . .

The stairs were narrow and steep and as he went up them, the wind and the rain played havoc outside while he, himself, made no sound at all and hardly breathed.

There was nothing but a shambles in the sitting-room. The smell of stale tobacco smoke still clung to faded fabrics touch alone identified.

The kitchen was no better though smaller, but then there was the overpowering scent of really good perfume behind a closed door that opened only with difficulty.

He touched spilled rouge on a littered dressing-table, said silently, Kid, I'm sorry I was too late. His stomach lurched and he fought down the sickness death now brought all too frequently in a rush.

Wet through, his matches only disintegrated. A bedside lamp lay on its side. The shattered spine of its electric bulb warned him the cord had been ripped out and used, ah *merde* . . .

Against the smell of the perfume was the stench of faeces and urine.

He turned away and clenched a fist, sucked in a breath and cursed Boemelburg for not giving them a break. A day off even.

Gagging, he threw up. Couldn't have stopped himself. Gasped, 'Louis . . . Louis, why the hell aren't you here to take care of this for me?'

Louis . . . Louis . . .

When he found a box of matches among a heap of torn lingerie on the floor, he took two out and struck them simultaneously. The room was in chaos, the mattress had been flung up and out of the way.

Madame le Trocquer's grey-haired head had been jammed so hard between the coiled bedsprings, their flaking black and rusty barbed ends had torn the withered cheeks.

Blood was everywhere beneath her head and on her face and lips. The frayed brown lampcord was wrapped so tightly around her neck, the flesh was puffy on either side of it. Her nightdress was torn down the back, a last attempt at escape.

The wheelchair lay on its side behind the door – she'd been rushed in here hard and had been pitched out, then the chair had been flung aside.

With a startled curse, Kohler shook the matches out and plunged himself back into darkness. The Captain was in jail, or was he really there? The Préfet had gone home to Vannes, or had he? Baumann and the others had been after the girl . . .

The pianist was where? he asked. God alone knew. The Tumulus of Saint-Michel, the Préfet had said. A brief-case . . . Papers of agreement for the Captain to sign, perhaps a portion of the missing money, a show of good faith.

6,000,000 francs . . . 'The caves,' breathed Kohler. 'Paulette must have somehow gone over the edge of the cliff on that path I found.'

Had she fallen into the sea? he wondered. Would daylight find her floating face down or washed up among the kelp and hanging from some rock? Boulders always made one hell of a mess of bodies. It didn't bear thinking about. No, it didn't!

Finding candles in the debris was not easy but when he had them, Kohler forced himself to examine the girl's bedroom.

The crew would have been looking for their money. Hence the wreckage. Girl things were everywhere. Snap-shots but only a few of them. Dresses, skirts and blouses but few of these as well.

She hadn't had much and what there was of it hadn't been very good.

'Then why was her door locked?' he asked, seeing the splintered wood of the jamb and wondering where the girl must have kept the key.

A box made of that paltry crap they called cardboard these days, had been ripped open and its parts flung aside, the red ribbon too. A box for dolls. The money? he asked. Was this where she had hidden it?

Louis would have to examine the corpse and the room – the shop and the rest of the flat. The Frog was good at things like that. He'd *talk* to that . . . that poor woman and ask her questions only he could hear answers to.

But on the surface it looked like the woman had held out for as long as she could and then had led them to the daughter's bedroom and that cardboard box. She hadn't been dead long. Maybe an hour at most, maybe half an hour.

'Paulette,' he said and went out into the rain and the wind. Louis was at the house by the sea but was there time to get to him? They both knew things the other desperately needed. Again he had to ask himself, Am I missing something?

A final look up the darkened, rainswept street revealed a pair of headlamps suddenly staring at him.

Blinded by them, he leapt aside.

Hélène Charbonneau was beside herself with worry over the child and her husband and could no longer find the heart to look the Chief Inspector in the face. Everything was going wrong. Everything.

Prisoners of the house and the storm, they waited. There was now no sense in leaving the house and trying to hide. No sense in anything.

St-Cyr drew in a breath. Somehow he had to convince her to tell him everything. 'It is a race now between the Captain and his crew, madame. Herr Kaestner must at all costs keep the truth of his love affair from the men. They, in turn, must find it out to discover why their money went missing and why their Dollmaker paid so little attention to its absence.'

Her voice was bitter. 'He has taken Angélique as a hostage. That is why he has left me no choice. Don't you see that if I do not kill myself, he will have to hold Angélique until I do? It's the only way.'

It was now nearly 5 a.m. Berlin Time. They had been over things again and again but in spite of what had happened, he found the woman still reticent. She had been there at the time of the murder – yes, of course – and had heard but sworn she had not seen the killing. Le Trocquer had confronted her with the doll when she had caught up with him on the tracks after having left her bicycle in the shed. He had told her in no uncertain terms exactly what he intended to tell the Captain and had thrust the doll at her as evidence.

Aghast at what Angélique had done, she had backed away in terror and had tried to plead with him for her life and that of the child and her husband but he would have nothing to do with her. 'You are all finished. *Finished!*' he had cried.

Stunned by his hatred, she had stumbled back and had fallen. She had then backed away from him on her hands and seat and, still not knowing what to do, had stood in despair and had heard the switch-bar as it had hit the rails.

There had been no sign of her husband nor of the Captain, she had said and had sworn she wasn't lying. 'The tracks . . . the bend in the line . . . I dropped the doll. I had cut my hand rather badly and when I went forward to see what had happened, I could hardly find the will to put one foot ahead of the other. You must believe me. You must! I only saw that he was dead. *I did not kill him!* I didn't! I *didn't!*' she had shrieked.

'And then?' he had asked gently. He had not reminded her that she had left the tracks and gone out on to the moor.

She had buried her face in her bandaged hands and had wept. 'I . . . I stepped on his glasses. I heard the glass disintegrate under my shoe. He . . . he made no sound but I knew he never would again because I had seen a boy lying just like him in that street in Berlin. Adèle . . . Adèle and I had got out of the car to help the boy but . . . but the Brown Shirts, they . . . they wouldn't let us touch him. I had seen others too,' she had said, 'on the road that day from Paris.'

'Did you and Herr Kaestner ever use that shed?' he asked, startling her back into the present.

'In which to have sex?' she blurted, looking up and across the kitchen table at him.

The grief in her eyes was almost more than he could bear. 'You know that is what I mean, madame.'

'Then never!'

'Yet you knew it well enough to leave your bicycle there.'

Must he keep on badgering her like this? 'Only because Johann had told me of it and that Yvon often left his bike there. I had never been to the clay pits before. I had to ask my way several times. Someone might remember.'

'And you never saw your husband or Herr Kaestner there on that day?'

'Never. I touched nothing but the glasses. I left the doll exactly where I had dropped it – I panicked, yes? and I ran in tears, not knowing what to do or what was to become, not just of myself, but of Yvon and Angélique whom I dearly loved and still do.'

Her distress only made the sincerity of her appeal all the more convincing. He wanted so much to believe her but she could well be protecting the husband.

'Madame, your husband's bicycle. Was it in that shed?'

It was a question she ought to have anticipated but found difficulty answering and had to take her time. 'N . . . no. Yvon . . . Yvon must have . . . have left it somewhere else – up by the standing stones perhaps. I did not see him. He . . . he could well have gone home.'

'But, madame, we know he didn't? He picked up the doll.'

'Yes . . . yes, he did, didn't he?'

'Kaestner gave you and your husband lots of time to get clear. That can only have meant he was not protecting either of you but giving himself time to decide how best to deal with the matter.'

She was frantic. 'He'll kill Yvon because he will have to. He'll kill Angélique. I know he will even though he likes and admires her very much. He can't afford to let her live unless I kill myself and even then . . .' She went to wring her hands in despair and only just stopped herself. 'Will he fling her from the cliffs? Is that what he'll do?'

They had not mentioned the Préfet for some time. St-Cyr thought to do so. Victor had known of that shed yet had tried to hide the presence of the bicycle tracks from them. Had he known of the cigarettes the Captain sometimes gave the pianist? Had he used them? He also had every reason to want the shopkeeper dead and to then blame the Captain so as to hide behind that blame.

But now? St-Cyr asked himself. What will he do?

'Your husband, madame. Please, I must ask you to tell me truthfully. Did he kill Monsieur le Trocquer? You are hiding something from me. I sense it, yes? I feel it. I want so much to help.'

Anger tightened all her features, making the tears glisten. 'And I have already told you I saw no one out there at that place. *No one, do you understand?*'

Had Charbonneau done the killing? Everything in her seemed to suggest he had.

'Yvon Charbonneau overheard the two of you, madame. He heard the accusations and later removed the doll and tried to hide it. He watched as the shopkeeper died or he did it.'

'And if he didn't?' she asked beseechingly.

'Then until I get the four of you in a room, I am not going to know which of you killed him.'

'Or even if it wasn't any of us but someone else perhaps? Some member of U-297's crew who would realize right away exactly the difficult position his Captain was in? A man who would say nothing about it to anyone and would keep his own counsel. A man who would then do everything he could to protect not only his captain and U-297's reputation, but himself most especially.'

'Did you see this man?'

'I went out on to the moor but something drove me back to the railway. I . . . I sensed I was not alone and that it was not my husband who watched me as I took my bicycle from that shed and hurried away.'

'Explain this, please, madame. You "sensed" another?'

She gave him a look so naked he shuddered. 'Yvon must never learn of it. He would only feel responsible. He would only blame himself for what happened.'

'Please, madame, I must have your secret.'

'I felt as I had in that street in Berlin on *Kristallnacht*. Instinctively I knew I would be raped and then killed.'

The party was over, the dance floor empty and the chairs all upside down on the tables. There wasn't a soul about. Badly shaken and drenched to the skin, Kohler stood alone. He tried to light a cigarette but . . . ah *nom de Jésus-Christ*! his hands shook too much.

'I'm getting too old for this,' he grumbled. 'I'm cracking up.' Louis and himself had been on the wrong side of the Occupying Authorities far too many times to let it happen again. Distrusted, despised and reviled by both the SS and the Gestapo in France *and* the fucking Resistance, they had best tread warily and overlook a few details.

'Like a certain car that nearly ran me down,' he said bitterly. 'One of ours. Herr Kaestner. I'm certain of it. Question is, Who let him out of jail? Baumann and the others or Elizabeth Krüger?' Had she had a spare key to slip the Captain? he asked himself and said, 'Ah *merde*, she might have.'

There hadn't been time to get more than a glimpse of that car and oh for sure it would be impossible to prove that it really had been Kaestner, but . . . 'He was alone.'

Nature called and automatically he started for the toilets only to stop, to wonder if Death's-head and the others had caught up with Paulette le Trocquer and had brought her back.

Was she lying in there on that wet-tiled floor in a swill of puke, soggy cigarette butts and spent condoms? Had she been taken to some cave, or had she managed to get away from them?

A pretty thing in her black leather skirt and turtle-neck sweater . . . he still had her shoes in his pockets and idly he drew them out only to realize what an idiot he was to even have them anywhere near himself if she was dead. *If.*

The Gestapo would only seize on them and have him arrested for her murder no matter the evidence. The men of

U-297 would all swear he had been after the girl. Louis would not be able to save him, not this time.

'Don't get yourself in such a panic,' he said.

The stage curtains were open and bunched at the sides. Carefully he set the shoes out of sight then sighed and said, 'I'm going to have to do it. Louis isn't with me.'

The door to the toilets was stained and cold. Of cheap wood and flaking, greasy white paint, it yielded all too easily for comfort. The sour stench of splashed urine, bad drains and cheap perfume rushed at him. There were no stalls, just an L-shape to the room with the men's urinal trough to the right, the sink down at the bend and . . .

When he found her right at the back of the room, Paulette le Trocquer was slumped and kneeling with her head over one of the toilets. Her knees were apart, the toes that had fought so hard for purchase and escape were slack against the hard, wet floor. Her skirt lay two metres from her next to the wall beside the sink, the slip and underpants and stockings were scattered in the slime. The turtle-neck sweater – soaked right through by the rain – had been pushed up to her armpits. Hairs stuck out from beneath it. Her brassière strap had been cut and now its ends hung loosely at the sides, the skin so bluish white and grey and cold, he had to force himself not to turn away.

How many had gone at her? he wondered sadly. Had they made her drink brandy and beer, a half-and-half on top of wine – was that why the toilet? Had they even bothered? One girl and six or eight men. Death's-head for sure. The boy Erich Fromm and others. 'Yes, others,' he said. 'They'd have held her,' and reaching down into the toilet, gently lifted her head by the hair thinking to pull her out only to realize he had better not.

'Louis . . . Louis . . . ah *nom de Dieu, mon vieux*, why aren't you with me?'

Bruises marked those places she had struck – the outer thighs, the buttocks and knees also.

Others marred the back of her neck – thumb-marks,

fingermarks as she had been shoved face down and held, not throttled. She had thrashed her legs and had tried so hard to stop it from happening. An hour . . . had she been dead an hour?

When he saw himself in the fog of a cracked and peeling mirror, Kohler was taken aback. He could still feel her hair and how cold it had been. He knew he must not touch her again yet he wanted to cover her. She looked so forlorn and lonely in that mirror, a kid . . . just a kid.

Outside, in the rain, it was still dark. His two sons were dead at Stalingrad and suddenly he wanted to be with them at home in better times, but the girl was dead and so was her mother,

It was nearly thirty kilometres to the house by the sea and when he reached it in darkness still, no amount of banging at the front door could arouse the occupants. *'Louis,'* he cried out. *'Louis, it's me.'*

The wind took his words and flung them up at the eaves and into the hammering rain.

9

The beam of the torch flashed round at timbered posts and scattered straw. The shed beside the railway spur was empty. There was no sign of the child nor of Yvon Charbonneau. Kerjean was grim and gave the shrug of a policeman thwarted by the odds and fate.

'Hélène, I am so sorry. A night like this . . . I had hoped at least for Yvon. The alignment, the clay pits, the treasures he uncovered when digging up the briefcase . . . I had thought he might have returned since he was not at any of the other places.'

He shook the water from his cap and cape and shone the torch momentarily up into St-Cyr's eyes. 'Ah, pardon,' he said. 'A bitch of a night, eh, Jean-Louis? At this time of year one tries to force the dawn but the sun remains in bed for as long as it wishes.'

It was now 6.30 a.m. Berlin Time, 5.30 the old time and still two and a half hours before there would be light enough to dispense with torches. When Kerjean, in the little Renault the Germans had allowed him to keep, had picked them up at the house, there had been no chance to let Hermann know that, contrary to all protestations, the Préfet had headed for Lorient and this shed, discounting entirely that the Sûreté had advised most strongly a visit to Quiberon. No chance, either, to tell Hermann that someone else could well have seen the murder or committed it. Someone from U-297's crew perhaps . . . *Merde*, this case, he said to himself. One must go so carefully, especially when unarmed and without back-up.

Kerjean forced a smile that was both awkward and uncertain. 'Still we are together, eh? I'm glad I did not stay in Vannes to rest up as your partner insisted, but turned around when I got there and came straight back. Angélique will be all right, Hélène. Come now, you must not worry. Herr Kaestner . . .'

'He's desperate, Victor. He'll do something. He *has* to,' she said.

'Now listen, the less he does, the better off he is. A man like that, he is like the cobra in the basket, isn't that so? One goes carefully past or does not move at all but never . . . never, Hélène, does one allow the hypnotism of the self, eh? Never.'

'Victor, a moment, please,' cautioned St-Cyr. 'Is Herr Kaestner aware that you borrowed the money to allow your son and several others to escape?'

'Hélène . . . ?' managed Kerjean, startled. All the fears of just what such a thing would mean were in the look he gave her.

'I had to tell him, Victor. I had no other choice.'

'Herr Kaestner cannot possibly know, Jean-Louis. No one knew but myself and . . .'

'And who, Victor? Who?'

Ah damn Doenitz for demanding that a detective be sent from Paris. Any other would have suited but no, it had to be Jean-Louis and his friend.

'All right, so I put the squeeze on that shopkeeper. That doesn't mean I killed him.'

'I didn't say you did. I asked who else might know you had borrowed the money.'

'Only Hélène, my son and his friends, and . . . and perhaps Paulette – that girl, Jean-Louis. What am I to do, eh? Run while I can? Hélène, did you not think of the consequences? Did you not consider my family, myself, the others . . . others whom I must protect?'

He had said too much and apologized. 'Paulette and . . . perhaps her mother, Jean-Louis. I . . . . I really do not know. It was a dilemma for me. So much money was required. A fortune. I could not let my son and his comrades be taken. As it was, things were difficult enough. That cave in which they hid. The Côte Sauvage . . . Few knew of it but . . .' He shrugged to indicate the futility of it all. '. . . but I could never be certain they would not be discovered. I had to feed them and keep them quiet. They could not show their faces – strangers still stand out in little places like Quiberon. All through the summer I sweated and the only thing that kept me going, apart from the hope of seeing my son safely away, was you, Hélène, and the walks we had, the friendship of two lost souls from such totally different backgrounds.'

There was little they could do and oh for sure it really was one hell of a dilemma. Hélène Charbonneau reached out to the Préfet and, startled by her gesture, Kerjean gently took her bandaged hand in his. 'I am sorry,' he said. 'I had hoped and prayed you and your little family would be safe and that someday soon, Yvon and you . . . well, madame, you know how I felt. I . . . I hated seeing Herr Kaestner take advantage of you but . . .' He shrugged again. '. . . neither of us could object.'

'But did Herr Kaestner realize this?' asked St-Cyr. 'Please, I must slip right into his mind so as to think like him. He knew of the telescope, Victor – Angélique would have shown it to him. He'd have looked through it on several occasions.'

'He knew of my visits, Jean-Louis. He . . . he misinterpreted them as did others, the local gossips.'

'Ah, yes, but did he not use those visits and then the real reason for them to force Madame Charbonneau to continue in his company? Did he *know*, Victor, and in knowing, keep that knowledge to himself and use it for his own ends? When he finally learned of the missing money, he was not overly concerned, yet it had supposedly been missing for at least eight weeks, though the loss was not revealed to him until the 5th of November when U-297 returned from duty.'

'One of the *sardiniers* did not return on the 3rd of November,' said Hélène Charbonneau. 'Johann would have learned of this on the 5th – everyone knew by then. Victor, you yourself had to investigate. The German authorities wanted arrests. You had to pacify them as best you could.'

'And Kaestner simply put two and two together,' breathed St-Cyr, 'and added your little *tête-à-têtes* on the beach or at the house. But,' he paused to search her out, 'did he know of it right from the start? Your stepdaughter, madame. Please, I realize it is very difficult for you to answer, but would she have told Herr Kaestner of Préfet Kerjean's interest in that telescope?'

'If she did, I . . . I cannot hold it against her.'

'What will he do, Jean-Louis?' asked Kerjean, aghast at what lay before them.

'He will take everything in, Victor. He will coolly analyse the situation and then he will make his move but, please, the sardines migrate north and the season here is late. In summer there would have been a few fishing boats – yes, of course – but not the fleet of twenty-six you wanted to watch so closely. You were worried about Herr Kaestner and his relationship to Madame Charbonneau. Too much was at stake and you could not afford to have anything go wrong. You called, you walked, you talked and finally you realized you had best take her into your confidence since she was already indebted to you and could be trusted.'

'I needed to watch the patrol boats and how they checked the fishing boats. I could not depend on others. There were also the comings and goings of the submarines. Their routine was constantly being altered. They were always met and guided in but I could never find exactly where it would happen or how many boats would go out to them. If he knew of the security leak then Herr Kaestner is as guilty as myself of its breach, though I doubt very much he realized the full extent of things until after the 5th of November. Now, please, a moment your-self.'

Kerjean took out the Lebel Model 1873 six-shot revolver the Germans had allowed him with only six cartridges. 'One for me,' he said. 'For you the cyanide, Hélène. It . . . it is the only thing left.'

'Then let it keep for a little, eh?' said St-Cyr.

Sadly the Préfet shook his head. 'Others depend on me not to tell the Germans what I know, Jean-Louis. As a section head in the Resistance, I must take this final responsibility.'

'Victor, don't, *please*,' begged the woman.

The beam of the torch faltered. The gun wavered, now towards the floor, now towards them but to one side and then . . . 'A moment, Victor,' said St-Cyr. 'Let her step outside. I'll tell the Germans she and I went along the tracks to the alignment to look for her husband – perhaps he called out to us. Yes . . . yes, that will suit. You were checking the shed. We heard a shot . . .'

'People will think I killed le Trocquer,' said Kerjean sadly. 'They will not understand that the Dollmaker has simply won another victory. He has chosen to sacrifice security so as to trap me into revealing everything I know to their SS and Gestapo.'

'A moment! Let her step outside.'

'Yes . . . yes, of course. Forgive me.'

She turned and stopped and bowed her head in grief and said, 'Victor, bless you for trying to help us. May you be with God.'

The sound of the hammer as it was placed on the half-cock came to St-Cyr. 'The torch, Victor.'

'The torch . . . ?'

St-Cyr took a step. The gun went up, a fist came in and up hard . . . hard under the chin. The shot shattered the con-fines of the shed. The woman shrieked and ducked her head.

Out cold and flat on his back, Kerjean lay on the straw. 'I

must not make a habit of this,' said St-Cyr ruefully. 'Please, I am really very sorry, but I simply could not let him kill himself.'

'*I did not want him dead.*'

She was frantic. 'But you must admit his death would have helped you greatly.'

'I . . . I don't know what you mean?'

'Madame, I think you do. Now let us find my partner and get this business settled before someone really gets hurt. There still may be a chance, slim though that is.'

Just beyond the turn-off to the house, the standing stones of Kerzerho were close, grey-green and drenched, tall and damned unfriendly. No more than two or three metres apart, and some just as high, they had been set out in awesome rows perhaps four thousand years ago. The stones cut across the main road to Plouharnel – there were 1,129 of them – and the noise roared up from among them like the chant of ancient savages.

'*Turmluk ist frei. Boot ist raus!*' Hatch is free. Boat is up! '*Ich hatt' einen kammeraden.*' I once had a comrade.

The shouting and the singing fell off at last and the two lorries stared at each other through the rainswept darkness of the lonely road where history watched and engines throbbed.

'Ah *merde*,' breathed Kohler. It was Death's-head and the others, and for all he knew, the tarpaulined back of the lorry held the rest of the crew.

'It must,' he said to himself. 'The noise was too loud to have been coming just from those four in the cab.'

Without taking his eyes from the driver, he reached across the seat to drag towards himself the string bag of skulls he had gathered from the pianist's study. He had searched the house for Louis, for a sign of anyone, and finding none, had taken the skulls but was now not so sure it had been a good idea. 'The stones won't like it,' he said. He was not superstitious, not really but . . .

212

'All right, you bastard,' he said, finding the cook grinning at him from behind the other windscreen, 'I'll defy the gods and their druids and give you my little present. I'll see what you do.'

Perhaps three metres separated the two lorries. A door opened and one of them got out into the rain to hang on and steady himself. Dishevelled, and doubtlessly stinking of puke, piss and beer, the boy Erich Fromm wavered, then drew himself up and took a step towards the other lights. He paused to wipe the rain from his face and to stare myopically at the Gestapo who had come to arrest him for his part in the rape and murder of Paulette le Trocquer, to say nothing of her invalided mother.

Taking another step, he threw a hand forward to steady himself. '*I didn't want to do it!*' he cried out, or something like that, and, fountaining up his guts, clutched his stomach and bowed his head in shame.

The rain parted the pale, short-cropped blond hair and coursed down the raw-boned, pimpled face. 'You're just a kid,' swore Kohler. 'Hey, you're not the one I want.'

Getting out into the rain, he went to the boy. 'Look, I understand how it must have been. They held you. They brought you up to her and put it in, so okay. What's done is done. Now go and get into the back of my lorry. Try to get some sleep while I sort this out.'

He had to help the boy. The bed of the lorry was too high and the kid, though he tried, couldn't possibly climb up.

When he had finally pushed him in and had tied the tarpaulin down, Kohler heard the others coming forward. They met between the headlamps. Thirty to one . . . were the odds that high? *Ach!* Did he really have to take on the whole crew?

Shoulder to shoulder and crowded, they formed a phalanx behind their cook and Otto Baumann and the Second Engineer.

Though pissed to the gills and still clutching bottles, they were rapidly sobering.

'You're blocking the road,' said Death's-head.

Kohler wanted to wipe that stupid grin from the lark-eyed bastard and saw again in memory that poor girl's head face down in a toilet.

Rain soaked the Kaiser moustache, causing it to droop, and poured from the black peak of Otto Baumann's forage cap.

'Why aren't you fellows sleeping it off in Quiberon?'

Was Herr Kohler serious? 'Duty calls,' said Baumann. 'U-297 has to be stuffed, Inspector. She wants it in her. She's greedy for it. All hands are to help. Our C.-in-C., Herr Freisen, waits for nothing and no one.'

So be it. 'Then what about Paulette Trocquer, eh, and what about her mother?'

The rain stung his face but did not seem to bother them at all.

It was Death's-head who, the grin vanishing, said, 'She went home, I suppose. Our loss is her gain, perhaps. Who's to say?'

'As for the mother, Herr Kohler,' said the Second Engineer, 'why do you ask us? An old hag in a wheel-chair?'

'Fine. I'm arresting the three of you and the boy for the murders of Paulette le Trocquer and her mother.'

He was really serious about it. 'And that of the shop-keeper?' asked the cook. The others stared at the Gestapo's loneliest detective.

'You boys let the Captain out of jail. I saw him in his car at the shop after I found the mother.

The surprise was genuine – or was it? The lark's touch of insanity leapt into Schultz's dark eyes. 'But Vati is in the lock-up. Otto, here, has the key.'

'Then why isn't he with him?'

'Because our Dollmaker sleeps and whoever takes the lorry back will be bringing him his breakfast.'

'You're lying.'

An angry murmur went through the crew. They pressed

closer. Baumann held them back with outstretched arms. 'Where is your partner?' he asked.

Was the party about to get rough? 'Not at the pianist's house. I've been trying to find him.'

'What about the woman?' asked Death's-head. The grin became a leer.

'What about her?' asked Kohler evenly.

'Nothing. We only wondered how she was getting on without our Vati's cock.'

The bastard. Hadn't they had enough?

'The child,' asked Baumann, 'and the father, please, Herr Kohler. Where are they?'

'With the Préfet, I think. The woman, too, and my partner.' He damn well didn't know where they were, but what the hell, there was no harm in trying, or was there? 'Kerjean did say something about looking for the husband in one of the tumuli.'

One of the passage graves. 'Which one?'

This had come from the Second Engineer. 'Look, I don't know, do I? I sent Kerjean home to Vannes but he must have gone to the house instead. Oh, that reminds me. Hang on a minute. I've brought your cook a little present.'

'Don't think of leaving,' cautioned Baumann. 'Not now. Not when you've just accused us of murder.'

'I won't. I'm only going to the cab. It's on the seat.'

'And this, my friend, is pointing right at your guts. It's loaded,' said Baumann. 'Please don't make me guilty of murder.'

At 7.30 a.m. Berlin Time, it was very dark and cold in the rain, and the hammering of the droplets on the backs of St-Cyr's bare hands stung so much, the uneasiness within him only increased.

For some time now Victor Kerjean had remained silent. That he wanted his gun back and felt betrayed was all too clear. Now he poured gasoline into the Renault's fuel tank while the Sûreté, who had his gun in a pocket, cupped hands about the nozzle and the opening so as to keep out the rain if possible.

There had been three jerry cans crammed into the tiny boot and only one of them had been full.

'Jean-Louis, Hélène will only tell the Nazis about my son – they'll make her. She's done for anyway, isn't that so? Let us take her back to the house. She can write a farewell to her husband and the child. Please, I beg it of you. The lives of too many others are at stake. Our work . . . The Germans won't be staying long. The invasion will come.'

The refuelling came to an end. Hélène Charbonneau heard St-Cyr desperately trying to fit the gas cap on. At last he succeeded, then the two of them stood out there while she sat alone inside straining to hear what they were saying about her.

'Victor, I have a murder to solve and until that is done, I cannot . . .'

'You *cannot*? You who call yourself a patriot? Oh *mon Dieu, mon ami*, don't try to play the pious, big-city detective with me. Give me back my gun and let me present the truth to her.'

The jerry can was heavy and as a weapon it would be eminently suitable. Kerjean was quick, tough and muscular. The blow that had knocked him out had been lucky and totally unexpected.

Now it would not be so easy. 'Potassium cyanide? How, please, did she come by it, Victor? Rat poison, is this what you are thinking as a way of explaining the coroner's report which will have to be done?'

'No one will care. Do you think Kaestner will? Hah! he *wants* her dead.'

'And you, Victor?'

Why must Jean-Louis make him say it again? Was Hélène listening? Was that it, eh? 'Me also, of course. There are my wife and my daughters, yes? And my grandchildren – I've eight of them, did I tell you? Eight. Four boys and four girls and two more on the way.'

'Let us be patient.'

'*Patient!*' The jerry can slammed against the car and rang hollowly. 'You ask for patience when time waits for no one?'

'Kaestner may believe she has already taken the cyanide. To him, she has no other choice, and this may well be our only chance. But there is also my partner, Victor. Hermann will certainly have come up with something and until I have a chance to talk with him, no one is taking cyanide or shooting themselves, and that, my friend, is final.'

Kerjean turned abruptly away and in the darkness and the rain, and with his dark overcoat and cap, it was so very difficult to see him. St-Cyr hesitated. He heard the can hit one of the others. The tyre iron? he wondered. Was Victor reaching for it?

There was only the sound of the rain. Hélène Charbonneau held her breath for as long as she could. What were they doing out there? she asked herself. It was not fair – nothing was. Victor had been a good friend but now . . . now. Yvon knew things the Germans would want to know – Angélique did too – and what was Victor to do about the two of them? Kill them? she demanded.

Ah damn that lousy shopkeeper, she cried and clenched her fists. Ah damn Paulette. Why could that girl not have tried to understand that things weren't as they seemed, that Angélique had been upset but hadn't realized the truth?

She pressed the back of her bandaged left hand hard against her lips to steady herself. Victor was right. She should kill herself. It was the only solution. Dead, there might be a small chance for Angélique and Yvon. She had to think of them and that was what Johann had tried to tell her.

'Victor . . .' she heard the Sûreté saying. 'Victor, please don't try anything foolish. Let us find the husband and the daughter, then let us see where things lie.'

Only the rain gave answer, and when she rolled the window further down, the droplets struck her face.

'Jean-Louis, I am warning you. As a section head of the *Front de la Libération de la Bretagne*, I cannot fall into their hands.'

'You won't. If I have to, I will shoot you. You have my word on it.'

The boot was closed.

'Then let us find the father and hope the Captain is looking for him too, and will have the child with him.'

They got into the car but now Victor sat behind the steering wheel and the Sûreté was forced to get into the front beside him and she had to think, was it clever of Victor to have done this? And she had to sadly nod and say, Yes . . . Yes, it was.

'We will try the Dolmen of Crucuno first, Jean-Louis,' he said, 'since it is much closer, and then, I think, The Tumulus of Saint-Michel.'

Three kilometres east of Plouharnel and the road to Quiberon, rain flooded the narrow, darkened streets of Carnac. Schultz spared the village little. Jamming the accelerator down, he gave the lorry all it had on the only hill worth mentioning in the whole of the Morbihan. All too soon, though, the beam of the headlamps cut an angry swath across the white-plastered front of a small hotel whose giant letters gave THE GRAVE OF THE DRUIDS – THE TUMULUS OF SAINT-MICHEL – and poured water off each of them.

Ah *merde*, sighed Kohler, not liking it one bit.

His own lorry soon screeched to a halt beside them and both raced their engines and trained the beams of their headlamps nakedly on the hotel in spite of the black-out regulations.

At last the portly owner got the message. Timidly the door opened and, on seeing that it really was the Germans, he stepped out to stand in the rain, shielding his eyes from the glare.

The maroon velour dressing-gown with its jade-green

218

collar and cord had to have been left by some down-at-heel Count of Monte Cristo more than fifty years ago. The beige felt slippers were too big and didn't even match each other. 'Messieurs . . . ?' began the man doubtfully – at least that's what he must have said but no one heard him.

His chubby cheeks were pale, the dome of his head bald, the ears rather small behind sidewhiskers and under the monk's tonsure.

Schultz gunned the engine hard, then switched off but left the lights on. The other lorry followed suit. Silence now intruded, joining the incessant hammering of the rain.

'He's getting wet,' offered Kohler.

'So what?' snorted Schultz.

'You're the Gestapo,' murmured Baumann. 'You do the honours, Herr Kohler. Tell him we're tourists and haven't got a lot of time. Tell him we're sorry to have interrupted his sleep but that death waits for no one and he should have been up and at work anyway.'

'The Préfet's car isn't here, Otto,' hazarded Schultz.

It wasn't. 'Give me back my guns,' breathed Kohler. 'I don't feel right without them.' *Verdammt*, what was he to do?

'And here we thought the Gestapo invincible and equal to every situation?' quipped Baumann drily.

'Piss off.'

The muzzle of the Luger jabbed him in the ribs. 'Give him Schultz's present. Maybe that will loosen his tongue.'

With the string bag of skulls dangling from his left hand, the Gestapo's detective walked into the lights to stand in the rain and throw his shadow over the hotel.

A big man, he was formidable.

'Listen, those boys mean business. Is there anyone in the tumulus?'

'The tumulus . . . ? But . . . but it is closed for the season, monsieur? The hours, they are from . . .'

'Kohler, Gestapo Paris Central. Just answer the question.'

There were at least six skulls in the bag and as the

Gestapo raised it higher, they, too, threw their shadow on the wall.

'Préfet Kerjean was here earlier but . . . Monsieur Charbonneau, he was not in the tumulus and the Préfet, he . . . he has told me to lock the door and let no one in.'

That was fair enough and what a good cop would have done. 'Where was he headed when he left you?'

'To Vannes . . . to his house. Monsieur, has anything happened to Monsieur Charbonneau? The Préfet, he has searched the tumulus most thoroughly in spite of my telling him the door was locked all day and Monsieur Charbonneau could not, after his last visit, have left the side entrance open for himself as he sometimes does. The Préfet, please, he has not said why he . . . he was looking for the pianist.'

'Someone wants him for a concert at the Santé.'

'The Santé . . . ?' Paris's largest and most crowded prison.

The others must have got down from the lorries, for the man drew in a ragged breath and could not take his eyes from them. 'So many,' he stammered.

'It's just a party. Give me the key and whatever candles you have. Here, hold this and I'll pay you up front. That way you won't have to worry.'

5,000 francs changed hands from a bundle the Gestapo dragged out. 'It . . . it is too much,' stammered the man. 'I have no change.'

'Don't worry. It's my treat. Look on it as a tip and if my partner arrives, tell him I'm in there. Tell him to do something and to go about it carefully.'

The crew approached and soon they too threw their shadows on the hotel. Quickly the owner crossed himself and, thrusting back the bag of skulls, disappeared into the house for the key.

The damned thing must weigh a good two kilos, thought Kohler. 'Exactly what kind of a door is it?' he asked doubtfully.

'An old one. A big one.'

Behind, and to one side of the hotel, a long, vine-covered pergola that might have been deemed quaint in pre-war days, led to the door whose great iron studs and hammered surface looked not only medieval but impregnable. The vines had lost their leaves and simply got in the way. The lock was stiff, the door took two of them to budge it and another to swing it aside.

Christ! The burrow behind it was lined with upright stones too heavy for fewer than eight or ten strong young men to have heaved into place. It was roofed by the same.

Grey and grey-green, the tightly fitted stones revealed signs of mitring which made one marvel at the skill of its builders. The stones were cold and damp and mossy and when he let a hand trail respectfully down the surface of one of them, Kohler swallowed hard. He'd have to duck. There was little enough room. His shoulders were wide. The floor was paved with blocks, or was it gravel? Dry in any case and all but level. Perhaps he could find some gentle rise, perhaps he could . . .

'You first,' said Baumann. 'Here, give me the key. Death's-head will keep it.'

Were they going to lock him in? wondered Kohler. 'The Préfet isn't here and neither is the pianist.'

'We'll see, since there are two entrances. If not, we'll have a trial of our own without them. Just you and ourselves. You'll tell us what we want to know and we won't tell you anything.'

'Then give me a light. My eyes aren't so good when it's pitch dark.'

'Quit stalling. The passage goes in to the centre of the tumulus. Graves open off it but are sunk a little into the floor. There is also a cross-cutting passage to the left and then, a little later on, one to the right which leads to the side entrance. The passage we are in makes a circuit in the centre with communal rooms opening off it, and it is in these rooms that there are several cremation pits.'

'You've been here before.'

'When one leaves the sea, what else is there to do?'

The *Blechkoller* of U-boatmen, that tin-can claustrophobic neurosis, was foreign to most of them or perhaps they were simply used to it and bolstered one another. Every once in a while the long line of men, stooped and otherwise, would stop to listen hard or laugh and make jokes until silenced by the others. In the damp and musty hush that followed these outbursts, the wind would whisper and sigh as it sought the ancient passages or found some hidden fissure it just had to explore.

Were its sounds parts of the pianist's symphony? he wondered. The entrance passage did, indeed, pass portals that led to cremation pits in rooms across whose walls and floors the torch beams erratically fled.

One long passage did lead to the west – Baumann shone his torch along it. The stones were grey and silent and forbidding. The floor, trod by ancient feet from across the millennia, brought with the thought of them, the sound of stone hammers cracking the charred bones of their brethren to burn them better and free the greasy marrow.

The smoke would have been thick and pungent with the stench of burning flesh. It would have crept along the roofs of the tunnels or hung there for days. Soot was everywhere above him, now that he looked for it. All too soon, though, the fears and superstitions of the crew got the better of them and they searched in silence, conferred seldom and then but softly, ghosts of another time and with candles instead of flaming torches or stone lamps.

A little farther in, another long passage went east into that same pitch-dark and uncertain void. But had both of these lateral passages once broken out at their far ends so that the rays of the rising and setting sun would have been seen directly but only at one precise time of year? The tumulus must be huge.

At a distant shout from one of the men, they discovered that the other entrance door was locked, but for how long had that been?

'We'll wait here,' said Baumann softly. 'We'll know soon enough if there's anyone else.' Anyone but the spirits of the dead, thought Kohler, the spirits of men, women and children who had once lived and worked and played and fashioned tools of flint and then of copper and had dragged their dead in here.

Schultz took the string bag from him and, grinning, set each of the skulls in wall niches where once the stone lamps would have been placed. They would have a trial and they'd find out what he knew but then what? wondered Kohler uneasily. On Thursday, in another forty-eight hours, they would put to sea taking their Dollmaker with them and no one the wiser as to the whereabouts of this half of the partnership, particularly if they locked the owner of that hotel and his family in with him.

St-Cyr was not happy. Ah no, most certainly. With the first grey touches of dawn, the rain had ceased. Now dense fog had come in to blanket everything and give to the alarm of foraging gulls and ravens a special sharpness.

Something was attracting them. Kerjean had heard it too, and so had Hélène Charbonneau but more than this, far more, was the Préfet's having not stopped where he should have, and the woman's alertness to the unannounced change of plan.

The Dolmen of Crucuno was a good one and a half kilometres behind them and that is where Kerjean had said he was taking them to look for her husband.

Tense and wary, she sat in the far corner of the back seat, directly behind the Préfet but visible to him in the rear-view mirror, for he had turned it so as to see her. Though it must hurt her to do so, she was clutching the door handle as if ready to bolt and run at the slightest sign.

She was afraid of Kerjean and must have overheard them talking about her.

Kerjean knew it too.

'Hélène, why not stay in the car,' he said, looking at her

in the rear-view. 'It may be the child the birds have found. It may be your husband. Until Jean-Louis and I have had a look, it could be anything.'

She didn't answer. With the back of her other hand, she rubbed the side window clear then stared emptily out at the moor.

Desolate and all but hidden beneath the fog, its scattered clumps of heather, gorse and stunted hawthorn gave shades of grey and brown to the ever-present silvery tufts of wind-twisted grass and boulders with mosses and lichens on them.

'Hélène . . .'

'I heard you, Victor. Why, please, have we stopped here? This place soon becomes marshy. There's a bog and then a fen of several hectares with an open space of water in the middle.'

Must she be so difficult? 'You know I have often found your husband there, Hélène. You know he swore he could hear parts of his symphony and that the Veneti and those from long before them used to throw offerings into its centre and to sometimes make sacrifices.'

'Sacrifices? Sacrifices for what?' she said harshly. 'My *husband*? Don't you mean Yvon? Don't you mean the man you cared enough about to watch over him for me?'

'Yes. Yes, of course.'

'What have you done with him?'

'Hélène, you are overwrought.'

'*Am* I? You were there at the clay pits on the day of the murder, Victor. You came to the house to warn me of trouble but you did not offer to go with me. You said you mustn't, that I would have to handle le Trocquer myself. *Me*, Victor. *Me!*'

'Jean-Louis, don't listen to her. She doesn't know what she's saying.'

'I know it only too well, Inspector. A package of American cigarettes? A crumpled handkerchief in the straw? My handkerchief. Mine!'

224

'Madame . . .' began St-Cyr.

Bitterly she looked at him. 'Angélique is aware of this place and will have told the Captain of it. My husband often took her with him both to hear the "symphony" and to gather sphagnum moss and the leaves of what the old fishermen call Labrador tea. Berries too, and other things. She is very close to her father and understands him better even than myself but she is also with the Captain and may be under his spell.'

'Hélène . . .'

'If you have killed my husband, Victor, I will tell the Germans everything. I know about your Resistance. Everything, do you understand?'

The gulls cried and the sound of them grew as she pushed open the door and bolted from the car.

'Ah *merde*,' breathed St-Cyr. 'Victor, I must ask that you . . .'

'Jean-Louis, I did not kill le Trocquer nor did I kill her husband. I swear it. She's crazy. She's all mixed up. Oh for sure, it's understandable but . . .'

'But, what, Victor?'

'But if the gulls and the ravens have got to his corpse we had best find her before she finds him.'

'Then stay close. Don't let us become separated. You first, then myself.'

'And the child, Jean-Louis? What if it is the child they are crying over?'

In less than twenty metres, the car and the road were lost to them. Kerjean asked again about the child but St-Cyr did not answer. Instead, he let only the sound of the gulls and the ravens come to them. Victor could well be guilty. Certainly he had been playing a very dangerous game. And what of Paulette le Trocquer and her mother? he asked himself. What of those empty jerry cans? Had he gone to Quiberon to settle the girl and her mother once and for all? Had he then returned to the house and taken the woman and this detective on to the clay pits so as to give himself an alibi?

Kerjean moved again, and he followed the Préfet for some distance. There were cairns half sunk into the peaty soil. Sometimes only a single, small menhir, perhaps not placed by the ancients but in far more recent times, marked the route.

Frequently they both stopped and listened hard but beneath the crying of the gulls and ravens, there was not even the patient dripping of water.

So muffled were the sounds at ground level, the birds had full dominion but then, suddenly, her voice came loudly and from all directions hollowly echoing. *'Yvon . . . Yvon . . . darling, please forgive me. I was so afraid the Captain would have us all arrested.'* Arrested . . . arrested . . . *'I could not tell him to leave me alone.'* Alone . . . alone . . . *'Darling are you out there?'*

Ah damn, where the hell was Kerjean? Why had he not kept his eyes on him?

'Yvon, is Angélique with you?' You . . . you . . . *'Did you meet up with the Captain?'* The Captain . . . the Captain . . . *'He took her from the house, Yvon.'* The house . . . the house . . .

St-Cyr went forward but was soon up to his calves in springy, water-soaked sphagnum moss which grew in low mounds and humps with leatherleaf, Labrador tea and cranberry and sometimes stunted black spruce. And to the damp salt smell of a cold sea, came that of rotting vegetation, of peat, black water and methane, and the sense of someone near but never seen.

Nom de Dieu, de Dieu, he said to himself, why could Hermann not have been with him?

He would only have bitched about getting his shoes and socks thoroughly wet! He would only have blamed his partner for being so stupid as to have let the Préfet out of his sight!

The humps and hollows grew more difficult but soon there were sedges, feather mosses and tall, coarse grasses, the beginnings of the fenland. 'The gulls are out there somewhere,' he said.

Everything wept moisture, everything was shrouded in fog. Stunted black spruce were spindly like the bones of a fish and often clublike at the top with a witch's broom of many shoots.

He fell. He went down on his hands and knees. His shoes were in danger of becoming lost with the sucking of the bottom muds. He almost called out, *Kerjean, where are you?*

He almost said, *You leave her alone.*

When he arrived at a bit of staging, a dock of sorts up on pilings and none too solid, there wasn't a sign of anyone. Only the fog and the beginnings of open water that was ringed by rushes now sear.

The tightly knotted painter with which the pianist had tethered his punt had been cleanly cut. 'Last night,' he said and knew he was right.

The gulls were out over the water. The ravens had no place to land except on the punt.

Kohler swallowed tightly. The chamber, deep in the Tumulus of Saint-Michel, was large enough and roofed by massive slabs that were held up by standing stones of several tonnes. He sat all alone before the men on a large, flat rock – had it been a megalithic butcher's block? he wondered. His feet were sunk into one of a scattering of cremation pits – shallow, round holes about a metre or so in diameter that had been dug into the floor perhaps four thousand years ago. They'd been excavated more lately, of course, but . . . *Ach!* There were still bits of charcoal and charred bone. He noticed a molar and tried not to concentrate on it, looked up suddenly.

Death's-head Schultz had his Walther P38 in a pocket, the Second Engineer had Louis's Lebel, and Baumann still had the Captain's Luger.

Among the thirty or so men who were gathered, those who had one of the thick, greasy candles held it before them in a clenched fist, and the light . . . the light not only flickered hauntingly across their faces but those of the others, and they all cast shadows on the roof and walls behind them. The stench of grease, soot, smoke, sour wine and beer, puke and sweat was close on the damp, cold, musty air just like in a submarine.

They were definitely not friendly. Grim-faced, stolid and silent, they were almost as apprehensive as himself. After all, he was Gestapo, was one of them, and mock trials, no matter how much of a joke they might claim them to be, were nothing to fool with should word get back to Berlin. Things could also go wrong. Ah *Gott im Himmel*, what was he to do?

Having searched and found no sign of Charbonneau, they wanted answers. They were about as much in the dark as he was. They genuinely needed to find out what the hell had been going on. Their Captain, their Vati, was being blamed for something he maintained he hadn't done. Paulette le Trocquer had been gang-raped and murdered and the Inspector was saying their cook, the Obersteuermann Baumann, the Second Engineer and Erich Fromm were responsible. The girl's mother had been killed. The money – some of it their own – was still missing.

'Let's face it,' grimaced the prisoner, 'that sweet little bit you guys nailed in the toilet would have told you every-thing, Death's-head. The question is, why don't you tell the rest of us?'

His head bent forward uncomfortably lest it hit the stone roof, the cook grinned and let his lark's eyes dance over the prisoner. 'We're asking the questions. You are doing the answering.'

'Then ask. Let it be between the two of us.'

'Otto, he hasn't understood.'

Baumann sighed. 'We found the girl just as you did, Herr Kohler, the mother also. Now, if we didn't kill them, who did?'

'Your Vati?'

Baumann dragged out the key to the cell and waved it

reprovingly. 'He's locked up. I myself saw him into the cell last night after his brief visit to the party.'

'And there's no other key? Don't be a *Dummkopf*. Quiberon's *gendarmes* would have had a spare. The Préfet . . .'

'The Préfet,' said Death's-head, still grinning. '*Bitte, Herr Detektif. Bitte.* Why would Préfet Kerjean release our Dollmaker when he believes him guilty of murder?'

'I didn't say he did. I only meant there could well have been two keys and that, given the opportunity, Fräulein Krüger could well have palmed the other one and passed it to the Captain.'

'The Fräulein Krüger . . . ? But . . . but how was she given that opportunity?' asked Baumann.

'Were there two cell keys hanging on the wall of that piss pot *gendarmerie*?' countered Kohler. He had got them talking. At least that was something.

Baumann thought about it. The Obersteuermann raked over the leaves of the past few days. The arrest, their demanding to take charge of Vati, the telexes to and from the Lion in Paris, the Préfet's backing down. Kerjean had vehemently argued that the Dollmaker was his responsibility yet had let them guard the Captain. '*Ja*, there may well have been two keys.'

'Good. Now we're getting somewhere. Question is, did she give that key to the Captain because I damned well saw him in a car outside that shop. He nearly ran me over.'

'Yet you do not believe he killed Madame le Trocquer?' asked Baumann. 'Why, please, is this?'

'Yes, why?' demanded Death's-head. 'Why blame us when you know Vati was there?'

'Because you bastards were looking for your money. You smashed the place up. The dollmaker wouldn't have bothered.'

'Unless,' said Baumann, half in thought and half in doubt, 'unless he had wanted to make it look as if someone else had done it.'

I.e., the crew.

'Were all four of you always together at the last?' asked Kohler, wishing he had fags to pass around. Tobacco was the great pacifier. 'Well?' he asked.

'Not always,' admitted Baumann cautiously. 'But we were together when he found the girl on her knees and then found the mother.'

'Before or after I did?'

'Before. You were still looking for us in the rain. We went straight from the Club to the shop and in a hurry.'

'No sign of the Captain?'

'No sign of anyone.'

'Would the Captain have killed them – did he have a reason, damn it?'

A reason . . . A reason . . . Herr Kohler had raised his voice and the passages had echoed it back.

Baumann threw Death's-head an uncertain look. The lark's glimmer vanished. Kohler caught the drift and said, 'Schultz, you had better tell us about the doll Angélique Charbonneau left in that shop. Maybe then we'll all understand why you wanted to find the pianist so badly. You were going to kill him, too, weren't you, eh? You were going to shut him up before he spilled it all to the others.' He indicated the rest of the men.

'Otto, he's lying. He's just trying to get us rattled.'

'Am I?'

Only the sound of the pianist's symphony came to them and they listened for it to a man.

'Death's-head, the doll,' said Baumann.

'The woman dropped it on the tracks. I saw her backing away from le Trocquer. I heard him shouting at her.'

'Good, that's very good,' sighed Kohler. 'Now tell us the rest.'

'She couldn't speak. She was too terrified. Her eyes were on the bend in the tracks. We both heard that iron bar come down. I swear we did. Then it hit the rails as it was thrown aside.'

'Where were you at the time?'

Damn Kohler. Damn the Lion for demanding that a detective be sent from Paris. 'Among the stones of that alignment.'

'Where was the pianist?'

'Nowhere near. I didn't see him, if that's what you're asking. I only saw the woman. She didn't see me. Not once. I made sure of that.'

'What about the Captain?'

'Vati was still in the clay pits or in the watchman's shed. Vati wasn't anywhere near the site of the murder. I would have known, yes? From where I was standing, I would have seen him.'

That too was good, but Death's-head still had the Walther P38 in a pocket, and that was bad. Kohler let his gaze move slowly over the men. He drew in a breath and nodded curtly at Baumann. So be it. 'You're lying, Schultz. The Dollmaker was there. During our second interrogation, Herr Kaestner told me he had overheard shouting, an altercation in French, and had seen the woman standing between the rails.'

The lark's eyes didn't rise to the bait. 'Vati was only trying to protect her. He still doesn't know I was there.'

Nor did any of the others until now. 'Then that only leaves you, my friend,' said Kohler.

'And the Préfet, and the pianist and the woman,' countered the cook, laughing at him. 'If Kerjean is so sure Vati killed le Trocquer, why not ask yourself, did Kerjean not also want that shopkeeper dead?'

'Did you see him there?'

Were detectives always so stupid? 'If I had seen him, I would have said so right away.'

'Providing you hadn't killed the shopkeeper and were certain you wouldn't be accused of it.'

Baumann interceded. 'Vati says he and the woman never met in that shed beside the tracks, Herr Kohler, yet there was one of his cigarette packages in it and the woman's handkerchief?'

Kohler spoke his thoughts aloud. 'The Préfet let my partner and I find them all by ourselves. He denied there were any bicycle tracks yet he must have seen them . . .'

'Forty on the Captain? Do I hear forty,' quipped the cook. 'I think the odds have just gone down to twenty on our Dollmaker, sixty on the Préfet, and ten each on the woman and her husband.'

'But what about yourself?' asked one of the crew.

'Yes, what about the doll, Schultzi? Why that doll?' asked another.

'Yes, why that doll, Death's-head?' asked Kohler. 'What was there about it that made you keep from the others that you had been there?'

'Nothing. Vati had been accused. I knew he couldn't possibly have done it. Like him, I merely waited to see what you and your partner would come up with. If Vati was to be convicted, I'd have come forward but admit it, Herr *Detektif*, you and the French judges would only have thought I was lying to protect him.'

The doll . . . what the hell had there been about that doll to make the cook so evasive and to make Kaestner pick up the pieces and refuse to yield them until certain he could not only do so but that the time was right?

It was Baumann who said, 'Death's-head, you had better tell us.'

'Otto, there's nothing to tell. It was just a child's doll. A nothing doll. What else could it possibly have been?'

The look of death perceived sought him out. 'Then why, please, did le Trocquer take it with him, and why, please, did he give it to the woman when it was the Captain he was going to see?'

Ah yes.

Trapped, Schultz flicked a glance to the right and left. He was near the entrance but perhaps four or five of the men were in the way behind him.

'Don't even think of it, Death's-head,' said Baumann. 'When we went after Paulette, you were the first to go for her and the last to rejoin us. You could have gone back to the Club. You could have killed her to shut her up but about what, please? This you had best tell us.'

The cook was a big man but he was going to need help. *Verdammt!*

Kohler waited. Schultz tried to grin but succeeded only in wetting his lower lip. He would need a flying wedge to get him through that door, then the legs of a gazelle and the lungs of the damned.

'I . . .' stammered the cook. 'Look, I was only trying to protect Vati. It . . . it was nothing. Nothing!' he said, his voice breaking.

'Take his gun,' said Baumann.

It was now or never. Kohler launched himself from the cremation pit and threw himself at the cook, carrying him into the men behind. They fell, they fought. Fists pummelled him. He pushed, he grabbed a leg, an arm, a neck . . . A burning candle rolled away. They were in the passage . . . the passage. 'Run,' he gasped. *'God damn it, go while you can!'*

Seized from behind, Kohler was carried forward in a rush as they pelted after the cook. He bucked. He hit the stone walls and tried to stop the men, tried to shake loose of them in the darkness going down the tunnel . . . down it . . .

Someone cried out and fell. Others fell on top of the man and soon they were all shouting, all trying to scramble up and he was free and running . . . running towards the light of day, the light . . . Fog . . . was it fog?

Schultz was right behind him. The bastard had darted aside into one of the rooms and had tripped the others. Now the cook reached daylight and they slammed the door shut and threw their weight against it.

Breathlessly Schultz tried to fit the ancient key into the lock before it was too late.

Kohler did it for him.

The cook grinned hugely but he still had the pistol and now it was pointing the wrong way. There was fog everywhere.

'Let's find the pianist and the woman,' said Death's-head, catching a breath. 'If they're alive, I'll tell you about the doll. If they're dead, I won't.'

'And what about the Préfet?'

'What about him, eh? You're the detective. You tell me.'

10

St-Cyr stood still. The woman – he was certain it was her – took another patient, careful step. Only with difficulty did the bog relinquish her foot. It made sucking noises and of these she was very conscious.

He cursed the fog. He asked, God, why must You do this to me, a simple detective?

God only gave him the sucking noises and, over the open water in the middle of the fen somewhere back there behind him, the crying of the gulls and ravens.

A punt, he said. A body. Blood, death and torn flesh had drawn the birds. The woman no longer called out to her husband. She knew what awaited her.

There had been no sign of Kerjean. It was as if the Préfet had vanished from the face of the earth or had been swallowed up by the bog.

She took another step. Sphagnum squished. Water as black as strong tea and stinking of rotten eggs, bubbled up to icily swallow her boots. When she found the spiked and spindly trunk of a blackened spruce rising up from the peat, she ignored the pain in her hands to frantically pull it free – strained at it, tried so hard she had to rest.

She went on and he could not understand her doing so. The tree trunk only made her progress more difficult by catching on things. Twice she fell and stifled her cries by burying her face in the soggy moss. Once she went down so hard, she lay there between the mounds of sphagnum and leatherleaf and he did not see her for some time.

Then she pulled herself up and dragged the trunk free.

Her long dark hair was awry with twigs, moss and mud, her face and hands bore smears of peat and blood, the bandages were gone, the coarse black woollen overcoat was soaking wet and very heavy yet she did not shed it.

Quite by accident or design she crossed the path but did not take it. instead, she stood off some distance straining to hear and see all that was around her. The fog swirled. He hid among the scattered cranberry and stunted spruce and saw her only now and then.

Satisfied that she wasn't being followed, she made her way towards the road but always kept the path well to her left.

When she fell to her knees with a cry and cast the only weapon she had aside, he knew something was wrong. Frantically she dragged at the peaty muds. She dug her feet in, sat back and, stiffening her legs, pulled hard at the thing. He heard her gasp. She gave a ragged sob, then said not loudly, 'Yvon, I never wanted this to happen.'

The bicycle's rear wheel was so bent and twisted, it took all her remaining energy to pull and pry it free until at last, it stood above the surface of the bog.

He waited – everything in him said to go to her, that she needed help and comfort, but he could not do so.

Kerjean had approached from the other direction. He had hardly spent a moment in the bog. He had known the bicycle was there. He had *not* known she would find it.

'An accident, Hélène,' he said and his voice, muffled by the fog, had a judgemental finality to it that was only reinforced by the eerie crying of the gulls and the deeper, harsher cawing of the ravens. 'I found it on the road. I thought it best to hide it here since your husband . . .'

'Yvon, damn you. *Yvon!*'

'Since your husband intended to kill himself.'

'*Why?*' she asked, the word torn from her. Anguish, pain and disbelief were in her voice, hatred too. 'Yvon had no reason to kill himself, Victor. He had every reason to live for Angélique's sake.'

'He tried to kill St-Cyr.'

'You know that is not true. He was only trying to protect Angélique. Yvon didn't even know about that damned doll until Monsieur le Trocquer confronted me with it. My husband didn't want people to find out what his daughter had done to me. He . . . he was afraid the inspectors and others would see it and he couldn't have that, could he?'

She was desperate. 'Where is Jean-Louis?' he asked.

'Nowhere near. There are only the two of us.'

'You should have taken the cyanide. It would have been better.'

'Better? Better than what, please? Your hands on my throat? My face in the mud until I can struggle no more? I know too much. You cannot let me continue to live.'

'Please don't be difficult.'

'You wanted Yvon to kill himself so you hid the bicycle you had smashed with your car. You let him crawl all the way out there to his boat. Was he badly hurt, Victor? Was he bleeding, damn you?'

Sacré nom de nom, thought Kerjean, why had Jean-Louis not called out? 'Hélène, I searched for Yvon. I tried to find him and found the bicycle at the side of the road. I swear it, but I could not have stopped him even if I had found him. He was insane and you know it. He was always hearing the ancients and their whispers. This place was very sacred to them, sacred to himself also. Yes . . . yes, don't deny it. A relic, he called it, from the Ice Age, from that time of much colder climate. He wanted to be buried here and unless I am very mistaken, we will find him in that little boat of his still clutching the boulder he intended to take to the bottom with him.'

'Yvon did not kill Monsieur le Trocquer,' she said harshly and, catching up the blackened tree trunk, wielded it to defend herself.

Kerjean found a cigarette and lit it. He made no move to approach her. He calmed himself and as he did so, the tree trunk was gradually lowered until its end dug itself into the bog beside the bicycle.

She looked like a witch, a hag, as pagan as the rest of the place. He finished the cigarette in silence and when it was done, pushed it well into the peat. Then he took a step towards her and said, 'Hélène, please let me help you.' Another step followed and another – the peat was sucking at his boots. It wasn't any easier for her to move. Frantically she tried to pull the tree trunk free but it wouldn't come . . . it wouldn't.

With a cry that was more of the distant past than of the present, a blurred brown shape rushed out of the fog across the tops of the hummocks to leap at Kerjean and grab him from behind and drag him down . . . down into the bog. They fought. Something green and sharply pointed was raised up in two fists. A bronze spear point . . . A . . .

St-Cyr fired two shots into the air and all at once the gulls began to scream while the ravens went to silence.

'Yvon . . .' she said. '*Chéri* . . .' The words were ripped right out of her.

'Monsieur, please put the weapon down. Please do not force me to shoot you.'

Kerjean was face down. His arms were bent to give purchase. Involuntarily the hands clutched at the peaty mud and it squished between the futile fingers.

'He thought I had been badly hurt and would surely kill myself,' said Charbonneau, 'and I let him think it. I cut up a goat I stole from a nearby farm and made a sacrifice of it to the gods of this place. I knew he would have to come back here and I waited.'

'Please drop the spear point.'

'Yvon, do as he asks.'

It was Kerjean who said, 'Kill me, Yvon. Don't let the Nazis take me.'

Schultz was not good company. Oh, he grinned and thought it all a great joke locking his buddies up like that, but from the Tumulus of Saint-Michel to the alignments of Kerzerho, a good eight kilometres, the muzzle of the Walther P38 had never wavered. Not for one second, and through the damnedest pea-souper Kohler had ever experienced.

He geared down one more time, put the lorry right into low-low and eased the Freikorps Doenitz's lumbering old sow among the standing stones.

The megaliths ghosted grey and ancient and a hell of a lot like some witch doctor's phalluses, and he had to wonder if this wasn't what the bloody things represented. 'Not astronomical sight lines but peckers!' he snorted richly. 'The fountains of youth to dazzle all the tribe's females and make the old druids randy!'

It didn't even get a rise out of Schultz. 'Cat got your tongue?' he asked.

'Just find the house by the sea and find the woman and her husband.'

'So, tell me about the doll, eh? Give me a break.'

Kohler was just fucking about. 'Not until we know they're dead. If they're not, you can forget it.'

'Then I'll never know? That isn't fair. Hey, how was Paulette? I meant to ask, and bugger that crap about your trying to help the Dollmaker. You had her, Schultz, and you killed her and I'm going to make it stick.'

The shot shattered the side window and nearly put them into one of the larger stones. Kohler jammed on the brakes and shook his head to clear it. 'I'm deaf, damn it! Deaf, you son of a bitch!' he roared.

To prove it, Schultz fired again. 'All right . . . All right, you win. Was she juicy? Was she just begging for it, eh?'

'I didn't kill her and I didn't kill her mother either. She was already dead when I found her.'

Somehow he had to get that gun away from Schultz. 'You're lying. You raped her and then you killed her.'

'I might have but I didn't. Now shut up and keep driving.

Don't try to put us off the road. You do and it'll be the last thing you ever try.'

They started up again. He had to keep him talking. 'Admit it. You knew that shopkeeper. You'd been working a fiddle with him and trying to get a hand up Paulette's skirt. When the pianist and Angélique went into the shop, and you saw that doll the kid had – you saw it, my friend – you put two and two together and went to see what would happen. That can only mean you knew well beforehand exactly what le Trocquer was going to do with that doll.'

'What if I did?'

Kohler brought the lorry to another halt. 'It makes you an accessory to murder but I happen to think you were there to stop that shopkeeper from ever meeting up with the Captain. I'm right, aren't I?'

The engine idled – it was a bit rough. Ah damn . . . Schultz had raised the pistol and taken aim at the Gestapo's forehead.

'One neat little hole and no more problems,' he said. 'Your dossier and that of your Frog friend tell me few will regret your passing.'

Kohler wet his throat. 'Look, I . . . I was only casting about for answers. Doenitz wants this thing solved. Mueller in Berlin is on the line to my chief in Paris all the time. He and Boemelburg are old friends.'

Several seconds passed. The cook was going to kill him. *Ach Du lieber Gott*, had it come to this?

'Paulette was a tease, a virgin. She kept it locked up like the Bank of France. Her old man always figured she was up to mischief, but the truth is, Herr Kohler, she was as pure as the new-fallen snow.'

'She wanted out into the big world. You offered a chance but she wouldn't go all the way with you.'

'She wanted an officer. She was "worth it", she said. She wasn't going to give it to just anyone.'

'Even though you'd brought her all sorts of little treasures? Silk stockings, perfume, underwear and . . .'

'Condoms,' grinned the cook. ' A nice big box of them.'

It was coming now. Kohler tried to prepare himself for the bullet. Louis, he said to himself, Louis, where the hell are you?

But Louis wasn't with him, and Schultz was right. No one at the rue des Saussaies in Paris, the former HQ of the Sûreté Nationale and now that of the Gestapo in France, would shed a single tear. Least of all Boemelburg who would only say, I told you so. Someday it was bound to happen.

Giselle would cry and would go into mourning for about a week. Oona would shed blue-eyed tears and try to comfort the girl. One blonde, the other black-haired. Day and night. Half Greek, half Midi French and twenty-two, Giselle was the sweetest, most gorgeous thing in Paris, but Oona, who was forty and lovely too, wouldn't be able to stop her from going around the corner to console herself at Madame Chabot's with the other girls. Whores all of them. Real patriots too. The rue Danton and a house for Frenchmen only, even though the money was not very good and he'd won his way into their hearts in spite of being one of 'the others', one of *les autres*.

Kohler let go of the steering wheel and switched off the ignition. Gingerly he raised his hands. 'Why make it messy for yourself? I'll get out. I won't argue.'

Schultz shook his head. 'You forget the Préfet. You forget your side window. Someone had to break it. Not me. I'm just here to protect Vati.'

'The others will tell Louis I was with you.'

'They won't say a thing. Vati won't let them. Vati must know all about the doll by now, but I'm loyal to him, Herr Kohler. He's our Dollmaker. He's the only one who can bring us home.'

In single file, and tightly grouped, the four of them made their way through the fog. St-Cyr brought up the rear. The Préfet's gun was in his hand. Would they ever reach the car? Would one of them not try to bolt and run or take the revolver from him?

Kerjean was immediately in front, then the woman. The pianist, who knew the bog best, was in the lead but would he take them on a wide detour so as to stall for time, would he lose them and slip away?

He had set the spear point carefully on a hummock and had gingerly raised his hands in surrender. As he had got up, the Préfet had said, 'Why didn't you do as I asked?'

Charbonneau had replied, 'Don't ask when you already know the answer.'

No one had spoken since then. Exhausted, afraid, each had kept their thoughts but which was the killer of le Trocquer, or was that person still absent?

There were so many questions and all of them raised others. Worst of all perhaps was his not being able either to sit down quietly to think things through, or to meet with Hermann to bounce things off him and get his feedback. They worked as a team yet were forced by circumstance and this blasted terrain, this . . . this pagan landscape, to work largely alone. Each half of the partnership would know things the other half did not.

The last time they had been together, a little more than twenty-four hours ago, they had helped with the bomb damage in Lorient and he had told Hermann of his two sons and had used their deaths to make him see things from Kerjean's point of view which had not been fair. Ah no, most certainly, but war makes even the best of friends from opposite sides think first of their own kind, stupid though that is and always has been.

He had told Hermann of the telescope and the Préfet's son. He had asked him to say nothing of it. 'Victor's a good man,' he had said. 'Don't blame him for wanting to get the boy out of France.'

Hermann had wanted to know if the shopkeeper had been aware of the escape. He had said he wanted to look at the Dollmaker's report on the state of the crew.

Had he found a report on the Captain? Had the Doll-maker been in Paris for some kind of medical assessment – was that why Kaestner had gone straight to the clay pits with such an urgency it defied rational comprehension? Surely the day after New Year's would have sufficed? U-297 wasn't putting to sea immediately on his return. Yet he had sent messages on ahead to tell others where he would be on a day when the pits would be closed and only the watch-man would be present.

Baumann had taken the message to the Charbonneaus. Both had known of its contents as had the child.

Angélique, wanting to put a stop to the love affair, had got her father to take her to Quiberon the day before the murder to buy some candlesticks from the man who would then take the doll she had left in the shop and go out to confront the Captain with it. The child had known of the shopkeeper and had seen so clearly what he would do. The man had delivered messages to their house.

'Kämmer and Reinhardt . . .' he muttered, his voice well muffled by the fog. Hélène Charbonneau had caught up with that shopkeeper who had then thrust the doll into her hands. She had backed away in terror until out of sight and had stood and dropped the doll at the sound of . . . of another voice, yes, yes, a sharp accusation of its own, then a skull's crushing, perhaps a gasp, perhaps only the sound of the switch-bar as it had hit the rails on being cast aside.

But had she told the complete truth? Was she still trying to protect the husband, just as he had been trying to shield the daughter by hiding the briefcase and the doll?

She had had ample reason to kill le Trocquer, so, too, had the husband, and if she had lied before, could she not still be lying?

Quickly he ran through the sequence of events: the confrontation, the receiving of the doll, the backing away, the challenge to le Trocquer from behind, then the killing, the dropping of the doll and, a few minutes later, the hesitant viewing of the body and escape, after which the husband recovers the doll and the Captain then finds the bisque.

But had it been like that? Were there not other pieces to fit into the thing? The Préfet for one?

The line had come to a stop. The Renault appeared out of the fog, sitting just as they had left it, at the side of the road.

'Jean-Louis . . .'

'Victor, I am asking you to trust me, even as I am now asking you, madame, and you, monsieur. Either one of you killed le Trocquer or none of you. We will return to the house but I must ask that you give me your word not to try anything.'

'What good is the word of a killer?' asked Kerjean bitterly.

'You will sit in the back, Victor. Madame, get in the front passenger's seat. Monsieur, please drive carefully. This gun will be on the three of you and I will not hesitate.'

'Then Victor will only try to get you to kill him,' said the woman sadly.

'And that is why, madame, I must put these bracelets on him. Préfet, I am sorry for the humiliation and the apprehension they will cause, but I cannot have you dead before giving the guillotine its final answer.'

'You're a fool! You always were a stuffed shirt! Answering the guillotine? Pah! Then ask yourself about the Dollmaker. Ask what he would do?'

The handcuffs were secure. 'I already have and I know exactly where he is.'

'And Angélique?' asked the woman. 'Where is she? Please, you must tell me. I'll never forgive myself if anything has happened to her.'

'At home among her dolls on the *chaise-longue* where you were to have poisoned yourself.'

The sound of the car was lost in the fog but then it came to them again and Schultz heaved a grateful sigh. 'The Captain,' he said. 'We'll let him decide what to do with you.'

The cook rolled down his side window. The sound of the car grew at a bend. It was negotiating the first of the alignments. Almost imperceptibly Kohler began to lower his hands towards the steering wheel. Anything was worth a try. There was a Beretta strapped to his left calf and just itching to be fired. 'Look, why not get out, eh? He'll squeeze right past us. He'll only think you boys were too pissed to continue and decided to sleep it off.'

Schultz hesitated. He couldn't seem to make up his mind, but at last he said, 'Don't try anything. You first. I'll follow. Take it slowly.'

'Just let me tie my shoelace.'

The cold muzzle of the pistol was pressed hard against the back of Kohler's neck. Some glass fell from the side window and they both heard it hit the running board as the door opened.

Once on the road, Death's-head made him raise his arms. 'Now we wait and you can count the seconds.'

The car came on but the sound of it seemed to come from all directions until, suddenly, there it was out of the fog with its headlamps staring at them and its engine still ticking over.

'Hey, I've seen that car before,' quipped Kohler gratefully. 'It's Préfet Kerjean but he's not at the wheel.'

Schultz didn't like it. 'Get back in the lorry! Don't fuck about.' He grabbed an ear but it refused to budge.

'The woman's with her husband. My partner's getting out. If you shoot me now, my friend, he'll nail you right between the eyes. Fog or no fog, that one can hit a flea on a whore's ass at twenty paces and not even touch the skin.'

'All right, we'll see what they have to say.'

'Then let me tie my shoelace. I wouldn't want to trip and have you hot shots start firing.'

'Hermann, is that you?' came the call of a blind man who could see well enough.

'Yeah, it's me. That shoelace is busted again. Ah *Gott im*

Himmel, Louis, the lousy bastards who make them should be shot.'

Schultz felt the Beretta jammed under his chin. '*Don't*,' breathed Kohler. 'We wouldn't want to spoil our dinner, especially not when we've got the cook with us.'

The chicken soup was good, the tinned ham from Alsace superb when fried with chopped, boiled potatoes, green onions, tomatoes and a sprinkling of basil. Not turbot or sole or oysters, ah no, of course not, thought St-Cyr, but beggars could not quibble. Schultz had had the ham and the dried soup mix, both staples of U-boat fare, in a box under the seat of the lorry. There was real coffee too, not the meagre three beans of authenticity Vichy doled out on top of every bag of the ersatz stuff that, even though it was so lousy, was still labelled 'coffee' and still rationed to half a kilogram per month per family.

Everyone had partaken of the meal, some not tasting it at all but eating it as people did these days, never knowing if it would be their last or someone would steal it hot off the plate.

They had cleaned themselves up and wore dry clothes that had been parcelled out by the pianist. Now the lines above the kitchen stove were once more heavily draped, and his shoes dripped the last of their run-off on to the hot iron.

Hélène Charbonneau's hands had been attended to. The child sat between her and the husband. Schultz was beside Hermann who would translate when necessary. The Préfet was at the other end of the table from the Sûreté. Out of deference, the bracelets had been removed.

Now all were waiting for the Sûreté to begin. He would light his pipe and take the time to contemplate each of them with one notable absence, that of the Captain.

The woman met his gaze steadily and did not flinch, so much so, that he could but find admiration for her and wanted to say, Be at peace. My partner and I will help you all we can.

But, of course, he could not do so. There were now two further murders to consider.

Unable yet to view the bodies of these latest victims, he could only trust to Hermann's incomplete remembrances of them.

Contrary to what both he and Hermann had come to believe, when faced with the gravity of the situation, Yvon Charbonneau had revealed an acceptance of reality that was sobering and far from the symphony he heard and the megaliths he searched.

Kerjean did not turn away from meeting his gaze either. They were three very formidable adversaries.

Death's-head Schultz was the fourth. Only Angélique bowed her head and moved her lips silently in a prayer for absolution.

'Good. Now let us begin,' he said, removing his pipe just long enough to motion at them with it. 'The key to this whole business is that one must think as the Dollmaker did. One must have the Allied freighter or troopship right beneath the intersection of the cross hairs.'

Kerjean asked for a cigarette. Charbonneau lit it for him. Schultz, if ever such a man could do so, remained impassive.

'Herr Kaestner,' said Louis, 'could not allow the crew who held him in such high regard, to find out that he had been having a love affair – excuse me, please, madame, for calling it that – with a Jewess, no matter how intelligent, kind or beautiful she was.'

'Death's-head couldn't have them finding it out either,' snorted Kohler, watching them all closely.

'Ah, yes,' acknowledged the Sûreté, 'loyalty to one's captain is to be respected and it is much to your credit, Herr Schultz, that you kept what you saw on that doll to yourself. Believe me, it is.'

Both hands were placed on the table as if to lift it out of

the way. 'If you're trying to grease me with margarine, forget it. There is still a higher court even than Gestapo Mueller in Berlin. I also didn't kill anyone.'

'Please, a moment, yes? Don't be difficult.' Again St-Cyr looked round the table at each of them. 'Herr Kaestner knew of the telescope, isn't that correct, Angélique?'

The whispered yes was barely audible, her fingers studied with a concentration that begged forgiveness. She had really done it this time, she thought. Oh *mon Dieu*, but she had!

'Then on the 5th of November, he knew for sure of the real reason for my visits to this house,' sighed Préfet Kerjean sadly.

'Money was missing,' said the pianist with a gravity that implied complete understanding and awareness of the outcome. The dark brown eyes were much saddened by life's little realities and looked down at the table as if puzzled but accepting of them, tragic as they were.

St-Cyr could still not help but imagine him at some concert.

'A lot of money,' said Hermann gruffly. '6,000,000 francs we still haven't seen.'

'And aren't likely to,' grunted Schultz in good enough French. They were all surprised. 'What did you do with it, Préfet?'

'Paulette . . .' began the child, her voice so faint it broke.

'Paulette knew who had "borrowed" the money,' went on Schultz. 'She wasn't about to say and she died to keep her silent, didn't she, Préfet? Vati wouldn't have killed her. We didn't, so that only leaves you. And don't tell us the pianist rode that beat-up old bicycle of his all the way to Quiberon. You drowned her, you smug bastard. You killed her and her mother.'

Men like Schultz were always liars. 'She was violated repeatedly. Did I do that also?' asked Kerjean.

Tough . . . *Nom de Dieu*, he could be a brawler when needed, thought St-Cyr.

'I'm not so sure she was violated,' hazarded Kohler apologetically. 'Hey, I didn't take a look where I should have. I just assumed she'd been.'

'The child,' hissed Madame Charbonneau. 'Her ears, messieurs!'

'One of the *sardiniers* did not return,' whispered Angélique, and never mind her hearing things she shouldn't but knew all about. 'Money changed hands. A lot of money.'

'Angélique . . . *Chérie*, you must not speak. Herr Schultz is . . . is not one of us,' pleaded the woman desperately.

The cook grinned and let his eyes dance over her. 'In that you are correct, madame. Vati didn't know what you were but now he does.'

'And that,' sighed St-Cyr, 'is exactly what I meant when I said we must think as the Dollmaker would. He learned of the missing money and the absent *sardinier* – every one of U-297's crew heard of it when they returned to base on the 5th of November. He knew of your repeated visits, Préfet, of your interest in using the telescope. He decided to wait. He would not be too concerned about the missing money until he had gathered all the information needed and had the target clearly in focus.'

'And was within 500 metres of it,' breathed Kohler. 'Just what he would have done had Angélique not taken that doll into the shop, we'll never know.'

'The Star of David,' said Préfet Kerjean sadly.

'The yellow star,' replied Schultz with a grin as he again sought out the woman, though she found within herself the will to look steadily at him.

St-Cyr flicked a glance at Hermann. Hermann never let him down. Always he was ready – seemingly relaxed, the Walther P38 in its shoulder holster once again, the Beretta he had pocketed in Provence on another case, resting untended on the table before him as if forgotten.

'Préfet,' said the Sûreté suddenly, 'you searched for Monsieur Charbonneau and many times brought him home.'

249

The gun was being used as bait, even a fool could have seen this, thought Kerjean. 'I did it as a friend, Jean-Louis.'

'Yes, but you also did it to keep tabs on Madame Charbonneau and the Captain. My question, though, and it can be answered by her husband also, is did the two of you ever share a package of American cigarettes?'

'Several times,' said Charbonneau. 'We were both given them from time to time, myself most often.'

'Good. And did you ever leave a handkerchief in Victor's presence, madame?'

'I shed lots of tears. I did not know if I could stand things much longer.'

'Please just answer the question.'

'Then hundreds of times. Will that be enough?'

He ignored the bitter outburst. 'Monsieur,' he asked of Charbonneau, 'where did you leave your bicycle on the morning of the murder?'

It was coming now, and she did not know if she could stand it.

They exchanged a glance, the two of them, then Charbonneau said, 'In the shed where I always left it when I went to that place.'

'And the Captain knew of this?' he asked.

'Yes. We . . . we spoke now and then. I knew he was seeing Hélène but . . .'

'But you could not have openly challenged him for fear of trouble even though you hated him for what he was doing to your wife. You needed somewhere quiet.'

The pianist turned to look at the woman and as he did so, his hand went out to cover hers. 'Hélène, you must forgive me. I should have talked it out with you. Together we could have explained things to Angélique.'

'I *don't* need anyone to explain things to me!' seethed the child, scowling at the table.

'I think you do,' cautioned the Chief Inspector quietly. 'Let us hope we have the opportunity but let us return to that shed.'

Drawing on his pipe, he gave it a moment. Schultz had sat up stiffly and that was good. Charbonneau had pushed himself away from the table a little. 'Madame, you arrived in great haste. Automatically you went into the shed because you knew your husband always left his bicycle there.'

'Yes. I . . . All right, I left mine leaning against his. There, does that satisfy you?'

'Hélène . . .' blurted the pianist, his look so desperate it flicked to the pistol and for a moment he could not tear his eyes from it.

'Madame, the man you heard challenging Monsieur le Trocquer spoke French, did he not?' asked St-Cyr.

The depth of sadness in her eyes said, Please don't betray us.

'Yes. I . . . I didn't hear all of it. I . . . I can't say how fluently it was spoken.'

She threw a glance at Schultz. Kohler had to shout inwardly, Bad French, madame? Was that it, eh?

Schultz had twice let his gaze pass swiftly over the Beretta, weighing up his chances. But so, too, had the Préfet and the pianist.

'What, please, did you hear?' asked Louis.

She must not tell him. 'I . . . I can't remember. I'm sorry but . . . but it all happened so suddenly. I was terrified. Monsieur le Trocquer would not listen to me. He was going to tell Johann. I knew I would be sent away, that no matter how much Johann might once have felt for me, he would not only hate me but loathe the very thought of having ever been intimate with such a one. I'm not vermin. I'm just a human being like everyone else.'

'Schultz, take that grin off your mug or I'll wipe it clean.'

'Hermann, *please*! Let's get to the bottom of this.'

'The Dollmaker killed him, Jean-Louis, and that is why I arrested him,' said Kerjean gruffly.

They looked at each other. 'Ah no, Préfet, not quite. Please, you had much to hide and to protect, and Monsieur le Trocquer, in exposing Madame Charbonneau to the Dollmaker, could free himself of the loss of the money and only expose yourself. You warned Madame Charbonneau of trouble but refused to assist her in any way because, Victor, you were in too much of a hurry. You knew she would try to find her husband but you also knew they would not silence that shopkeeper before he spoke to Herr Kaestner. They were far too gentle, far too soft for such a thing, isn't that correct? Remember, please, she did not know of the doll until confronted with it.'

Ah damn the Sûreté, damn Doenitz. 'You will never prove I killed him.'

There was that curt nod Kohler knew so well. 'You didn't tell us of the shed, Victor,' went on the Sûreté. 'You claimed not to know of the bicycle tracks. You let us find the handkerchief and the cigarette package you placed in that shed so that we would be led to the affair between the Dollmaker and Madame and would suspect the Captain or the pianist but not yourself. Never yourself. You "borrowed" the money, but kept that to yourself and Madame Charbonneau. You argued with that shopkeeper violently, I believe, just as Paulette told me. You tried to warn him off but he refused to listen. He had now the opportunity to get back at you for putting the squeeze on him, and he wasn't about to let you forget it. Not for a moment. Paulette must have overheard the whole thing.'

'I did not kill that girl, Jean-Louis, nor did I kill her mother. The Captain was at the shop when Madame le Trocquer died. Herr Kaestner had a spare key to that cell of his and the use of a car.'

'But no one knew of that key except yourself, Victor, and the Fräulein Krüger – she can be asked. When confronted with the matter, she will tell us. But in any case, I think you left it handy and she picked it up. You came back for it probably, but she denied knowing where it was.'

'Pah! You're crazy. The Captain killed them to protect his . . . his precious sense of "honour".'

'No, Victor. The Dollmaker knew exactly what you would do. He needed the mother and daughter dead – yes, yes, of course – to protect his reputation. He did leave his cell using that key after the others had returned him to it from the party. He found the body of Paulette and then that of her mother. Before this, he went straight to this house to leave a little something for Madame Charbonneau. Please, I have it here and fortunately it did not get wet.'

Opening the crumpled handkerchief he had used to protect it, St-Cyr tumbled the tiny white pill on to the table.

There was a moment of silence as they all looked at it.

'He then went back to his cell, Victor, knowing you would also take care of Monsieur Charbonneau because you had to.'

'I didn't kill anyone, Jean-Louis. I'm not a murderer. *I'm a policeman*, damn you!'

Mentally St-Cyr ran through the sequence: the woman's catching up with Le Trocquer on the railway spur, her backing away, the altercation she overheard – the Préfet – the killing, her dropping the doll at the sound of the switch-bar, her tremulous viewing of the body and race to leave the area all the time feeling someone else, someone she did not know but only sensed – Herr Schultz – was watching her.

The husband quickly recovered the doll and the brief-case. The Captain, having caught sight of the woman or perhaps her husband, came along the railway spur to set his satchel aside and then find first, the fragments of bisque. He left the tracks and then found the body. He waited. He turned in the alarm twelve hours later. He knew the woman and her husband had been there but he also was convinced Kerjean had taken the money.

'You did it, Victor.'

'Then give me my gun and let me finish myself.'

He shook his head. 'You would only kill Herr Schultz so as to gain his silence and then try to kill my partner for the same reason. Lastly myself and . . .' he paused, 'since there are only four cartridges, it would be a toss-up between the couple but as Monsieur Charbonneau, with all his bicycle riding and digging, is the far stronger of the two, you would kill him and then deal with Madame. Even Angélique would not survive. The cause you support is greater and while one can sympathize, one cannot condone your actions. That, please, is from another police officer.'

'Schultz will only tell the others, Jean-Louis. Hélène has no chance and neither have Yvon and the child.'

'But Schultz will not say anything? Please, he's far too intelligent and far too loyal to his captain. He'll keep the secret so that U-297 can put to sea with their Dollmaker. Only then will they stand a chance of coming back.'

It was Kohler who said drily, 'He'll also make a bundle, Louis. Unless I've missed my guess, our cook put all his money on the Préfet.'

The lark's glimmer was there. Schultz fanned out the betting slips he took from a pocket. 'That's good,' he said, 'but I still want our money back or it's no deal.'

'Hermann, shoot him. I'll kill Kerjean and we'll say it was a toss-up. Doenitz won't care so long as he has the Captain.'

They would do it too, thought Angélique. She just knew they would. 'Messieurs,' she managed, 'is the rest of the money not in Monsieur le Préfet's car?'

The kid should become a detective, thought Kohler but he wouldn't wish it on anyone, especially not these days. Schultz just wasn't going to budge. Ah damn.

Pulling out his wad of bills, Kohler peeled off a few thousand francs for possible expenses and reluctantly slid the rest across the table.

Schultz pocketed everything and said, 'Now take care of him.'

Kerjean hesitated. He got up and lunged for the pistol. He had his hand on it. The shot rang out. The child shrieked. The stepmother yanked her close. The pianist held the woman.

Blood ran from the Préfet's forehead as he lay on the table before them.

'Madame, I am sorry it could not have happened outside,' breathed the Sûreté. 'He was a good man, caught in a vice, and I will regret for the rest of my life that I had to be the instrument of his death.'

So might the Resistance. '*Merde*, Louis I need a drink.'

Hermann always had to have the last word and it would be unkind to remind him that it was not a day for alcohol. Or was it?

The train to Paris was again delayed. St-Cyr, his feet up on the opposite seat next to Hermann, eased his back and shut his eyes. One slept when one could. Hermann unfortunately was a resonant snorer. The Benzedrine had finally worn off.

'He mustn't take any more of it,' he said softly. 'He'll never make it through this lousy war if he does.'

U-297 had not put to sea on Thursday as scheduled and they had had to wait a full twenty-four hours after that before the boat had gone out with the tide to disappear at last beneath the waves.

Though far from the complete sum, the money had put the cook back into favour with the men. The C.-in-C. Kernével had accepted their report as had Doenitz. Perhaps they liked its tidiness, perhaps Herr Freisen simply was relieved at not having to go to sea and the Admiral pleased that the Dollmaker would.

They hadn't seen Kaestner, and the Captain hadn't bothered to find them. With luck U-297 would go down with man and mouse and the woman and her husband and the child could at last live in peace. For now, though, all they could do was wait. They could not go back to Paris in hopes of losing themselves in the crowd, they dare not ask to leave the Forbidden Zone for fear of arousing suspicion.

Like so many these days they were trapped, never

knowing if and when the rifle butts would smash against the door to cries of, *'Raus! Raus!'*

The Bavarian's eyes half opened at some sudden thought and he murmured, 'Is it really okay, Louis? Is the kid happy?'

'Yes. She's with the stepmother and her father, Hermann. They're together at last.'

'Good.'

Hermann took a deep breath. He sighed and said, 'I can hardly wait to get home. I hope Giselle hasn't left me. I hope Oona's still there.'

He drifted off and was lost to him again, and St-Cyr had to wonder about his partner's use of 'home'.

'Paris has become that to him,' he said to himself. 'The divorce will go through. His wife will leave him for another. His sons are dead.' He paused.

'The megaliths remain.'

He let his mind linger on them but they had not been the dawn of European civilization. For that, one had to go back in time much further to the caves of the Dordogne and to those of Spain, to Lascaux and Altamira and other places. Yes, other places.

And a shabby trunk full of artefacts that had been discovered by an all-too-willing buyer in a shop in Paris.

And a woman of thirty-five and a boy, a young man of twenty – had he been twenty? One spoke of both boys and young men in the same breath – bathing at twilight beneath a waterfall and all but hidden by the trees.

Naked, the woman had reminded him of Marianne. An absolutely gorgeous figure but . . . but a sensuousness, an earthy desire, a hunger that had troubled deeply for he had never thought of Marianne as being like that. Never.

Yet his dead wife had revealed it with another, though that had happened a little later on and he had been too busy and away too much to have noticed that the sands of his second marriage were rapidly sinking under him.

Again he thought of that woman and the boy. Like

forebears of another time, they had welcomed the water to their splendid bodies and had let it pour over them, laughing, kissing and fondling each other until, up from the ground, the smell of old leaves and mould had grown damp.

Then he had heard them making love in the cave and again it had made him think of Marianne who was now but a memory.

When he awoke with a start, it was just as a stone hand-axe was descending on his forehead. He cried out, '*Hermann!*', scaring the hell out of his partner.

'Last summer,' he gasped. 'That business of the cave and the film crew. That actress.'

'*Verdammt!* You don't want to give me a heart attack, do you?'

'No.'

'Then go back to sleep. How many times must I tell you that business is over and done with and best forgotten?'

But it would not leave. Had they arrested the right person? Had they settled it as they should have? A stone-killer . . . a stonekiller . . .

Rudely he was shaken awake and frantically he searched for his ticket only to be confronted with a telegram.

Swallowing, he read it.

SANDMAN STRIKES AGAIN. BODY OF HEIRESS FOUND IN BIRDCAGE AMONG DOVES NEAR CLAY-PIGEON SHOOT BOIS DE BOULOGNE. REQUEST IMMEDIATE ACTION. REPEAT ACTION. IMPERATIVE VILLAIN BE APPREHENDED. REPORT 0700 HOURS DAILY. STURMBANNFÜHRER BOEMELBURG CONCURS AND PLACES YOU BOTH DIRECTLY UNDER MY ORDERS.

HEIL HITLER.

My orders . . .

It was from General Ernst von Schaumburg, Kommandant

von Gross-Paris. Old Shatter Hand himself. Rock of Bronze to his staff. A Prussian of the old school.

A birdcage, sighed St-Cyr. Was it coincidence or simply God laughing at him?

Author's note

Recent radiocarbon dates give ages of up to 4000 BC for some of the megalithic remains of the Carnac area. Within the time frame here, however, a maximum of 2000 BC was generally accepted.

The real U-297 was sunk on 6th December 1944 off the Orkney Islands by HMS *Loch Insh* and HMS *Goodall*. The characters in this novel are totally fictitious as are the events, and none were drawn from that boat or any other, though I do hope they have that sense of being.

Other Titles in the Soho Crime Series